A few snowflakes landed on my sleeve, glittering on the purple material of my dress like tiny pieces of frozen lace. Shivering, I brushed them off, but more fell to take their place.

"I'll go back in and get our coats." Lila glanced at the sky. "That horrible man isn't going to forget that Winter attacked him. He did bite him badly, didn't he? I've never heard of a collie biting before."

"Neither have I, but I'm sure some of them do."

"Winter has made an enemy all right." Lila reached over and touched my shoulder in sympathy. "And I'm afraid that you have too, Jennet."

Winter's Tale

by

Dorothy Bodoin

A Wings ePress, Inc.

Cozy Mystery Novel

Wings ePress, Inc.

Edited by: Lorraine Stephens
Copy Edited by: Elizabeth Struble
Senior Editor: Lorraine Stephens
Executive Editor: Lorraine Stephens
Cover Artist: Pam Ripling

Wings ePress Books
http://www.wings-press.com

Copyright © 2004 by Dorothy Bodoin
ISBN 1-59088-672-0

Published In the United States Of America

December 2004

Wings ePress Inc.
403 Wallace Court
Richmond, KY 40475

Dedication

To the memory of my parents,

Nicholas and Helen Bodoin

One

As I walked up to the Caroline Meilland Animal Shelter, in a swirl of blowing snow, I saw a Christmas tree in the bay window of the old white Victorian house next door. It was a massive balsam, whose branches filled the entire window, and the multi-colored lights wound around them shone like individual jeweled beacons, still and brilliant.

With Christmas a week away, festive decorations livened up the little hamlet of Foxglove Corners, but here, a block beyond the Corners, the deserted park across the street and the animal shelter were in plain white dress.

The Christmas tree was the only bright touch in the stark, monochromatic scene. Shiny ornaments weighted down its branches, and icicles dripped and sparkled among the decorations. I was impressed. I had stopped decorating with tinsel several years ago when the city of Oakpoint decreed that it had to be removed from discarded trees.

I couldn't resist one more admiring glance at the lights in the window, before setting my grocery bags down on the porch and ringing the doorbell. I was no more ready for the holiday than I ever am, but instead of going Christmas shopping, I had stopped at Blackbourne Grocers to buy an assortment of treats for the shelter dogs.

Letty Woodville opened the door. "Hello, Jennet," she said. "What's all this?"

As she bent down to pick up one of the grocery bags, a splattering of wet snowflakes landed on her gray-streaked hair. She peered inside, politely pretending to be surprised. I knew that she couldn't be. I had brought several such bags to the shelter on previous occasions.

Before I could answer, a small black puppy raced toward the entrance. With her left hand, Letty lifted it high into the air to prevent it from running out into the street. She stood in the entrance, awkwardly balancing grocery bag and squirming canine baby, managing to hold on to both competently. The pup was now chewing the sleeve of her long denim dress.

"Meet Charcoal," she said.

I reached out to pet his silky head. "I brought some rawhide chews and dog treats with real bone marrow for your foundlings."

"How sweet of you. I'll put them in their Christmas stockings." She looked up at the sky. "I wonder if it's going to keep on snowing."

"According to this morning's forecast, only flurries. The wind makes it seem like more."

I pushed back my hood and stamped the snow off my boots on the doormat before following Letty inside.

"I hope we'll have a white Christmas," she said, voicing a sentiment I'd heard several times already today. In fact, I'd said something similar myself.

"You look like you could use some help," I said. "Is it all right if I…"

Letty handed me the puppy before I could finish my request. With her free hand, she closed the door. Then she smoothed her chewed sleeve and ran her hand through the melting snow on her hair.

I held the little canine body close to my face. It was so soft and incredibly warm that I felt the winter chill stealing away. I breathed in the sweet puppy smell and whispered his name and friendly nonsense to him, while he licked my cheek earnestly. He was new since my last visit. When his squirming grew frantic, I set him down, and he scampered away.

"Lila will want to see you," Letty said.

I picked up the other grocery bag and followed her through the dining room into the kitchen where Lila, Letty's older sister, was rummaging through boxes stacked on the countertop, table, and floor.

It looked like an ordinary afternoon at the shelter, but something was troubling me. The place was unnaturally quiet. I listened for the usual raucous barking that would make conversation difficult. All I heard was the rustle of tissue paper.

I slipped out of my turquoise parka and laid it on a chair. There was scarcely room for the grocery bags, but the kitchen was a comfortable, welcoming place. With her silver hair wound in a bun and her plump form wrapped in a voluminous apron, Lila lent a nostalgic, grandmotherly touch to the clutter. I always felt at home here.

"Why is it so quiet?" I asked. "Where are all the dogs?"

"Including Charcoal, we only have four right now," Lila said. "Two are outside exercising in the yard. Come see the little stray Crane brought us yesterday."

Quietly, she approached a crate set in a far corner of the kitchen. She lifted the edge of the beach towel cover and spoke softly to the small brown dog who cowered inside the safe haven, ears laid smooth against its head, dark eyes wary.

"Hello, Brown Dog," Lila said.

The responding snarl might have come from a much larger, more ferocious animal, but Lila didn't flinch.

"This little one must have been abused. She trembles when

we try to touch her and won't eat. She snaps at the other dogs, but I'll gain her confidence. You'll see. I know the secret."

Letty said, "Lila can work wonders with dogs. She always had the gift."

"Did you say that Crane found her?" I asked, as Lila replaced the makeshift cover.

It was a pleasure to hear his name and to speak it. I hadn't seen Foxglove Corners' favorite Deputy Sheriff Crane Ferguson for a week. While he kept the peace in and around Foxglove Corners, I taught English in Marston High School in Oakpoint, Michigan, sixty miles away.

Our meetings were all too infrequent and brief, but the future looked brighter. Tomorrow morning I would meet him for breakfast at the Mill House, and a few days later, Christmas vacation would begin for me. For Crane, there would still be long hours of patrolling the country roads; but for a while, I would be available when he had a free hour or two.

"Crane saw her shivering by the side of the road," Lila said. "She almost got away from him, but if he hadn't brought her to the shelter, she'd surely have died."

The Caroline Meilland Animal Shelter was the best place Crane's frightened stray could have landed. Founded as a memorial to my friend, the slain animal rights activist, Caroline Meilland, it was a homey no-kill shelter that had opened only last month. A portrait of the vivacious, chestnut-haired Caroline hung above the mantel in the shelter's living room. It always reminded me that something of Caroline still lived on in Foxglove Corners, helping the animals.

"Do you mean that until Crane brought this dog to you, you had only three strays?" I asked. "The last time I was here, I saw at least a dozen."

"That's right," Letty said. "We found good homes for them, but since then the stray population seems to be declining."

Lila added, "Before Brown Dog, we only had two. During the night, someone tied a shepherd mix to our porch with a note, asking us to find a good home for him. You'd think they would have included his name."

"It makes no sense," Letty said. "At this time last year on the farm, we had twenty dogs. Now we have the room and the money to keep many more. People must be taking better care of their pets these days."

"Maybe in an ideal world," I said. "Not the one we live in."

The low number of dogs in the shelter was difficult to understand. There were always lost or abandoned dogs roaming the countryside. They were either too weak to survive or soon grew too strong, becoming a threat to both humans and other animals.

I supposed some people assumed that their castaway dogs would find new homes if they left them on a country road to fend for themselves. Sometimes they did. More often, the dogs died of starvation or were killed by predators.

"Well, Christmas is coming," I said. "Some unfortunate holiday puppies often wear out their welcome before the needles dry on the tree. I predict you'll soon have a full house."

Lila said, "Speaking of Christmas, I'm going to decorate our tree this afternoon, if I can only find the box of lights. Letty brought our decorations in from the farm yesterday. Come see the gorgeous Fraser fir we bought at the Christmas tree farm over on Silver Oak Road."

She led the way into the dining room where a tall, perfectly symmetrical Fraser fir stood in the bay window.

"That's the stage my own tree is at," I said. "I won't have time to decorate it until school is out."

At that moment, Charcoal dashed into the parlor, dragging a long, fuzzy red stocking. He shook it furiously while Lila regarded him with fondness.

"In the company of such unbridled energy, I feel almost young again. We're going to have an open house between Christmas and New Year's Eve, Jennet. I hope you can come."

"That's a wonderful idea. This is the only no-kill shelter for miles around, but it's in a fairly isolated location. People may not know you're here."

"They're going to have a story about the shelter in the *Maple Falls Banner*," Lila said. "Our pictures are going to be in the paper, too."

"That should help. I'll be sure to watch for it." I went back into the kitchen for my parka. "Well, enjoy the lull. You may soon have more charges than you can handle."

Charcoal had fallen into an instant slumber with his treasured red stocking under his head. I hated to leave the shelter, but I had been away from my own dog long enough. She needed her dinner, fresh water, and her afternoon walk.

I buttoned my parka and pulled the hood up over my hair. "Your neighbors' Christmas tree is gorgeous," I said. "That bay window makes a perfect frame for it."

Looking puzzled, Lila glanced toward her own bay window that looked out on an empty lot. Letty asked, "What neighbors?"

"The people next door," I said, wondering at her question. There was no house on the left side of the shelter, and the Foxglove Corners Municipal Park occupied the entire block across the street. What other neighbors could there be?

"You must be mistaken," Letty said. "The house next door is empty. No one has lived there since we've been here."

She was emphatic, and now I was confused. I'd noticed that the two houses were similar. They probably had matching floor plans. The window in the shelter's dining room faced the bay window of the neighboring house.

Casually, I walked to the window with every intention of

proving Letty wrong. New neighbors must have moved in while she wasn't looking or was away at the farm. And the first thing they did was set up a Christmas tree?

I looked. The bay window was there, with decorative gingerbread trim that also adorned the small front porch, but the only tree in my view was a young maple growing too near the house.

Through the window, I had a clear view of an empty room, partially shielded from the eyes of the infrequent passerby by three ecru panels.

I didn't say anything. What was there to say, after all? I must be obsessing about Christmas trees to imagine one fully decorated and with environmentally unfriendly tinsel at that. Teaching boisterous teenagers is stressful at any time, but especially in the days before a holiday—perhaps more so than I'd imagined.

"Let me know when you set the date for your open house," I said. "I'll be there, if I can."

Lila walked to the door with me, thanking me for my donations.

I said, "I see that it's stopped snowing. It's still cold, though."

I'd left my new silver Taurus across the street in front of the park. It was the only car in sight. This was truly an isolated place, but that could be a good thing, especially when the shelter was filled. There would be no close neighbors to complain about barking dogs.

"Come again," Lila said, "but please don't keep bringing things. It's thoughtful of you, but we have so much now. Our benefactor makes sure of that."

After Lila closed the door, I stood on the porch for a moment looking at the park with its trees spreading long, leafless branches over the old swings and slides—all of it deserted.

Then I turned to look at the window where I had seen the Christmas tree. It wasn't there. Nevertheless, I walked up to the house, past the porch and the maple tree, and peered inside. Behind the curtains I saw plain gray walls and a hardwood floor—nothing else.

Good Lord, was I losing my mind? A little stress couldn't create a decorated Christmas tree out of the thin air. Or could it?

I tried to summon a few happy thoughts. If I had to have an hallucination, make it a seasonably appropriate one, like a Christmas tree. Or better still, a blond deputy sheriff with silver streaks in his hair and frosty gray eyes that could blaze with sudden warmth. That was an apparition for any season.

Considerably cheered, I drove home to my green Victorian farmhouse where my own dog and my undecorated tree waited for me.

Two

When I arrived at the Mill House the next morning, Crane was deep in a cozy conversation with Susan Carter, the pretty blonde waitress who has a not-so-secret crush on him. The Sunday edition of the *Maple Falls Banner* lay at his elbow, unfolded but ignored.

Susan held a coffeepot in her hand, but Crane's cup was already full. She was an accomplished young waitress who excelled in hovering and lingering. This morning her face was flushed and her eyes were unusually bright. I wondered if she might be coming down with something.

"Here she is now, Susan," Crane said when he saw me. "You can bring our orders any time."

Susan bestowed one of her fleeting smiles on me and retreated.

"That girl sure is something," Crane said.

"She's something indeed."

I slid into the booth across from him and allowed myself the pleasure of contemplating his face for a long luxurious moment, marveling at how he provided his own brightness, even on the most overcast of mornings. With or without sunlight, his fair hair and gray eyes shimmered. It was as if someone had sprinkled him with glitter.

Crane rose and came around to my side of the booth to take my parka. He hung it on a nearby peg and returned, pausing on the way to greet an elderly couple sitting at a table by the window. He was a true Southern gentleman, albeit one transplanted to Michigan soil a generation ago. Sometimes I heard the faintest hint of a Southern accent in his voice—like now.

"Doesn't the Mill House look cheerful?" he asked.

I looked around, finally focusing on something other than Crane, and noticed that I had stepped into a world of red. Since last Sunday, the restaurant had burst into full Yuletide bloom.

Crimson cloths covered the tables, and red poinsettias had replaced the traditional centerpieces of wildflower bouquets in jars. More of the plants in various sizes lurked on the counter and in corners. Next to the cash register, a tabletop tree, decorated with gingerbread cookie ornaments, added a final festive touch of holiday décor. I wondered if the tree was real—if it was live or artificial, that is.

"The place is brimming with good cheer," I said. "You're still coming to have dinner with me on Christmas, aren't you? I hope you won't have to be on duty."

"I'll be off. I worked all through the holidays last year. The Christmas before I went back to Tennessee and had a grand old-fashioned celebration with my family."

"Do you mind not visiting your relatives this year?" I asked.

Now it was Crane's turn to look at me, which he did for a long time. After what seemed like an eternity, he said, "No. I may go for a week in the spring."

I relaxed. Crane had given me many indications that I was important to him, but none of them were of the permanent kind. Forging relationships was never easy. The fates had arranged to send this perfect man to me. Why should I assume that the rest would flow along smoothly to an inevitable end, whatever that would be?

Crane said, "I'll bring our dessert. My Aunt Becky sent me a fruit cake made from an old family recipe and an Old Dominion pound cake laced with bourbon."

"How kind of her. So you'll have something from the South for Christmas dinner."

"My aunt looks out for me. I told her that the sweetest girl in Foxglove Corners invited me for dinner on Christmas. She told me to thank you for taking me in and to wish you a Merry Christmas."

Crane's compliment was typical of his own innate sweetness, but, at the same time, I didn't suppose there was a surplus of girls in Foxglove Corners. Technically, at twenty-nine, I wasn't a girl. Susan Carter was a girl.

Still, as my friend, Leonora, always told me, 'Don't analyze the compliments men give you. Just thank them.' So I only smiled and said, "If you talk to your aunt again, thank her for the cakes and wish her a Happy New Year. What's new in the *Banner* today?"

He handed me the first section and pointed to an article on the front page. "This should interest you."

I read the headline above the picture of a child and a dog: 'Reward Offered for Lost Pet.'

Crane said, "A child up in Maple Falls came home from the hospital yesterday to find her dog gone. It looks like Halley, the same color, with the same markings, only smaller. What are they called?"

"Shetland sheep dogs? Border collies? A mix?"

"Something like that. The dog's name is Cinder. Anyway, this little girl has cancer, but it's in remission now. She's grieving for her pet. Her father offered a two hundred-dollar reward for its safe return. There'll be no merry Christmas for her unless that dog comes home."

Since Crane had told me the facts, I didn't read the story, but I looked again at the picture. The child had short curly hair and a happy smile. Her arms were wrapped around her dog who looked like a miniature version of my own black collie, Halley. Apparently her hold on Cinder hadn't been tight enough.

"I hope they find the dog," I said.

"If they don't, I'm sure somebody will come forward and give her a new one."

In the festive surroundings of Christmas red, our conversation had turned as gloomy as the dark morning. Where was Susan? Usually Crane commanded excellent service, no matter how crowded the Mill House was. Nothing would restore the holiday atmosphere more quickly than an old-fashioned country breakfast.

"What did you order for us this morning?" I asked.

"Buttermilk pancakes and country ham. Is that all right?"

"It's perfect," I said. "I hope it'll be ready soon. I'm so hungry."

As if she had overheard me, Susan came out of the kitchen bearing a large tray. As she set the items Crane had named in front of us, she said, "The cook found some frozen blueberries to mix in the batter just for you, Deputy. Tea or coffee this morning, Ms. Greenway?"

"Coffee, please," I said.

Without delay, Crane poured maple syrup on his pancakes and began eating them, and the stack started to diminish. I concentrated on cutting my slice of ham into pieces, neatly trimming the fat and rind, and moving them to one side of the plate.

It's now or never, I thought. If you're going to ask him, do it now.

"Do you believe in ghosts, Crane?"

My question took him by surprise, as I thought it would. He didn't answer right away but looked down at his plate and impaled a piece of pancake with a fork. He lifted it slowly to his mouth and chewed it, regarding me all the while with cool, appraising gray eyes. I couldn't imagine what he was thinking, but it seemed as if he'd slipped into slow motion.

"Why do you ask?" he said at last.

"Answer me first. Please."

"Well, I don't rightly know if I do," he said. "For now, let's say that I might. My Aunt Becky believes in them. For what it's worth, she had an experience with one when she was young, but she doesn't like to talk about it, even with me. I'm getting us sidetracked. Tell me why you want to know. Did something unusual happen?"

"Yesterday I saw something that wasn't there. I wanted to tell someone who wouldn't think I had lost my mind."

Crane had stopped eating and was waiting for me to go on.

"I think I saw a ghost yesterday, or rather a ghost tree." Then I told him about the apparition in the bay window of the old Victorian.

"The funny thing is that I saw tinsel on the branches," I added. "Nobody decorates with tinsel these days. I haven't even seen it for sale in the stores."

"That's significant. Your tree may belong to an earlier era."

All of a sudden, my experience didn't seem so worrisome. Crane was listening to me. He believed me.

"I guess tinsel isn't nearly old enough to qualify as antique, but you're not telling me what you think. I was positive I'd seen the tree, but when I looked again, it wasn't there. I went right up to the window and checked again, just to make sure."

"This house is on Park Street, right?"

"Yes, next door to the animal shelter."

He was in no hurry to deliver his verdict. He stared at what remained of his pancake stack while I waited. At last he said, "It seems like I read a story in the *Banner* some years back about a haunted house on Park Street. It was more like a house with a curse on it. As I recall, anyone who tried to live there met with some misfortune. Let me think."

While Crane set about collecting odds and ends from his memory, I felt heartened enough to begin on my own pancakes. I knew that he seldom forgot any sensational story, especially if it had happened in Foxglove Corners. When he spoke again, he had more details.

"The owner had a death in the family and suffered a nervous breakdown or heart attack. When he recovered, he moved up north but held on to the ownership of the house and offered it for rent. It's in good condition with a deep lot and a park across the street. Over the years several people tried to live there, but something always went wrong in their lives.

"I can't remember any more except that in the late sixties a reporter set out to investigate the so-called haunted house. He died under mysterious circumstances the same day the story was printed. He was trapped in a forest fire, I think."

As Crane related the strange tale, my apprehension about my mental health turned to avid curiosity. If the house was supposed to be haunted, perhaps I wasn't the only one who had seen the disappearing tree.

"Do you think this is the same place?" I asked.

"It's possible. You look up the address, and I'll research the background. In the meantime, I don't want you to go near that house. Nothing is going to happen to you, if I can help it."

"That's a nice sentiment, but it's a little dictatorial," I said. "With the fascinating information you gave me, it's unlikely I'll stay away from it. So the answer to my question is that you do believe in ghosts."

"Anything is possible. Remember, we're not sure yet that it's the same house. Even if it is, it shouldn't affect Lila and Letty. How's my little stray, by the way?"

Thinking that he was referring to me, I was momentarily startled. Then he held up his right hand, and I understood. An angry red scratch stretched from the middle of his palm down to his wrist.

"She won't eat and isn't very friendly, but I see you found that out. They've named her Brown Dog. Lila and Letty are assigning names according to color."

"Lila will be able to calm her down," he said.

"There are only four dogs at the shelter. I can hardly believe it."

"That's odd. It's not unusual for me to see four abandoned dogs in one day. That's a part of my job that I really don't like, taking strays to the pound. You know they'll probably be euthanized there, but feral dogs are as great a threat as wild animals. Now that I can drop them off at a no-kill shelter, I don't mind catching them."

I reached across the booth to touch the scratch. "Be careful. You don't want to have to get rabies shots."

"I had a friend who did. It wasn't fun."

"Neither is rabies."

He glanced at his watch. "I'm going to be late, but before I go, I want to ask you something."

He brought a magazine, the *Michigan Traveler,* out from under the *Banner* and handed it to me. He had opened it to a lavishly illustrated photo story about a place called Snow Lodge.

I scanned the article, admiring the pictures of the rooms. They were all country comfortable and enticing, each one with its own fireplace.

"Are you going traveling?" I asked.

"Maybe I am. Will you come away with me? It's the perfect place for a winter weekend getaway. The author says so."

He said the words as if they all began with capital letters. My imagination added the missing adjective—romantic. Romantic Winter Weekend Getaway. Next to "I want you to be my wife, Jennet. Will you marry me?" this was the kind of invitation I had wanted to hear from Crane for a long time.

So, yes or no? I didn't have time to think, but I didn't have to think. "When?" I asked.

"Right after New Year's Day. I'll have two days off. You'll still be on vacation then, won't you?"

Swiftly, I counted. "I don't have to go back to school until the fourth of January."

"Will you go?"

Incredibly, he sounded shy. I thought I had already given him my answer.

"I'm sure Camille will take care of Halley. She's offered to before."

"Then you'll come with me?"

"Yes, I will. It sounds wonderful."

Once again, he consulted his watch. "Good. I wasn't sure. Jennet, I have to go."

He drew a ten-dollar bill out of his wallet and set it under the syrup pitcher. "Wait. We won't be here again until after Christmas, will we?" He added another ten.

I looked on, bemused. Susan would be pleased. No, Susan would be flabbergasted. Or maybe she wouldn't. I suspected that she knew Crane well.

I thought that I did, too, considering that our friendship was still relatively new. He was usually predictable. Our dates had a wondrous sameness about them that rarely varied, but this morning he had surprised me with his ready acceptance of my supernatural experience and by proposing a winter weekend getaway.

Romantic Winter Weekend Getaway, I corrected myself. It was a lucky sign for a happy new year.

Three

On Sunday afternoon, I decorated the railing of my front porch with balsam roping. As I attached a red velvet bow to each post, I breathed in the rich scent of the fresh branches and admired the festive contrast of the ribbons against the light green color of my house.

My black collie, Halley, lay on the porch watching me, her head resting on her front paws, her eyes fixed on the old yellow Victorian house across the field and up the lane. Every now and then, she snapped to attention.

Camille Forester, my neighbor and friend, lived there with her dog, Twister, the black Belgian shepherd mix who had stayed with us in the fall during Camille's extended European vacation.

Like the bows, Halley was attached to a porch post on her big dog tie. In spite of two semesters of obedience school, she had never mastered the recall, except when the command was given by Crane, whom she adored, or when I had a tasty treat in my hand.

She was staring at the woods to the left of Camille's house now, frozen in a pose so breathtakingly beautiful it made me wish I had my camera handy. I didn't see anything. Sometimes I found her surveillance a little unsettling. Usually I told myself that some wild creature, detectable only by a canine, was out there.

I knew Camille was home. I wanted to tell her about the phantom Christmas tree and Crane's invitation. I couldn't go to Snow Lodge with Crane unless Camille agreed to take care of Halley. I never doubted that she would, but naturally, I had to ask her first.

"Would you like to go for a walk?" I asked Halley. "Do you want to see Twister?"

Halley yelped her answer and sprang to her feet, always ready for an activity we could do together. I exchanged the tie for her leash and then went back into the house for my key and locked the door on the way back out.

Foxglove Corners was a fairly safe place to live. Many people left their doors unlocked, except when they left for the day or at night. I'd only lived in the country for six months, though. I always made sure that nobody could get into my house and looked cautiously behind me when darkness came.

A light snow had fallen this morning, leaving a powdered sugar covering on the ground. That was possibly all we were going to have of a white Christmas this year, but the countryside had a fresh, new look. Halley and I turned onto Jonquil Lane, making the first footprints in the snow, and soon we reached Camille's gate.

The yellow Victorian was the only genuinely old house on Jonquil Lane. It had a soft buttercup color that glowed in the light and a magnificent wraparound porch encircled by perennial beds in the other three seasons. Now, in its wintry setting, it resembled a giant pineapple cake frosted with marshmallow icing.

Twister was barking on the other side of the door, which sent Halley into a similar frenzy. She tugged at her leash, and when Camille opened the door, she leaped at Twister, wild with joy at their reunion. She nipped playfully at him. I unfastened her leash, and the two dogs set out chasing each other madly through the house.

Camille wasn't perturbed by this display of canine exuberance. Since our first meeting last summer, she had undergone a dramatic change. With her gray-streaked honey blonde hair cut short and fashionably styled, she looked younger than her fifty-five years and happier than I'd ever seen her.

She had applied soft blue eye make up this morning, and over her pink striped shirtwaist dress, she wore a long red apron. These provocative words tumbling down the front: "Come, woo me, woo me, for now I am in a holiday humour and like enough to consent."

"What a marvelous apron, Camille! May I borrow it?" I asked.

"Certainly, but there's no need. I bought another one like it for you. Come into the kitchen and tell me the news. I'm having a baking day."

"Two things are new. The best thing first—Crane."

I followed her into the enormous country kitchen, where almost everything except the appliances was blue or covered with blue gingham. Something was baking in the oven, but the aroma wasn't immediately identifiable, nor was it particularly tempting.

"What do you mean Crane is new?" she asked.

"He invited me to go with him to Snow Lodge for a few days after Christmas."

"Oh, Jennet, that's a lovely place, close to Lake Huron, very secluded and romantic. You aren't hesitating, are you?"

"No, of course not. I want to know if you'll take Halley around the second or third of January."

"You know I will. Twister misses her. Well, Snow Lodge

and Deputy Sheriff Crane Ferguson. I almost envy you, Jennet."

Like many other women in Foxglove Corners, Camille was one of Crane's admirers. Their numbers were legion.

I glanced at the cookie cutters scattered on the table. Two racks containing numerous brown cookies in vague animal shapes occupied the center of the table, and several packages, wrapped in green and red paper, crowded the counter. They all smelled interesting, but not the kind of interesting that made me want to reach for a sample.

"Are you baking Christmas cookies?" I asked.

"Not exactly. I'm making treats for the neighborhood dogs. There's a package for Halley somewhere here and a bigger one for the dogs at the shelter. Will you deliver it for me the next time you go there?"

"I will. I'm going to stop by tomorrow after school."

In the light of a new day, I wanted to look through the bay window of the old Victorian again to see what was there—or wasn't.

"You said two things were new, Jennet."

"The other one is weird. When I was visiting the shelter yesterday, I saw a Christmas tree in the house next door. The next time I looked, it wasn't there."

"A supernatural manifestation!" Camille exclaimed. "How delightful. Tell me about it."

Neither Camille nor Crane seemed surprised to hear that I had come into contact with something from the world beyond, but then I should have expected this. I had known ever since moving to Foxglove Corners that things were always a little bit different here.

Camille listened in fascination as I described the apparition. I suspected that she was almost envying me again. Encountering a person or object from the other world doesn't have to be terrifying. It can be an adventure. After all, there was nothing malevolent about a Christmas tree.

"How in keeping with the season!" she said, when I finished my account. "Christmas and ghosts go together. Didn't you tell me the shelter is in that old white house on Park Street with an empty lot on one side?"

"Yes. Why?"

"I know the story of the house next door. Over the years, it's often been empty. The kids used to think it was haunted. On Halloween, they'd dare one another to visit it."

"According to Letty Woodville, the house has been vacant since they opened the shelter."

"It's likely to stay that way," Camille said. "Today most people want something more modern, without a reputation."

"Crane told me that whoever tries to live in the house meets with some misfortune."

"Not everyone," Camille said. "I know a woman who lived there for years after she retired. Nothing bad happened to her. Eventually, she had to move to a nursing home, but by then, she wanted to go. Some of the tenants had troubles over the years, but tragedies happen all the time, often where people live. Surely a house can't be blamed."

I couldn't disagree with her, but if the house on Park Street had been the scene of a disproportionate number of tragedies, maybe something more sinister was going on.

Suddenly I had a chilling thought. "What if it was a forewarning of some tragedy of my own?"

"Nonsense."

Camille could talk about haunted houses as if they were commonplace, but she also had a strong realistic streak, the same kind Crane had.

"You're not moving into the house," she said. "You're only visiting the shelter next door. Do you suppose you have psychic powers in your genetic makeup?"

I could tell from her expression and tone that she was joking, but sometimes I wondered. "My mother used to have premonitions and dreams that were forewarnings, usually of death. I don't think she ever saw anything that wasn't there, though."

"Maybe you inherited something from her," Camille said. "The library is near the shelter. They may have back issues of the *Banner* on microfilm and maybe a file on the house. And oh—our resident author, Lucy Hazen, wrote a book about the house once. It's probably out of print, but I'm sure the library will have it."

"That's a good idea," I said. "I can ask her myself. While you were in Europe, Lucy Hazen and I got to know each other. She even said some complimentary things about Twister."

Camille was astonished. "She's always been so unfriendly. Talk to her then. I'm sure she did research on the house for her book."

I made a mental list. Return to the house on Park Street, go to the library, call Lucy Hazen. I felt that I was taking charge of my apparition.

"Where are the treats for the shelter dogs?" I asked.

Camille handed me two packages wrapped in bright red. The smaller one had a tag with Halley's name printed in green ink.

"She'll love these. Now, where is she? The dogs are awfully quiet. They should be in here where the cookies are. Halley!" I called. "We're leaving, Halley!"

We found both dogs in the living room. They had ended their play. Twister was sitting at the front window, staring outside at something that had captured his attention, and Halley was lying down nibbling at her front paw.

"What's wrong, girl?" I asked.

"Maybe she picked up a piece of ice," Camille said.

"Surely it would be melted by now."

Kneeling down on the hardwood floor to investigate, I lifted Halley's paw and ran my fingers gently over it. It felt rough and cold, the way it should, with sharp nails that would soon need trimming. There was no foreign object that I could feel or see.

Halley wagged her tail and gave me an imploring look, but as soon as I released her paw, she attacked it again with renewed ferocity. It might have been a rawhide bone instead of a part of her body.

"I can't imagine what's wrong," I said.

We still had to walk home. The distance was not great, but we ought to start before Halley damaged her paw. I put on my parka and fastened her leash to her collar. Then I pulled up on the leash, coaxing her into a standing position. She stood reluctantly for a few seconds but then sat down and started licking her paw again.

I was puzzled. "She was fine on the way over."

"I'll drive you home," Camille said. "If she's still bothered by it in the morning, you can call the vet."

As it turned out, the ride proved unnecessary. With a few final licks, Halley stood again and this time took a few steps. She appeared to be walking normally.

"There," Camille said. "It's all right. Dogs know more than we suspect about what ails them. They know what to do for themselves. Watch her on the way home. Can you handle both Halley and the cookies?"

I carried the packages in one hand and held Halley's leash in the other. It was awkward but manageable. We walked back home without incident, and that was the end of Halley's trouble. The next morning, she seemed to be all right.

Dogs were like that. Sometimes what seemed to be escalating into a major emergency resolved itself without a mad dash to the vet.

~ * ~

The halls of Marston High School overflowed with Christmas spirit, and no one was inclined to swim against the tide. Today, on the last full day of school before the Christmas recess began, most classes might as well have been already on vacation, except for the unfortunates in math who were taking a test.

I showed my world literature classes a Christmas movie with an essay assignment attached: Supernatural Elements in Classical Christmas Movies. Ironically, I had chosen the topic before my own encounter with a supernatural element at the house on Park Street.

As the day wore on, the Yuletide spirit turned into a fever. Students exchanged gifts, and in the afternoon, the choir traveled through the halls singing Christmas carols, while Coach Adam Barrett, dressed in a Santa Claus suit, followed them, flinging handfuls of hard candy into the classrooms. No one had seen the principal yet. He was probably in his office, finishing last-minute paperwork before the vacation began.

On the way home that afternoon, I took a detour into Foxglove Corners to deliver Camille's home-baked treats to the shelter. I passed the library, which was closed, and drove down Park Street. The neighborhood was as quiet as I remembered it, the somberness softened today by fresh snow cover.

I parked the car across the street from the shelter and looked toward the house next door. No Christmas tree lights shone in the bay window, but on the front porch, a man in a brown jacket stood on a ladder pounding a nail into the area above the front door. Beneath him lay a large wreath decorated with pinecones and a bright red bow. It looked as if the haunted house was about to have an occupant.

Four

Letty Woodville set the package of dog treats on the mantel where red candles flickered amid a collection of framed photographs.

"The dogs won't break into them ahead of time, if they can't reach them," she said.

As I explained that the gift was from Camille Forester, Charcoal tried to leap into my arms. I picked him up and made a fuss over him.

Two other dogs, larger but still puppies, were playing tug-of-war with a raggedy stuffed carrot. Of Crane's brown stray, I saw no sign. She must still be hiding in her crate.

"I see the house next door has a tenant," I said.

Lila moved one of the candles away from the package. "Not exactly. The owner, Henry McCullough, is in town for the holidays. We met him yesterday."

"Is he the man on the porch hanging the wreath?"

"No, that's his nephew, Fred. He helped his uncle move in."

I assumed there was more to the story, but apparently Lila had exhausted her store of information, except for one detail, the kind she wouldn't miss.

"There's a new dog next door. He's a collie."

People, a dog, a wreath on the door, and perhaps later a real spruce or pine. The supernatural aura was falling from the house next door like melting snow, but no amount of present normalcy could erase the fact that I had seen a phantom tree in the bay window.

Henry McCullough would be a far better source of information about his own house than any ancient *Banner* article or even Lucy Hazen. Lila or Letty could introduce us, and I should be able ask him about the house's history without mentioning the curse, just in case he was sensitive about it.

"How is Brown Dog?" I asked.

"I coaxed her to drink a little goat's milk this morning, but she still won't let me touch her," Lila said.

"At least she's taking some nourishment, but if she won't come out of her crate, her chances of finding a new home are non-existent. Thank heavens Crane brought her to you."

"She will," Lila said. "I need more time with her."

I set Charcoal down on the floor, where he promptly tried to take possession of the stuffed carrot.

"All three dogs have ignored that toy for days," Letty said. "Now they're fighting over it."

As I watched the mock battle begin, I reflected that life was never dull for people who lived with dogs, especially when the dogs were young. Not for the first time, I wondered if I should add a new puppy to my own household.

~ * ~

The first snowflakes began to drift down as I left the animal shelter. By the time I drove out of the Corners, it was snowing in earnest. I wondered if I should take the back roads home. They might become slick if the snow continued, but they would also be less traveled. If my car skidded, the chances were good that I would collide with bushes and trees instead of steel.

Still trying to make up my mind, I drove slowly along Silver Oak Road, watching for icy patches, turning my windshield wipers up a notch higher and wishing my bright lights were more powerful.

Suddenly I saw something in the road that shouldn't be there. Just beyond a 'Horse Country—Drive with Care' sign lay a large object half in my lane. I steered to the left and squinted, trying to see through the swirling snow.

It looked like the body of a large animal lying still in death while snow fell on its fur. The colors were wrong for a deer. The downed creature might be a pony then. Its silvery gray coat was partially covered with a whisper-light blanket of snow, and it wasn't moving.

I slowed down and tried to steer the car into a clear expanse that swept down to a cornfield. Instead I swerved on an icy stretch of roadway and made a series of swirling tracks in the snow, before coming to a stop on the opposite side of the road. I was some distance farther than I had intended.

Raising the hood of my parka over my head and pulling on my gloves, I got out of the car, but left the engine running. It was colder out here on this deserted road than it had been at the Corners. With the snow beating against my face, I walked back to where the animal lay.

A little daylight was still left, but the falling snow made visibility extremely poor. I approached the animal cautiously, realizing for the first time that it might be a dangerous wild beast, a large coyote, perhaps, who wasn't dead at all, only asleep. As I drew nearer, however, I saw that my guesses were incorrect.

As the animal moved slightly, lifted its head, and shook itself free of snowflakes, I saw that it was a dog. Moreover, of all possible breeds I might have chanced upon, this dog belonged to the one nearest to my heart. He was a collie with a thick blue merle coat. The colors blended so perfectly into the wintry background that I was amazed I had seen him at all.

I assumed that the dog was a male because of his size. I was accustomed to looking at a collie the size of Halley, who was a little smaller than the average female. This dog was larger than any male collie I had ever seen, which was why I had mistaken him for a pony.

The dog lifted his head higher still and turned to give me a beseeching look, the kind that only a dog in distress can give and no dog lover can resist. His eyes were dark and intelligent. They held the dazed expression of one who has seen the impossible happen but hasn't realized it yet.

His most remarkable feature was his head, with its strikingly distinctive markings. The left half was black, with tan shadings above the eye, while the right side was blue merle with black patches worked into the silver.

He was obviously a collie of high quality and someone's prized possession but because he wasn't wearing a collar, there was no way to tell to whom this gorgeous creature belonged. He had been wounded. Above his right eye, dried blood showed through a patch of snow.

I removed my glove and held out my palm to allow him to sniff my scent.

"Come," I said softly. "Can you walk? If you can, come with me."

I repeated my command. To my amazement, the blue merle rose and, without hesitation, followed me. He walked unsteadily, but he moved. It seemed that he gained strength with every step he took.

With the flying snow at my back, I was the one who lagged behind, marveling all the while at the novelty of a dog who came when called.

I kept a second crate in the back seat of the Taurus so that Halley could accompany me on road trips in safety. When we reached the car, I held the door open. The collie lifted himself up onto the seat, crawled through the door, turned, and lay his head down between his paws.

His dark eyes were trusting, and the next move was mine to make. When I turned to look at him a second later, his eyes were closed. He had fallen asleep.

As I stroked his damp head, I reflected that the entire episode seemed surreal, more like a winter night's dream than an actual occurrence. The dog in the crate was real, though, and he needed medical attention. I could take him home with me and try to tend to his wound myself, or I could take him to the animal shelter.

The last of the light was fading, and the snow was still falling. I longed to be home, but the shelter, with access to around-the-clock veterinary care, was the only sensible choice. Besides, if the dog was more seriously injured than I thought, I was closer to the shelter than my house.

I couldn't turn around on the narrow road, but I drove on until I came to a crossroad. Here there was no traffic, and I had more room to maneuver the car around on the ice. Soon I was heading back in the direction from which I had just come.

~ * ~

Letty Woodville rushed out to the porch to see what had brought me back to the shelter so soon after leaving it. Lila stood in the doorway with Charcoal in her arms. Behind her, the bright lights beckoned, promising warmth and safety. The rest of the block was dark and quiet in the falling snow.

"What a pretty dog!" Letty said. "But what an odd color he is and what an unusual face. Where did you find him?"

"On Silver Oak Road. He's been hurt, but I don't think he was hit by a car. He's unusually gentle."

I opened the crate, and the blue merle jumped down out of the car and walked to the open door where Lila stood. He sniffed the floor and stepped over the threshold into the hallway. Letty and I followed him inside.

As if certain of his welcome, he sniffed various corners of the living room and surveyed the excited puppy in Lila's arms with a tolerant look. Apparently oblivious of the other dogs barking in the kitchen, my foundling lay down on the rug beside the fire.

"His owner must be frantic with worry," Lila said. "He looks like a valuable dog. Someone will be searching for him."

"In the meantime, I'd like to name him," I said. "He was found in a snowstorm. Let's call him Winter."

"Winter he is," Lila said. "Let's get you a drink of water, boy, and something to eat."

I said, "Now, I really have to go home."

Letty walked with me to the door. "This is quite a coincidence."

"What is?"

"To have one lost dog and one dog found within an hour, and both of them collies."

"Whose dog is lost?" I asked.

"Luke, the dog next door. Henry McCullough just left. He came over to ask if we'd seen him. He's afraid that Luke may have been confused by the move and wandered off."

She shivered and pulled down the sleeves of her beige cardigan. "With all the snow and cold, this is no night to be a lost dog."

Five

I met Crane, by chance, on Silver Oak Road the next day at noon. His patrol car was emerging from one of the byroads I had taken last night on my long drive home. He waved as he passed me and pulled over to the side of the road. I steered onto the shoulder and parked behind him, thinking that I must be the only person in Foxglove Corners who didn't mind being stopped by an officer of the law.

I pressed the button to roll down the window and watched him walk up to my car. His slow smile traveled all the way up to his gray eyes, filling them with a summer's worth of warmth.

"This is a surprise, Jennet. I was just thinking about you." He frowned and moved closer to the car. "You aren't sick, are you?"

"No, I couldn't be better. It's Christmas vacation. We had a half day today."

"I forgot." He glanced at his watch. "Come have a bite to eat with me then. I'm due for a lunch break. Unless you're bound for somewhere special, that is."

I was, but my schedule was flexible, especially when Crane issued an unexpected invitation.

"We had our Christmas breakfast this morning, but coffee and a roll sound good," I said. "I'm going to skip lunch and go shopping for presents instead."

I was in a holiday-inspired good mood. The breakfast gathering of the Marston High School faculty was a festive tradition that could melt the heart of the most confirmed Scrooge. Afterwards, we had three shortened classes, which amounted to a scaled-down repetition of yesterday's pre-holiday revels.

The best thing about the day, though, the icing on the Christmas coffeecake, was this unexpected encounter with Crane and the knowledge that in a few more days he would be a virtual Christmas captive in my Victorian farmhouse—for dinner definitely, for the entire day, I hoped.

Lately, I felt as if there was an ever-lengthening stretch of days between the times I saw Crane. It hardly seemed possible that we'd had breakfast together at the Mill House only three days ago.

"There's a diner about five minutes up ahead," he said. "Follow me, but drive carefully. The road's slippery. I passed an abandoned car in the ditch a mile back."

Thus forewarned, I drove with extra caution, keeping a safe distance of three car lengths behind him. The road was slick but not so treacherous as the ones I'd driven on last night. Sliding into the patrol car of one of the sheriff's deputies was inadvisable, even if I could reasonably expect understanding and a measure of forgiveness from him, if it were to happen.

The diner was crowded. At least two dozen cars were parked in the small lot. It was rush hour, but for Crane, the time was immaterial. I knew that someone would always find room for him.

He got out of the patrol car just as I pulled up alongside him, the two of us claiming the last parking places. I'd managed to navigate the slippery road without incident but almost went into a spinout on the walk in front of the diner.

"Be careful," Crane said, catching me before I could end up on the frozen ground. "You have the whole season to survive.

This is only the second day of winter."

We found seats together at the end of the crowded counter. Crane ordered a large plate of steaming beef stew with biscuits and, for me, coffee and a cinnamon roll.

"I found the most incredible collie last night while I was driving home," I said. "He's a gorgeous blue merle."

Crane pounced on the one word in my account that I knew would attract his attention. "Blue?"

"Not cobalt or cornflower, but blue, yes."

"I thought all collies were brown like Lassie or black like Halley," he said.

"Blue merle is silvery gray with tan, black and white markings. It's one of the four recognized colors in the collie breed. The dog was hurt but not critically, at least I don't think so. I took him to the shelter. Letty is going to have the vet look at him today."

When I described the wound to Crane, he said, "It sounds as if someone hit him with a heavy object. Most people with an ounce of sense wouldn't try to hit a big dog. I wonder why I didn't see him. I cover every inch of Foxglove Corners every day, at least twice."

"He was probably hiding from you, although he was willing to come with me. Have you seen any dogs running free lately? Collies in particular?"

I was thinking about Henry McCullough's lost Luke. If anyone was in a position to watch for a lost, strayed, or stolen dog, that person was Crane.

"Not since I picked up that brown dog. Why?"

"There's another lost dog in the neighborhood. His name is Luke. Lila described him as brown with a full white collar and a blaze. That's a white streak running down the middle of his face. He has a graying muzzle, and he's about eight."

"I'll be on the lookout for a dog like that. Who lost him?"

"Luke belongs to Henry McCullough, the man who owns the haunted house. I haven't met him yet, but I will. One way or another, I'm determined to solve the mystery of the vanishing Christmas tree."

The admiration in Crane's eyes was unmistakable and a little surprising. Usually even a passing allusion to a new mystery elicited one of his familiar warnings not to meddle in dangerous affairs or to let the police do the work they're paid to do. Apparently, he didn't consider my planned otherworldly investigation dangerous.

"That's mighty fast detective work, Jennet," he said. "Tell me how you found out who owns the house."

"Well, I haven't done anything yet. Henry McCullough came back to his house for the holidays, and then his dog disappeared. Do you think it's the curse at work?"

"Could be, but people who haven't come within a yard of a curse are losing their dogs right and left lately. I'd say it's a coincidence."

"You don't think—" I broke off as a terrible thought surfaced. "What?"

"That somebody could be taking the dogs?"

"Like a dognapper? Maybe. I've been wondering that myself. It happens from time to time."

The thought of someone stealing Halley sent icy needles jabbing through my heart. "That scares me to death."

"We don't know for sure that's what's going on," he said. "It's not time to panic yet. I'll look into it."

The waitress served our order then. As I broke the roll in two, I decided to push the thought of dognappers to the back of my mind for now and enjoy this unplanned interlude with Crane.

"So you're going Christmas shopping this afternoon," he said. "I'm surprised you waited so long."

"I am, too. I've had days and days, and I don't usually

procrastinate. Now, time is running out."

"Are you sorry you agreed to cook dinner for me on Christmas?" he asked.

I glanced at him and saw a teasing gleam in his eye. His question implied that the idea was his, but I had issued my invitation weeks ago when he'd returned from deer hunting. About some things, I didn't procrastinate.

When I first came to Foxglove Corners, I dreamed about having the perfect country Christmas in my new house. I planned to decorate the porch with evergreen roping and have a real tree instead of the artificial tabletop version that kept its needles forever and its decorations in place through the magic of a glue gun.

I'd have a fireplace, too, with a real fire in it. My imagination added the expertise to build a fire which, at the time, I lacked. Outside it would be snowing, the soft, fluffy kind of precipitation that did no harm. Here my vision of the perfect Christmas faded.

I hadn't met Crane then, nor even moved into my new house. I had no way of knowing how incomplete my vision of Christmas Future was. In the months since Crane and I had met, I'd added several embellishments to it.

Tomorrow I'd have to go grocery shopping in order to prepare the elaborate dinner I planned to cook for him. Also on the agenda was a trip to the vet for Halley who was chewing her paw again.

"Cooking dinner for you is exactly what I want to do, which is why I invited you," I said.

Crane set down his empty cup, brushed crumbs into his napkin, and reached for the check.

"I'll try to see you before Christmas, if I can, honey. It'll just be for a little while, though. I'm on duty straight through to Christmas morning. Everything's quiet around the Corners now, but that can change at any minute, just like the weather."

I followed him outside, and he walked with me to my car, holding his arm protectively against my back. He waited for me to get inside and start the engine.

"You be careful now," he said, for the third time this day. "It's a skating rink out there. I've seen three accidents already this morning."

Leaving this alarming vision hanging in mid-air, he got into his patrol car and drove away, like his ancestor, the Confederate cavalryman.

I imagined him in a gray uniform, riding a tired horse through an unnaturally quiet countryside, his gray eyes wary and alert, as he waited for the enemy to show his face, while I…

My imagination faltered. Kept the home fires burning?

I wondered if I could find a very special Christmas present for Crane, something Southern.

~ * ~

Lakeville, Michigan, wasn't the best place to find a present with a Confederate flavor, but I roamed in and out of the little stores on the street called Antique Row aimlessly until, finally, I found a small shop next to the Green House of Antiques. Apparently Cheryl's Imports had opened exclusively for the holiday trade. I went inside and looked down to read the welcome scrolled in gold on the floor tiles: *Bring home gifts from around the world to make your Christmas merry and bright.* This was the kind of store I'd been looking for.

I stepped over the scrolling and joined the shoppers, one of whom was black-haired Lucy Hazen, Foxglove Corners' resident horror story writer. Looking elegant in a long black coat and gold earrings, she was very much in her element among the English teapots and tins of imported tea. As a diversion, Lucy practiced the art of reading tea leaves.

"Hello, Jennet. Are you finishing your Christmas shopping today?" she asked.

"I haven't bought a single gift yet. I'm looking for something Southern for Crane, something special."

"How about a book on the Civil War?"

"He already has a large collection of non-fiction and veterans' memoirs. Collecting Confederate memorabilia is his hobby."

"I suppose a calendar would be too impersonal.

"That would be as bland as a dozen handkerchiefs. Sometimes he wears a hand-painted tie with a scene of General Lee surrounded by his men. I'd like to give him something like that."

"Well, I don't envy you your search," Lucy said. "I'm sure he'll like anything you give him."

That sounded like the prelude to a farewell, and I remembered
that I'd been intending to call her. "You used an old white Victorian house on Park Street as a background for one of your books, didn't you, Lucy?"

"Yes, for *The Devil's Bell*. That was a long time ago."

"You must know something about the house then. Did you research its history?"

Lucy's eyes grew bright with curiosity. "Yes, thoroughly. I have extra copies of the book somewhere. I'll give you one. Now, why are you asking about the McCullough place?"

As I told her what had inspired my question, she fumbled in her purse for a pen and scribbled a few notes on the back of an envelope. Maybe she was considering using me as a character in one of her horror novels. If she did, I hoped she wouldn't have me come to a gruesome end.

"You're not the first person who's had an unusual experience in that house, but I don't recall anyone else seeing a Christmas tree," she said. "I'm leaving in the morning to visit my sister in Texas. When I come back, we'll get together and have a nice long talk. I want to take notes."

Lucy gathered her selection of teas, wished me luck in my search for Crane's present, and went on her way. I turned to browse among the gifts from around the world and soon found everything I desired in this one shop, including a tall, colorful beer stein decorated with a majestic stag for Crane. It wasn't remotely Confederate, but Crane loved to go deer hunting.

Then, with all of my purchases in one shopping bag, I left and drove to the shelter. I wanted to know the vet's assessment of Winter's injury and, more important, if anyone had claimed him.

As usual, Park Street was quiet, and the park itself was deserted. I walked to the shelter and rang the bell. Over the noise of the puppies yapping in the yard, I heard a different barking from inside.

When Lila opened the door, there at her side stood Winter, wagging his tail. His coat was fluffier and more lustrous than I remembered. He seemed proud of his appearance, as well he might be.

"Come in, Jennet," Lila said. "I've been brushing and brushing him, and he only grows more beautiful. He's an absolute joy to groom, not like those impatient pups."

I stroked his head. "You do remember me, don't you, Winter?"

I thought he wagged his tail a little faster.

"Come join us in the kitchen," Lila said. "You're just in time for coffee and cake. Henry is here, and he's been telling us the most interesting stories."

Six

Henry McCullough abandoned his narrative to rise to shake my hand. "How are the roads out there, Miss Greenway?" he asked.

"Please call me Jennet. They're a little slippery. You have to drive carefully."

"That's always a good idea. These days I like to look at the snow from inside where it's warm and safe."

His dark blue eyes had a youthful sparkle. In all other ways, however, Henry McCullough was very old, with the weathered skin of a man who has lived a lifetime in the sun. Over his white shirt he wore a dark red cardigan.

He sat at the round kitchen table with his hands wrapped around the coffee cup, as if he hoped to draw warmth from it. His right arm rested on a stack of papers.

Winter appeared at his side and nudged his elbow, and Henry obliged him with an affectionate pat on the head. Satisfied with the special attention, the big blue collie walked over to Brown Dog's crate and lay down alongside it.

Lila said, "That's where Winter likes to stay. He's the only one of the dogs she'll allow near her. I'm so glad you found him, Jennet."

"He's older and more settled than the others. The younger

dogs may be too boisterous for her."

"Doctor Randolph says that Winter is around four or five years old," Letty said.

"How does the vet think he was injured?" I asked.

"Probably by a blow to the head."

"That's what Crane thought."

I couldn't imagine anyone aiming a blow at Winter's magnificent head, or striking a dog for any reason. Still, I wasn't so naïve as to suppose that this never happened.

"Otherwise, he's all right. He isn't even undernourished. I don't know how long he's been lost, but he must have found food somewhere."

"Has anyone reported him missing?" I asked.

"Not yet. We posted a note in the animal hospital and notified the Humane Society and dog pound. We're going to put an ad in the Lost and Found."

"Later," Lila said. "After Christmas. There's plenty of time."

I knew how she felt. Henry moved his arm, and I glanced at his flyer. He'd pasted a picture of Luke to it and lettered 'Have You Seen This Dog?' in black marker across the top. The description of Luke matched the one Lila had given me. Henry was offering a five hundred-dollar reward for the return of his pet.

He said, "My nephew made twenty of these. I don't think it's enough."

"I'm going grocery shopping tomorrow," I said. "I'll post the flyers around town for you, if you like."

"Thank you Jennet. I'd appreciate your help. I think that Luke tried to find his way back to Maple Falls. He's never known another home. There's no fence around this house, but I wasn't worried. He never wandered far from where I was before."

Privately I thought that Henry's explanation for Luke's absence was unlikely. Wouldn't a dog's home be where his owner was staying? Henry desperately wanted to believe that Luke had followed the road up north to Maple Falls, a Lassie-Come-Home in reverse. There would be no kindness in dissuading him when I had no other version to offer.

"I know he'll come home," Henry said.

Lila covered his hand lightly with her own in a gesture of sympathy. "We'll do everything we can to help you find him."

As Lila took a coffeecake out of a bakery box and Letty fussed with the coffeemaker, a comfortable silence descended on the kitchen. There could be no better time than the present to question Henry about his house.

"Old Victorians have always fascinated me, Mister McCullough," I said. "I've heard rumors that your house is haunted. Does it have a particular history?"

My words hung in the air. The last sentence especially sounded foolish. No one said a thing.

Henry's expression was grave, and he was quiet for so long that I was certain I had alienated him. I wished I could take back the words.

Finally he said, "You must be psychic, Jennet. We were just talking about haunted houses."

He looked around him at the cozy kitchen, at Letty, who was reaching for another cup, at Lila, slicing the coffeecake, and finally at Winter, keeping his vigil by Brown Dog's crate.

"My house does have a history, but it's something I don't usually talk about because I need to attract tenants," he said.

I leaned forward, eager to hear what he would say next. This mystery was going to be easy to unravel. In a few minutes, I might have the solution.

"The house must be over a century old," I said. "Was it haunted when you first came to live in it?"

"So far as I know, there was nothing remarkable about it, except for its charm. I had fifteen happy years there with my family before disaster struck. I'm sure the haunting began with me."

While we waited for him to continue, he accepted a slice of coffeecake from Lila. Then, while Letty poured coffee for me and refilled the other cups, he resumed his story.

"My daughter, Andrea, was killed on Christmas Eve in 1956. She was on her way home from college for the holidays. It was snowing that night, and I was worried about her driving alone.

"The tree was in its usual place in the bay window. I was wrapping the presents, wondering why she was so late..." He broke off, as if he were remembering what had been in each one of those boxes intended for a daughter who had never arrived. "They're still in the attic, unless one of the tenants over the years moved them. I could never give them away.

"Her car skidded on an icy bridge and crashed into the water below. We didn't know about it until the next morning. She must have been killed instantly. That's the only fortunate thing. She didn't suffer."

"How terrible," Lila said.

"Yes, it broke my heart. Then, in the summer, my wife died. I decided that I was through with holidays and celebrations. A year later, I came home from work on Christmas Eve to find a tree in my house. It was decorated and strung with lights.

"At first I thought one of my neighbors had put it up while I was away, but there was something familiar about it. I'll swear it was the same tree we'd had the year before. I don't remember much about what happened afterwards. They say I had a mild heart attack. All I know is that when I came to, the tree was gone."

"So you imagined it?" Letty asked.

"At first I thought so. I was sure I was losing my mind. I didn't talk about it to anyone, but it was all I could think about. I began to wonder if Andrea had sent the tree as a sign to let me know that she was all right. That was when I started to read about haunted houses in Michigan."

"Did you ever see the tree again?" I asked.

"No, but after that first shock, I wanted it to come back. I'd convinced myself that in some way, the apparition was connected to Andrea. The next Christmas Eve I waited up all night, but it didn't appear. In all the time since, nothing out of the ordinary ever happened to me again."

"That's the strangest story I ever heard," Letty said. "To think we're living next door to a haunted house."

"How long did you live there?" I asked.

"For only a few more years. I wanted to move up north to be closer to my sister, but I couldn't bring myself to sell the house, so I rented it. The stories began with the first tenant. There were supposed to be places in the house that seemed colder than others, a scent of balsam floating through the air, and the sound of weeping—all the usual ghostly trappings. A few people claimed they saw a Christmas tree materialize in the bay window and then vanish."

"How did you know all this if you were living up north?" I asked.

"From the people who used to live in this house before it became a shelter. We kept in touch. It was always in the back of my mind to come home some day."

"What made you return now?" Letty asked.

"I want to spend one last Christmas in my house. I've always wondered if some day the tree would return. I'm stronger now, and I won't be alone. My nephew and his family are coming down to spend the holiday with me. But now I've lost again. Luke is gone."

Now was the time to tell him, I thought. Now, before he grew too despondent over losing Luke.

"I didn't ask about your house out of idle curiosity, Mr. McCullough," I said. "Last Saturday I saw the Christmas tree apparition. I particularly noticed the tinsel."

"Why didn't you say anything, Jennet?" Letty asked.

"I wasn't sure then."

Henry said, "So the haunting is still around. That tinsel, Jennet... Andrea and I could never agree about the proper way to place it on the tree. I did it the proper way, hanging one strand at a time. She'd throw it into the branches in bunches. I decorated the last tree alone. That's how I knew it was one Andrea never saw."

Lila was dabbing at her eyes with a tissue. "That's the saddest story I've ever heard. Well, Henry, if Jennet saw this phantom tree last week, maybe you'll see it, too."

"Maybe, but I'm not counting on it. I haven't seen anything out of the ordinary yet. All day I sit in my rocker at the window and watch the dogs when you let them out in the yard to play. And I wait for Luke."

He looked away from us, down at the picture in the flyer.

I said, "I'm glad I'm not the only one who saw the tree, but I still don't understand where it came from and why it appeared."

With a sigh, Henry gave his empty plate to Letty, who was clearing the table. "I guess we're not supposed to understand."

"Did the house get its reputation for being unlucky because of the haunting?" I asked.

"Partly, I suppose, but that was a separate rumor. There was no truth to it. My tenants' misfortunes were very run-of-the-mill, like failed marriages, a fall down the stairs, and bankruptcy, the kinds of things that happen to people every day."

I drank the last of my coffee. The desire to return to my own familiar world was sudden and powerful. As fascinated as I'd been by Henry's story, I felt disoriented now, almost as if I'd spent an hour in another time. The sight of the blue dog asleep beside the crate brought me back to reality.

I picked up the stack of flyers, got up, and gave Winter a farewell pat. He woke up and wagged his tail once.

"I may not be able to explain an apparition, but I hope I can help find Luke for you, Mr. McCullough," I said. "I have to be on my way. All of you, have a Merry Christmas."

We exchanged goodbyes, and Lila promised to contact me if Winter's owner came to claim him.

After hearing about Henry's experience, I felt a little better about having seen the phantom tree. Misery loves company, as does the fear of the unknown. If I ever saw a supernatural manifestation again, however, I hoped it would be a happy one whose significance I could easily understand—a gazebo decorated for a summer wedding, with garlands of roses and ivy, for example.

Seven

The patients who barked and meowed their displeasure at finding themselves in the waiting room of the Foxglove Corners Animal Hospital were an amusing bunch. There was a preponderance of large dogs today, most of them extremely vocal, and a few aloof cats hiding in their carriers. In a crate, two chocolate colored puppies alternated frolic with sleep, as they waited for adoption.

Set at a safe distance apart from the rest of us was something concealed in a large wooden box. Whether this was for its own protection or ours was unclear. Most of the dogs eyed the box with hostility.

"A snake? There's a snake in there?"

I heard the whispered words and occupied myself by trying to guess if the box really contained a reptile. Whatever kind of creature waited inside, I doubted that it was warm and fuzzy.

Holiday cards, illustrated with snapshots of the hospital's clients, adorned the walls of the waiting room. In one corner stood a Christmas tree decorated with bones and biscuits that couldn't be real because all the dogs ignored them. The tinny jingling of silver bells on the collar of a massive St. Bernard reinforced the holiday atmosphere.

Doctor Randolph, whom we were supposed to see, was in

emergency surgery, so our appointment was with Doctor Foster. This was my first visit to the animal hospital. Halley was a new patient. Until her recent paw-chewing obsession, her health had been excellent, and she had no shots or boosters due until the spring.

She lay at my feet, her delight in being with her own kind apparent. Every now and then, she tried to nip at a nearby wagging tail or lunge at someone who was paying her a compliment. Her antics made us the center of attention.

My grip on her leash today was so tight that my hand ached. I had finally realized something that should have been clear to me days ago.

As I'd posted Henry's flyers this morning, I'd seen numerous notices of lost dogs tacked to poles all over town. Two such papers were posted here on the hospital's bulletin board, among ads for pet sitting and grooming services and the newsletter of the Siberian Husky Rescue League.

One flyer in particular caught my attention because of the fuzzy picture of the black and white husky mix. Pepper, who had disappeared in the Wolf Lake area, suffered from seizures and needed medication. Her owner offered a reward of an unspecific amount for her return.

The high number of lost dogs had gone far beyond coincidence. Foxglove Corners was in the grip of a virtual epidemic. While we had been distracted by holiday plans, the dognappers had quietly moved into our area to ply their deadly trade.

I knew that the theft of dogs for sale to research laboratories was a lucrative business. Like some grotesque monster that thrived on the lifeblood of the helpless, the market was in constant need of fresh subjects. Research scientists were able to pay high prices for the dogs they acquired. An owner's reward was irrelevant to the dognappers. The scientists had more money in their coffers.

The dognappers were probably closing in on Foxglove Corners even as I sat here thinking about them. How many times had Halley stared into the woods beyond the lane at what I'd assumed was nothing? And why had I thought that her frequent low growling was directed toward some wild creature?

I'd read that dog stealers moved stealthily and quickly. To entice dogs to their doom, they used chunks of meat laced with tranquilizers and other lures. Dogs left unattended became prime targets. The thieves would be miles away before an owner realized that his dog was missing. No matter how many flyers he posted or rewards he offered, the pet would never be seen again.

In October, Caroline Meilland, the murdered animal activist, had posted pictures of emaciated laboratory dogs on her Wall of Suffering. Held fast in restraints, they looked as if they were already dead, but still, they were considered valuable for use in experiments. I hadn't been able to look at the pictures for long, but I 'd never forgotten them.

I thought about Luke, and a great coldness enveloped me. It was almost a physical pain.

By leaving Halley in her run unattended all day while I was teaching, I was putting her at constant risk. I didn't know how I could have been so careless with the dog who mattered so much to me. *My precious black collie.*

"Ms. Greenway? You can bring Halley in now."

Hearing her name, Halley turned her head. Her brown eyes were alert, and her ears tipped at a show-ring perfect angle. I turned, too

In the hallway that led to a series of examining rooms stood a smiling young woman. She had long flaxen hair and wore a white coat over her pink dress.

"I'm Dr. Foster," she said. "You can take Halley to Room

Two."

I led Halley past the closed door of Room One, from which came an indignant yelping. Dr. Foster followed us into the room, closed the door, and consulted the chart in her hand. Halley stood regarding her, wagging her tail in happy anticipation of some good thing.

"How is Halley today?" Dr. Foster asked.

"She's well, except there's something wrong with her front paw, the right one. She keeps chewing it. I can't get her to stop."

Her dark eyes suddenly wary, Halley watched as Dr. Foster approached her, but she relaxed when the young vet's hands began to move gently and expertly over her body. They came to rest on the troublesome paw.

"I've looked, but I can't see anything there," I said

"I can. Right here."

Working so swiftly that I'm sure Halley never realized what was happening, Dr. Foster removed the offending object as deftly as a mother might take a splinter from a child's finger.

"Here. It looks like a thorn."

"But the ground is covered with snow."

To prove her point, Dr. Foster held up the miniscule object. "Nevertheless, it's a thorn."

"That's what it looks like, but I don't understand. I've never seen any roses growing where I live."

"Well, it's gone now."

It was pointless to speculate how Halley had acquired a thorn in December or how long it had been lodged in her pad. I wondered why I hadn't seen it.

As Dr. Foster rubbed ointment into Halley's pad, she said, "You are such a good girl, Halley. She should be fine now, Ms. Greenway."

"Thank you, Dr. Foster," I said. "Ready, girl?"

Unmindful of her newly treated paw, Halley almost bolted out of the door without me.

I liked Dr. Foster very much. With her calm and gentle approach, she would be probably good with all creatures, even nervous or aggressive ones—even the snake.

"Our original appointment was with Dr. Randolph, but I'd like to see you again when I bring Halley in for her shots," I said.

Dr. Foster looked pleased. "I'll be looking forward to a return visit. We'll send you a card when her shots are due. There are some tasty bones for you at the desk, Halley. Ms. Greenway, have a Merry Christmas."

A few minutes later, as I stood in line waiting to pay my bill and trying to keep Halley away from the ferocious looking German shepherd in line with his owner behind us, an older man in a white coat, came out of the hall. He stepped up to the desk and began writing on a chart.

With his curly grayish-red hair and a tie in a busy holly berry pattern, he resembled an overgrown elf. When Dr. Foster joined him for a brief consultation, I realized that he must be Dr. Randolph finished with his surgery.

A visit to an animal hospital never failed to energize me, especially when the outcome was pleasant, but the feeling was short lived. On the way out, we passed the bulletin board with the lost dog flyers. In this season of good will, the specter of the dognapper cast an ominous shadow over Foxglove Corners.

Maybe one of the dognappers' tricks was to scatter thorns in the areas where dogs walked, hoping the irritation and pain would slow them down, making them easier to capture. Or was I being paranoid?

Set alongside my recent troubling glimpse into the supernatural, this new concern, with its grounding in the real world, was more immediate. I would have to deal with it swiftly, and I would need help.

~ * ~

"Do you think I'm being an alarmist?" I asked Camille later that afternoon.

We were sitting in her cozy country kitchen, surrounded by trays of golden pastries shaped like bow ties. Camille stood over them with a bowl of powdered sugar in her hand, giving them a liberal sprinkling.

The confections were *chrusciki*. They were featured in her new Polish Christmas cookbook that wouldn't be out until next year. I had come over in time to enjoy a preview sample.

In Camille's kitchen, all problems were manageable.

"I've heard about dogs vanishing in and around Foxglove Corners before, but not in recent years," she said. "I don't think you're overreacting, Jennet. You can't be too careful when your dog is in jeopardy."

I handed her the afternoon edition of the *Banner*. "Then there's this." The story was on the front page.

> *Collie Thefts Under Investigation*
> *Ellentown, Michigan—(AP)—*
> *Nineteen Ellentown residents have reported their dogs stolen in recent weeks, leaving town officials without an explanation.*
> *Katherine Curran of Animal Control doesn't understand why the stolen dogs were all collies.*
> *In nearby Maple Falls, five cases of dognapping have been reported in the past week.*
> *"All collies again," said Curran, "except for one Shetland sheepdog. It's a mystery."*
> *According to Deputy Sheriff Jake Brown, "It's like someone caught them all up in a giant net. We have no clues, whatsoever, at this time."*

"That settles it," Camille said. "Do you think Crane has read this?"

"I'm sure he has. He always reads the *Banner*. I don't think I'll see him before Christmas, but I'll ask him then. In the meantime, what do you think?"

"About the Ellentown disappearances?"

She had finished sprinkling sugar on one batch of *chrusciki* and was working on another. The table was getting a slight dusting of powdered sugar, as was the floor.

"There's the Twilight Zone explanation and the obvious one," she said. "I agree with you. It looks like a dognapping ring is operating in the area. As to why collies in Ellentown, I have no idea."

"As you can imagine, that detail struck terror in my heart," I said. "Deputy Sheriff Brown's figure of speech is quite creative, isn't it? I'd like to meet him. I wonder if Crane knows him."

"You can always ask him and have him introduce you, if he does."

"I guess I could. I think I know why so many of the missing dogs are collies. Besides Colliegrove, there are two other collie kennels within a radius of seventy-five miles of Foxglove Corners. They always have pet quality pups for sale. We're living in a rural area, and they're wonderful dogs on farms, or anywhere, for that matter."

I rested my hand on Halley's head. I found that I was petting her even more than usual, as if that alone could ensure her safety; and I didn't want to let her out of my sight.

I'd taken her with me on this brief late day visit to Camille. She lay beside her best canine friend, Twister. Both of them were as close to the *chrusciki* as they could get without actually begging, their attention fixed on Camille's sugar tossing activity.

I'd always felt safe when Twister stayed with me, but I knew that a determined dognapper could lure any dog into his trap.

"I can't see your run from my house, Jennet," Camille said. "Even if I could, someone might snatch Halley while I wasn't looking. It doesn't take very long. When you go back to school, you can leave Halley with me or, if you'd rather, leave her locked inside your house. I'll go over and let her out around mid-morning and later in the day."

Although I'd hoped Camille would make this kind of offer, neither solution was ideal, except as a temporary arrangement. Left inside alone all day, Halley would grow bored and lonely, but I was afraid that having two rambunctious dogs in the house all day might prove too taxing for Camille.

"I'd really appreciate that, Camille, but only as a temporary measure. I have to earn a living, but I don't have to teach in a school that's so far away. Next year, I might look for a job closer to home. That would cut almost two hours from the time I'd have to leave Halley alone."

"You don't really want to do that, Jennet, do you?"

"I love teaching at Marston, but I can't see any other way right now except to catch these dognappers and put them out of business."

She looked at me in amazement. "I can imagine Crane's reaction."

"We can start by making it a town project. The first thing is to make people aware of what's going on. If they make sure their dogs are never left alone, there won't be any dogs to steal."

"That'll take care of the pets," she said, "but what about the poor strays? They don't have anybody to look out for them."

Camille set the empty bowl in the sink and covered one of the trays with bright green plastic wrap. "I don't know how we can help them unless we can get them to the shelter. It's all too horrible to think about, but we have to stop the dognappers."

"We have our strategy for Halley's safety mapped out. I'm going to be home for two weeks, and I'll come up with a plan. Could you stop over sometime before Christmas and see my tree? I have a present for you."

"I'll come tomorrow, and try not to worry. We're forewarned. You know what they say about that." Camille handed me the covered tray. "Here's some extra dessert for your Christmas dinner. Crane loves them."

"When I first came to Foxglove Corners, I thought it was the safest place in the world," I said.

"It will be again."

As I walked home, holding tight to Halley's leash and managing both collie and *chrusciki* tray without a single mishap, I realized that I felt better, but only about Halley. Among the lost were Luke, Cinder in Maple Falls, Pepper, the husky mix who needed her medication, and countless other hapless dogs to find—if that was still an option.

Taking on the dognapping ring was going to be one of the most difficult things I had ever done. Already I knew what to do first. That night, I would write a letter to the Editor of the *Banner*.

Eight

Like miniature peppermints dropping into a candy jar, one by one the ingredients for my perfect country Christmas fell into place, except for the snow. There wasn't any to speak of. Only a trace of the last snowfall remained on the ground, held there by the cold temperatures, but the white shadings on the landscape were sufficient to create the illusion of a winter wonderland.

It didn't matter. With the last ornament on the tree, the turkey on its way to the oven, and Crane knocking on the door, my Christmas was complete. All I had left to do was slide *The Nutcracker Ballet* into the CD player.

Wearing his sheepskin jacket over a gray sweater with a falling snowflake pattern, Crane looked like the winter personified. His smile was as bright as a glimpse of the sun on a December morning. He was carrying the Christmas cakes, presents, and movies from the video rental store.

"You're up early for a man who's been working all night," I said.

"It was a pretty quiet night."

He set the cakes on the kitchen counter and slipped one of the packages under the tree. Then he unwrapped a new red collar and fastened it around Halley's neck, admiring the way its bright color contrasted with her fur. This done, he kissed me under the sprig of mistletoe taped to the Tiffany light fixture.

"Merry Christmas, honey," he said. "Mmm, you smell good. Sort of like a ginger cookie."

Then he held me away from him to read the quotation lettered on my red apron. A slow smile crossed his face.

"Come woo me, woo me, for now I am in a holiday humour and like enough to consent."

I felt my face grow warm. Was the provocative quotation too much? No, I decided. Definitely, absolutely no.

"Since you're not often in a holiday humour, I'm going to take you at your word," he said. "Now or later?"

"Later," I said. "I've got a dinner to get together first. Shall I make you some coffee or breakfast? We won't be eating until four or so."

"I had jelly donuts at home, but coffee would be good. It's cold out there. If you like, I could build a fire now and then later take Halley out for an extra long walk in the woods. Twister can come, too."

I filled the percolator and plugged it into the outlet on the stove. "That sounds like a good idea. So you had a quiet night?"

"More so than usual. Four ice skaters were reported missing over near Lost Lake. Their folks thought they fell through the ice."

"Did they?"

"It turns out they went for a winter hike in the woods and got lost. Eventually, they found their way back to the road. Mainly, I've been dealing with speeders. People drive seventy miles an hour and more on these country roads, like there's no one else in a car out there."

"Crime must be taking a break for Christmas," I said.

"So it seems. So far."

He sat down at the table, and Halley, who knew the words *walk* and *Twister*, sat beside him, alert and eager, waiting to hear more.

"Did you see the article in the *Banner* Wednesday about the stolen collies in Ellentown?" I asked.

"I did, and they ran a follow-up story about the girl in Maple Falls who lost her dog. Six people offered to give her a new puppy. She thanked them but turned them all down."

"You can't replace a dog like you can a stolen bicycle. About the Ellentown story, Crane, do you know anything more about it? Information the paper didn't print?"

"Not about the Ellentown collies, but I know Jake Brown. Do you want me to ask him?"

"Yes, if you would."

"You're thinking about Halley."

He dropped his hand down to pat her. She laid her ears smoothly back against her head and gazed at him expectantly.

"I've been thinking about her, too," he said. "It looks like the dognappers are in business again. You shouldn't leave her outside in the run all day. You're taking a chance."

"I came to the same conclusion."

"By my calculations, the thefts happened over the last two weeks. I haven't heard of any other new cases. Have you?"

"No, but they've probably already taken all the dogs they could get. Will they stop now, do you think?"

"There's no profit for them in stopping. More likely, they've moved on for a while. They tend to follow a specific route, from Maple Falls, then south to Foxglove Corners and now Ellentown. That's only thirty miles to the east of us. They keep moving."

"Then do you think they're gone?"

"For now, but sooner or later, they always come back. The next time they show up, we'll be ready for them."

"But what can we do now?"

"The FCPD is sending warning letters to all dog owners in the area and to grocers to watch for anyone buying unusually large amounts of dog food. If a patrolman sees a dog left alone in a yard, he stops and alerts his owner to the danger. I tracked down a man who was suspected of dognapping last year, but he checks out all right."

I hesitated before putting the unthinkable into words. "I hope that's not what happened to Luke. He's an old dog, and Henry McCullough has lost so much already. I feel connected to Henry because he once saw the phantom Christmas tree, but it's too sad a story to tell on Christmas. I wish I could find his dog for him."

"There's practically no chance of that, honey," Crane said. "Luke is probably in another state by now. Possibly he's changed hands several times. That's if he's still alive."

I thought Crane would say something like that. I knew he was right, but I tended to balk whenever someone claimed there was nothing to be done. Couldn't we hope for a Christmas miracle, even though Christmas was already here and, so far as I knew, Luke wasn't?

"I wonder if Winter escaped from a dognapper," I said. "That would explain his wound."

"Could be. He'd have to be pretty clever, though. You say that he is. The little brown dog must have met up with them, too."

The coffee was bubbling on the stove. I brought the mugs down from the cupboard and filled them with the steaming dark brew. The smell and taste of coffee in the morning was rejuvenating. Like Camille's blue and white kitchen, it reduced even the impossible to manageable size.

"Have you seen any more ghosts?" Crane asked.

"No, thank heavens. I don't want to."

"Well, then," he said, "you watch the turkey and I'll walk Halley for you. Aren't we supposed to be merry on Christmas? Tomorrow is soon enough to deal with dognappers and ghosts."

Crane was right, of course. He almost always was.

He finished his coffee and went into the living room where he set about building a fire. Halley pranced and whined around him. She hadn't forgotten his offer of a walk and was probably wondering why he was keeping her waiting.

In the meantime, I reviewed the status of my own projects in the kitchen. The turkey was in the oven where it would stay until mid-afternoon, demanding only occasional attention. The cranberries were cooked and cooling, and the Brussels sprouts and rice could wait until much later.

In honor of Crane's Southern heritage, I had baked cornbread muffins. They were neatly stacked in a star-shaped wire breadbasket. Finally, thanks to Crane's Aunt Becky, we had two cakes for dessert, along with Camille's *chrusciki*. Everything was nicely under control.

Why I had been regarding this Christmas dinner as elaborate was a mystery to me. It was simple, except for the stuffing, which had involved several steps as well as bowls, utensils and a frying pan to wash. Now when Crane came back from walking the dogs, I could join him at the fireside and enjoy our time together, while my dinner finished preparing itself.

Crane said, "If you're lonesome for ghosts, I rented us two movies for after dinner. *A Christmas Carol*, the George C. Scott version you said was your favorite, and *Scrooged*. That's the one I like."

"Every Christmas I watch at least one version of *A Christmas Carol*. I think the apparitions in the Scott movie are the best." I wondered if I was going to keep running into the supernatural even in my home and on this day.

Crane put the finishing touches on the fire and lit the

candles

on the mantel. When the flames were leaping and Halley had withdrawn to wait patiently by the kitchen door for her promised outing to materialize, Crane and I sat down in front of the fireplace, and he fell to reminiscing about his past Christmases in Tennessee.

"We always spent Christmas with my Aunt Becky in the Smokies. She lives in a log cabin, the kind I'm going to build some day. We used to cut down one of the trees on her land and decorate it with old homemade ornaments, nothing fancy. We'd hang greens in every room. All the aunts and uncles and cousins would be there.

"One year, Aunt Becky gave me a Lionel train, and my dad set it up around the tree. Then every year, she gave me a new boxcar for Christmas. I could hardly wait to open my present, even though I knew what it was. I'd play with that train for hours. I used to want to be an engineer when I grew up."

Crane gazed into the fire, as if he could see that cabin room in the leaping flames. "I still like trains. Whenever I see one, I stop and watch it go by.

"The adults would all sit around the fire and tell family stories. That's how I learned how our family fared during the War. Now my relatives are scattered all over the South and West, but most everybody gets together once a year for a Christmas reunion."

"I'm sure you miss them, Crane," I said.

But I hope you're not wishing you were with them now. This Christmas with you is going to be the best one of my life.

I didn't say the words out loud. I wanted to tell him this, but I didn't. Suppose he didn't feel the same way? I was surer of him now than I'd been even a few months ago, but sometimes my certainty seemed as far away as a memory of a childhood Christmas.

I remembered my own family opening presents around the Christmas tree. Now, only my sister, Julia, was left. She lived out West, but we kept our bond alive through telephone calls and infrequent visits. She had called early this morning to wish me a Merry Christmas, and I'd told her that Crane was going to spend Christmas with me.

"That's wonderful, Jennet. I'm looking forward to meeting him," she'd said.

Crane tossed a piece of leftover wrapping paper on the fire and stood back, staring into the flames. The warmth was wondrous and inviting. How had I ever lived without the luxury of a fireplace? I drew nearer to the fire and to Crane and encircled his waist with my arms.

"I'm so glad you're here," I said.

He covered my hands with his own. "Maybe I'd better take the dogs for their walk now."

~ * ~

When they returned from their hike in the woods, Crane announced that he was famished, and Halley headed for her water pail and lapped noisily for several minutes. Then she crawled into her crate and lay down, with her head resting on her empty food dish.

"What did you do to my dog?" I asked.

"She's worn out. I thought I'd have to carry her back. Twister wasn't any livelier. You and Halley can't be getting enough exercise now that winter is here. Did you give up walking?"

"No, but I don't enjoy being outside when it's cold. I don't take her so far."

"I thought we could go down the lane a ways after dinner," Crane said.

"It'll probably be dark by then."

I'm sure Crane didn't realize it, but I considered the entire day mine to orchestrate, and I had other plans. In my view, watching Christmas movies by the fire and other indoor activities were preferable to strolling in the bitter December cold for the sake of exercise.

"How about watching a movie until dinner is ready?" I asked.

"*A Christmas Carol*?"

"Whichever one you'd like."

He brought the tape in from the kitchen and slid it out of its case. "We'll play your favorite first. This year you'll see two versions of Scrooge."

Before joining Crane in front of the television, I slipped into the kitchen to double check on my dinner's progress. Nothing was burning, all was well, and we had hours of uninterrupted time together, that rare commodity. Nothing could find us here, neither the specter of an unruly English student, nor any outside force calling Crane back to duty. It was Christmas Day.

~ * ~

I handed Crane a knife and the platter. "I'm counting on you to carve the turkey."

"I can do that," he said and set to work, expertly transforming the bird into slices of dark and white meat neatly stacked on the platter.

While Crane carved the turkey, I brought the rest of the dishes into the dining room. Then, when everything was in place, I stepped back and surveyed the table with an unaccustomed feeling of pride.

I wasn't a natural cook, so when I managed to create a sumptuous meal and present it elegantly, I was always a little surprised. Everything had turned out cookbook picture perfect, even the gravy, that perennial challenge for a novice.

Crane set the heavy platter on the table and held out one of the chairs for me.

"Everything looks great, honey. Are we ready?"

"Yes, just let me get an extra serving spoon."

All morning I had been so intent on creating a perfect dinner for Crane that I'd forgotten to eat breakfast and lunch. I had set out plates of nuts, crackers, and dip for Crane, but I'd been too busy to sample them myself. Now I ate a generous portion of everything and decided that the meal was truly good. From time to time, I glanced at Crane. Apparently, he thought so, too. The corn muffins, I noticed, were a particular success.

After dinner, we brought the cakes and coffee closer to the tree to open our presents. I reached for a box wrapped in shining silver paper and handed it to Crane. "This is for you. I thought it was something you'd like."

When he lifted the beer stein out of the tissue paper, I thought it looked even grander than it had in the store.

"I do like it very much," he said. "This looks like the buck I let get away last month. And here's a present for you. Merry Christmas, honey."

He laid the small box in my lap. When I opened it, I found a sparkling crystal bracelet. Against the black velvet that lined the box, the stones glittered like stars.

"It's so beautiful, Crane," I said. "I think crystals are lucky."

I held the bracelet up to the light, but he took it from me and clasped it on my wrist. Gently, I touched the hard stones. They were surprisingly warm.

"I remember that crystal necklace you used to wear last summer," he said. "I always liked that on you."

"I'll take both of them with me when we go to Snow Lodge."

"When we go to Snow Lodge," he repeated. His words were heavy with the promise of a wonderful new turn in our relationship, a new beginning.

~ * ~

By five-thirty, darkness had fallen, but inside, all was bright. We had firelight, candlelight, and the small clear star-shaped lights that shone on the branches of the tree. We were alone in a private, secret world. While we were watching the ending of *Scrooged*, it started to snow.

Crane walked back from the window. "A little light snow. It won't amount to much, but for everyone who wants a white Christmas, there's one in Foxglove Corners tonight, even if it came a little late."

He turned off the television and pressed the VCR rewind button.

I'd long since taken off my red apron, but I could tell by the look in Crane's eyes that he remembered its invitation. 'Come woo me, for now I am in a holiday humour and like enough to consent.' No, I'm *certain* to consent.

"By any timepiece, it's later, Jennet," he said. "You must owe me at least a hundred kisses. Come and sit by the fire with me."

He reached out his hands. I rose and took a few steps toward him, drawn to the silver in his eyes as if by a magnet.

"You have a bit of green ribbon in your hair," he said.

I reached up to take it, but his hand was there before me, caressing my hair lightly and pushing it back off my forehead.

"Your hair still smells like ginger," he said softly, as he transferred the green ribbon to his pocket.

"It's carnation."

"Whatever it is, it smells good."

He pulled the chair closer to the fireplace, some might say dangerously close, but now nothing felt better on my skin than the hot breath of the fire. Through the window I could see the snow falling, still and white. I would almost be able to hear it, except for the crackling of the fireplace flames and the beating of my heart.

He sat down and pulled me onto his lap, and my arms moved
as if they had a will of their own, wrapping themselves around his neck.

"I was thinking that the best Christmas present of all would be you in my arms by the fire," he said.

"I'm here."

"When was the last time we really kissed?" he asked.

On Halloween night after my party, after everyone had gone home? No, there was that night in November before you left to go deer hunting, and one night a week later after the movie at the Carnival, and here in this room on the fourth night of December.

"I can't remember," I said. "I think it was in another season."

"Well, we're together now, honey, and at Snow Lodge we're going to have the whole weekend."

He reached for my left hand and lifted it. The candlelight and the firelight glanced off the crystals, setting them to sparkle like stars. The bracelet fell back a little from my wrist, and he raised my hand to his mouth and kissed it; then he turned it over and kissed my palm.

I moved my right hand across his face and mouth in a caress of my own. It was like touching fire. He pushed aside the long folds of my red dress, and I felt the sudden rush of heat from the flames and from his hand, as it rested heavily on my thigh.

Everything tonight, every single touch, made me think of fire.

The longing that held me in an iron vise was a familiar one. I had known that I wanted Crane five months ago, ever since that sultry midsummer evening when I had found my way into his arms by this very fireside.

No other man had ever come as near to my heart as this

roughhewn, gray-eyed deputy sheriff whose manner with me—
if not with the criminal element—was as gentle as a Tennessee
breeze.

The problem was that I wasn't sure how to carry this desire
over into reality, and I had done everything wrong. First, I had
taken a few steps backward, which I instantly regretted. Then
on another night, during a flame-heated encounter like this one,
Crane had done the retreating by suggesting a walk that
included Halley.

I remembered his words as clearly as if he had spoken them
tonight: "If we stay here now, I'm going to make love to you."

I wished I'd said, "Let's stay then." But I didn't, and I
couldn't go back and undo the past.

So the three of us had gone walking on the byroads of
Foxglove Corners, while a storm brewed overhead. Before the
summer was over, Crane had told me that, since he'd saved my
life, I belonged to him.

Surely, there was only one way to interpret that statement.
Of course, I could have disputed his claim that he had saved my
life, as it veered slightly from reality, but I didn't. I was no fool.
I liked the idea of belonging to him. At the time the power
dynamic implicit in Crane's statement didn't bother me. His
dictatorial nature was a part of him, and I liked the whole Crane
package.

We had weathered a few more storms since then, and now
we were in another season.

Setting thought aside, I kissed him, trying to show him what
I couldn't find the words to say. I kept kissing him and felt his
arms tighten around me in a grip that was almost painful. Every
individual part of my body began to dissolve in the relentless
onslaught of my longing and Crane's caresses.

I knew that he wanted me, too. I couldn't possibly be
mistaken about his desire. Was our first genuine romantic tryst

going to happen tonight then? After all, I was in a holiday good humour and like enough to consent.

"I wish it could be Christmas all year around," Crane murmured, as he lowered me gently to the floor. We weren't closer to the fireplace now, but it seemed as if the flames were reaching out dangerously close to my flesh, and the crackling of the fire was unnaturally loud, almost as if it were inside me.

But I was hearing another sound as well...

The annoying *beep beep beep* of Crane's pager brought me rudely into a different sphere, one considerably cooler. Saying, "I'm sorry, honey; I have to get this," he moved his hand from behind my shoulders.

As he listened to the caller, his expression became grave and his eyes cold. In a heavy voice he said, "I'm on my way."

And then with the briefest of farewells he was gone.

Nine

Crime hadn't taken a Christmas break after all. Crane didn't call that night. He wouldn't have told me what had happened anyway, as he never discussed official police business with me.

I heard the news on FGC Radio as I drove into town the next morning. While I had held the Deputy Sheriff of Foxglove Corners a captive by the fireside, in another part of the village, a shadowy murderer was snuffing out the life of one of its beloved citizens.

The victim was Dr. David Randolph, the veterinarian who had been performing emergency surgery while Dr. Foster removed the thorn from Halley's paw. An unknown assailant had robbed and strangled him in his own house on Christmas morning. Dr. Foster had found his body. Since there was no sign of a forced entry, it appeared that he had known his killer.

The story ended with a sad irony. Dr. Randolph, who loved animals so much, had no dog to protect him or sound the alarm. Earlier that week, he'd had to put his critically ill retriever to sleep.

As soon as I heard this alarming news, I decided to make a stop at the Mill House to buy a *Banner*. The next logical step was to go inside and read the paper in a warm place while sipping a soothing hot drink.

The morning was bitterly cold, the news chilling, and the last little bit of warmth that had remained with me after my interrupted fireside interlude in Crane's arms was gone. If only we had become lovers last night, I wouldn't be so aware of the arctic blast that enveloped me now as I made my way to the Mill House.

It was all about timing and Crane being one of the sheriff's deputies. Whenever something happened in Foxglove Corners, my claim on him always dissolved. But things were going to be different at Snow Lodge. I would have him all to myself then.

I looked for his patrol car in the parking lot, hoping to find him inside on his morning break. He wasn't there, but Susan Carter was. Her blonde hair was braided into a thick plait today, and her customary effervescence was as neatly contained as her hairstyle.

She gave me one of her fleeting smiles. "Are you alone this morning, Ms. Greenway?"

"Yes, and I don't need a table, Susan. I only stopped in for a hot drink."

"You can have a table anyway. We're not busy this morning. Take this one here." She led me to a booth with a view of the mill house and handed me a menu.

As I set the *Banner* down, Susan's eyes lingered on the headline. "Isn't it terrible about Dr. Randolph?"

"It sure is. It's frightening to think there's a strangler on the loose."

She touched her throat. "Crane will keep us safe."

"That's what I was thinking. I'll have a cup of hot chocolate, please, and a cinnamon roll." Seized by a spirit of wanton recklessness, I added, "With whipped cream and marshmallows in the chocolate, please."

When Susan left, I unfolded the paper and began to read its more detailed coverage.

This was the second murder of the year in Foxglove Corners, the first being the shooting of the animal rights activist, Caroline Meilland. Before that killing, Foxglove Corners had enjoyed a long stretch of peace and obscurity. There hadn't been a murder here in twenty years.

Gradually, my sense of safety was eroding. I could almost feel the ground giving way beneath me. First Caroline's murder, then the threat of dognappers, and now the presence of a strangler. We still had country quiet, but the peace was gone.

From the front-page story, I learned that Dr. Randolph was a native of Foxglove Corners who had practiced veterinary medicine in the same animal hospital for nearly twenty-five years. He had often provided pro bono veterinary services, and frequently visited the public schools as a volunteer lecturer. He had no known enemies. Still, according to the news account, he might have known his killer.

Next to the article was a picture of Dr. Randolph. I remembered him from that brief glimpse I'd had of him at the hospital desk. With his curly hair and holly berry tie, he had reminded me of a Christmas elf.

On the Obituary Page, I read that he was a widower with grown children. His daughter attended Michigan State's School of Veterinary Medicine, and his son was a practicing vet in the Upper Peninsula.

I folded the paper again and set it aside. Slowly, I drank my hot chocolate, savoring every sip. I was in no hurry this morning and had no special destination in mind. What had sent me out on the road was a restless spirit that was foreign to me. No doubt it was kin to the reckless spirit who craved whipped cream and marshmallows in her hot chocolate.

While I had thoroughly enjoyed the rare down time of my Christmas vacation—in particular, certain segments of it—I now found myself yearning to be on the move. So—should I visit the Green House or the post-Christmas sales at Warringtons, or both? Green's and Warrington's were equally appealing, but I realized that I didn't really want to go to either place.

Drifting aimlessly through my days wasn't my habit. By the

time I had drained my cup and finished the last bite of cinnamon roll, I had chosen a destination. If I visited the animal shelter, I could check on Winter and also find out if Henry had seen the phantom Christmas tree again. Also, I might learn more about the murder from Lila and Letty.

In other words, I was finally filled with purpose. Moved by the spirit of the season, I left a generous tip of my own for Susan Carter. Maybe that would convince her to stop flirting with Crane.

~ * ~

The roads to town were in good condition. Some of them were actually plowed. As usual, I appeared to be the only one going somewhere today, but that was fine. It was a pleasure to have the roads of Foxglove Corners to myself.

The sun was shining, and most of last night's snow had disappeared into the frozen ground. The little that remained glittered in the sunlight. It was as if someone had taken a giant sugar shaker and sprinkled the countryside with diamond dust. Lost in my contemplation of the winter-bright day, I almost passed the sign on the oak tree without reading it.

'Free puppies—This way!' A wobbly arrow pointed east. Wet snow had obscured the letters and the arrow, creating the impression that they were melting. But the words were still distinct, and they issued an unmistakable invitation:

Welcome, dognappers! Come and get them. Do with them what you will. You don't have to work to meet your quota. Just stop here.

Searching for a place where I could safely turn around, I drove on about a quarter of a mile until I found a wide private driveway. In minutes, I was heading back to the oak tree, following the arrow down a long dirt road to the blue-sided ranch house where the unwanted puppies awaited homes.

I parked behind a rusty beige station wagon and walked up to the porch. A large wreath with the traditional pinecones and red ribbon hung above the door. In the front yard, a giant snowball, the probable beginning of a snowman, had melted into a shapeless lump on the front lawn. Pieces of a broken sled lay on the porch, alongside a discarded jacket. In spite of the holiday wreath, my impression of the place was one of untidiness and uncaring.

The chunky young woman who opened the door wore faded jeans and a wrinkled white shirt with two missing buttons. From somewhere toward the back of the house, I heard children's voices raised in a heated argument.

She stared at me in an unfriendly manner. "Yes?"

There was nothing cordial in her voice either. I wondered if I had interrupted her in the middle of some important task.

I smiled. "Hi. I was driving by and saw your sign."

When she didn't react, I added, "Your sign for free puppies, the one on the tree."

That caught her attention, and she motioned for me to come inside.

"Yes, I have four puppies to give away."

"Could I see them please?" I asked. "Oh, my name is Jennet Greenway."

"They're back here. This way."

She led me away from the angry voices into a laundry room. Here, both the washer and dryer were running. The noise and disorder, along with the mixed odors of laundry detergent and dog, were overpowering.

In the corner I saw a child's playpen lined with newspapers and rags. Inside were four tiny bundles of light golden fluff in constant motion. As I knelt down in order to see the puppies more clearly, they scrambled over one another in a race to be the first to greet me.

"They're almost six weeks old," the woman said. "They're all alike, except for the one male. He's a little larger than the females."

"They're so adorable! Are you certain you want to give them away?"

She shrugged. "Sure. The sooner, the better. They're cute, but I can't keep them. I didn't ask for them to be born."

I forced back the comment I wanted to make. "Well, no, of course you didn't. You have no control over that. Do you own their mother too?"

"Yeah, Lady's around somewhere. She's a golden retriever. I have no idea what the father is."

"Aren't you afraid that someone might take one of your puppies and mistreat it?" I asked.

She looked at me in obvious confusion, as if I'd suddenly begun to speak in a foreign language.

"Why would anybody do that?"

She leaned over the side of the playpen, picked up the puppies, one by one, and put them down on the tiled floor. As soon as he was free, the male pup promptly darted toward the living room, whereupon the woman scooped him up and set him firmly back in the pen.

He began a frantic whining that made me long to pick him up and comfort him. In the meantime, two other puppies discovered a hard blue rubber ball, while the fourth one jumped up on me, balancing her tiny paws on my leg.

She was a pretty little creature, all soft and fluffy with fur the fresh yellow color of a spring daffodil. I picked her up, and she licked my face. She had only just seen me, but her dark eyes were filled with adoration.

"Since you don't want the pups anyway, could I take them all?" I asked.

Suspicion flashed in the woman's dark eyes, and they narrowed. "What do you want with four dogs?" she demanded.

"Well, they're all so cute, and I have plenty of room. Ten

acres."

"One," she said. "Take one."

"All right," I said. "It'll be this little golden girl. Now, are you certain you don't want any money for her?"

She hesitated, possibly wondering if she should have written 'Best Offer' on her sign instead of 'Free Puppies', but then she said, "No, I guess not. Another week, and I'll be paying to get rid of them."

I reached into my wallet and took out a twenty-dollar bill. "Please take this, for food, or to buy something for the others."

Quickly, she slipped the money into the pocket of her jeans. The transaction completed, I left the house with the puppy cradled in my arms.

Once I settled her in Halley's crate, she began to cry. I had taken her from a warm safe place to begin a journey to the unknown, and she was afraid. I couldn't do anything except talk softly to her and hope that my voice would reassure her.

Her misery lasted half the way to the Corners, until finally she grew quiet. I glanced in the rearview mirror and saw that she had fallen asleep.

"Don't be afraid, little one," I said. "You're going to a good place."

As soon as I dropped the puppy off at the shelter, I planned to call Leonora and Camille. I was sure they would be willing to stop at the blue house, choose a puppy, and take it to the animal shelter. If he wasn't too busy, Crane would probably volunteer to take the fourth pup.

The puppy was still sleeping when I arrived at the shelter. Gently, I lifted her out of the crate and walked to the porch, holding her as if she were a baby. She was awake now but suddenly still and quiet, like a living creature that had been turned to stone, a small garden statue in my arms.

Lila opened the door and stared. "Jennet! My goodness! What

do you have there?"

From somewhere in the house rose an instant canine clamor. The shelter dogs weren't sounding the alarm; they were welcoming a visitor.

"Her owner was giving her away, so I took her before someone with evil intentions could come along," I said. "Now you have six."

Lila took the small animal from me. "The poor thing. She looks too young to be taken away from her mother."

My charge was less rigid now that Lila was holding her. I remembered that Lila had a special way with animals.

Winter stood in the doorway, wagging his tail and eyeing the newcomer curiously. Letty, who was just coming in from another part of the house, didn't waste time on questions.

"Let's all go into the kitchen," she said. "Some nice warm milk is what this baby needs."

Now that the puppy's immediate fate was secured, I made a fuss over my last foundling who was nudging my hand as if to remind me of his presence. I stroked his shining blue coat and told him how beautiful he was. His fur felt and looked as if it had just been brushed.

"I'm so glad you still have Winter," I said. "Did you have a merry Christmas at the shelter?"

"Our Christmas Eve was very quiet and pleasant," Letty said.

"I thought I'd be homesick," Lila admitted. "I've never once been away from the farm for the holidays, but we had fun here. We met Henry's family, and the dogs kept us busy."

Her tone didn't convey Yuletide merriment, though. She seemed almost apprehensive.

"Did you hear about Dr. Randolph's murder?" she asked.

"I heard the news on the radio this morning. I guess times are changing everywhere. Do you know anything new?"

"Nothing at all. As long as we're surrounded by dogs, I feel safe." Lila lowered her voice. "But I was there, Jennet, at Dr. Randolph's house. It must have been just before he was killed. I only told the police—and Letty, of course."

"Good heavens, Lila! You were at the crime scene on Christmas morning?"

"I was delivering our Christmas fruit cakes," she said. "This year we have so many new friends. How could I have known that poor Dr. Randolph was about to get murdered?" She grabbed a tissue and dabbed vigorously at her eyes.

"You couldn't, Lila," Letty said. "I'm just glad you got out of there before that strangler came."

"I hope the police won't consider me a suspect because I was there," she said.

"What nonsense! They won't. I told you to forget about that."

"I don't want to talk about this any more—not now." Lila opened the refrigerator door. "We have a hungry new puppy in the house."

I watched her pour milk into a saucepan on the stove and turn on the heat. She worked briskly and effectively, bringing a small ceramic dog dish down from the cabinet, holding it under the faucet, and wiping it dry with a dishtowel.

"Six dogs should intimidate the most determined intruder," I said. "No one has to know they're mostly puppies unless they're out in the yard. The newscaster said that Dr. Randolph might have known his killer. Do you suppose he had an enemy?"

"That's impossible," Letty said. "Everyone liked him. I've never met a kinder man."

There was that word again. The murder of a kind man was difficult to understand. Now, if Dr. Randolph been generally disliked—the miserly town banker, for example—it would be different.

Lila poured milk into the dish and set it down for the puppy who lapped hungrily while Winter watched and licked his chops.

Actually, we were all watching this momentous event. The sound the little creature made drinking her meal seemed unnaturally loud.

"I'm going to ask my friends to take the rest of the litter, so you can expect three more pups. Have you heard about the ring of dognappers operating in the area?"

"Dr. Randolph sent us a letter before Christmas," Letty said. "We got one from the Police Department, too."

"You don't suppose that's what happened to Luke, do you?" Lila asked with a worried look. "I can't imagine a worse fate for a dog."

I saw no point in telling her that I'd had the same thought. "I hope not."

Letty said, "We'll take good care of the puppy, Jennet, and the others, if you bring them. I guess we'll be seeing Dr. Foster at the hospital now."

"You'll like her," I said. "I'm going to try to get the rest of the litter now. Wish me luck."

~ * ~

I called Leonora from my cell phone and explained the puppies' plight. I knew she had planned to fly back to Detroit on Christmas for a rest before her New Year's ski trip to Boyne Mountain. I hoped to catch her between flights.

She answered the phone on the sixth ring, but when I heard her voice, I realized that I'd awakened her.

"I'm sorry," I said. "I didn't know you'd still be sleeping. How was Vermont?"

"Wonderful, but cold. It's cold here, too. Next Christmas I'm going to Hawaii. Did your homespun country Christmas live up to your expectations?"

"It was even better than I hoped."

"Did Crane give you a diamond ring?"

"No, but he gave me a crystal bracelet."

"You're moving in the right direction."

"Do you think you could drive out to Foxglove Corners today?" I asked. "There's something I'd like you to do for me."

Leonora was always ready for an adventure, and I never doubted that she would be willing to take part in my rescue operation.

"Sure," she said. "What am I supposed to do?"

"I'd like you to pick up a giveaway puppy. Then we'll take it to the animal shelter. After we get her safely delivered, we can go looking for excitement, country style."

This was an inside joke of ours, dating from my first day in Foxglove Corners.

Leonora laughed. "That sounds like fun. Just give me a few hours. I'll be on your doorstep around one."

Next I called Camille. Helping animals in need was second nature to her, and she was eager to participate. I wouldn't be able to talk to Crane just now, but I had no doubt that he would probably phone me or stop by my house for a visit later. In all, it was turning out to be a very satisfactory day, although different from the aimless one I had started this morning.

Possibly the puppies might go to good homes in the area without our intervention, but it was more likely that the dognapper would chance upon the 'Free Puppy' sign and add them to his cache.

Caroline Meilland had once said, "Always remember that the smallest thing you do can make the greatest difference to all the creatures that share the earth with us."

That was something I didn't intend to forget.

Ten

Leonora's red Taurus skidded on a patch of ice and careened across the narrow, tree-lined road as she tried to regain control of the steering wheel. We came to rest at last in a high snow bank, only a few feet away from the wide trunk of a gnarled old tree.

"Well," I said, when I found my breath, "I guess we lived through that, but I don't want to do it again. Is the car all right, do you think?"

"Probably. This is a soft snow bank. It's a good thing there weren't any other cars for us to run into."

"We must be the only ones out driving in a snowstorm, but that's a mixed blessing," I said.

Hoping to see a sign of human habitation, I looked around, but we were alone on a deserted road bracketed with dense woods. "No one is around to help us, but we won't have to worry about being accosted. That's something."

Leonora put the car in reverse and accelerated in an attempt to break free of the snow bank. The wheels spun madly, but the Taurus didn't move backward. We were stuck, held·fast in a tenacious embrace of snow. Clearly we weren't going anywhere soon.

"What now?" she asked. "I can't believe I found the only

icy spot on the road. This is not my idea of excitement, Jen."

"I think you found the only snow bank, too."

We were stranded on one of those isolated country byroads with no name. Leonora had turned onto the scenic shortcut on our way home from the animal shelter where we had left the third puppy. Our rescue mission was now complete. A man had taken the male puppy before Leonora arrived. I hoped he was someone who only wanted a canine companion.

"I survived a few snow disasters in Vermont," Leonora said. "If I can master the slopes, I won't be stopped by a little snow-covered country road."

"Do you have a shovel in your trunk?" I asked. "I can clear the snow away from the tires."

"I'm afraid I don't. I never needed one before. You have a cell phone, though, don't you?"

"It's in my car."

She glanced at my large shoulder bag that lay on the seat between us.

"I don't suppose you have any food in your purse. A candy bar, maybe?"

"No, but we're in no immediate danger of starving. We'll freeze to death first."

"Seriously," she said, "what do we do now?"

Our answer came in the form of a light splattering of fresh precipitation on the windshield.

"Snow," Leonora said. "Of course. We're stranded in the middle of nowhere in the middle of winter, and it starts to snow again. I'm glad it's still daytime."

I didn't point out that we wouldn't have daylight much longer since it was already past five o'clock. I let her reference to midwinter pass. We weren't there yet. In our present situation, a little distraction would be better.

"This is a dilemma straight out of one of my old-time books:

Two girls find mystery and adventure when their car breaks down on a country road in a blizzard. Think of this as our real life adventure, Leonora."

I peered through the window, searching for a substantial piece of wood, a branch fallen from a tree, perhaps, something I could use to beat the snow away from the tires. Along the road there should be dead wood brought down by the high winds that had torn through Foxglove Corners earlier in the month.

I couldn't see anything but snow and stark, twisted trees. They formed grotesque shapes against a greenish sky filled with gray and orange clouds. None of the branches were within my reach.

"Do you see anything out there we could use in place of a shovel?" I asked.

"No, and I don't see any houses either," Leonora said. "Not anywhere. Only scenery. I'm sorry, Jen. We should have stayed on Spruce Road. Do you think there's a chance that Crane will come to our rescue?"

"That would be a nice development but an unlikely one. I think he stays on the main roads most of the time."

The unexpected snow had begun to fall at an inconvenient time. Usually, I never missed the weather forecast, but now that I was on vacation, I hadn't bothered to turn on the television. There was no place I had to be, even though I'd been in almost constant motion since leaving the house this morning.

This might be a passing snow shower or the beginning of a winter storm. With only the slightest chance that anyone else would pass this way, we had to take action quickly.

"We'll have to leave the car here and walk back to Spruce Road. If we're lucky, another car will stop and help us, or maybe we'll find a place with a phone so we can call a tow truck."

"Then we'd better start out while we can still see," Leonora said.

We got out of the car, and Leonora locked the door. I joined her and gazed down the road that had been our undoing. The snow was falling harder now. It felt more like a battering than a cool caressing. Soon it would chip away at our visibility, and the cold would sear our exposed skin.

Fortunately, we were both sensibly dressed in warm parkas with hoods, gloves and, most important of all, boots. Only our faces were at the mercy of the cold, but since our mishap had occurred shortly after we'd left Spruce Road, from this point, we would have only a mile or so to walk.

In spite of her warm clothing, Leonora was shivering. "Let's stay close together," she said.

I nodded. At first, we walked side by side on the narrow road. Soon I was trailing behind her and fantasizing about fireplaces, hot chocolate, and all warm and comforting things.

Leonora loved winter sports and was in top physical condition, whereas my usual winter exercise consisted of abbreviated walks with Halley. I suspected that our adventure would soon begin to lose its luster.

Before long, stinging sheets of snow battered our faces like a rain of sharp needles. The bitter cold found its way through the material of my parka. In spite of my lined gloves, a dull pain began in my hands and rapidly intensified. I moved my fingers, trying to ward off frostbite, and kept them in my pockets.

I began to think that I couldn't take another step. I did, of course, slipping on the slick surface, regaining my balance, and moving slowly forward. Eventually we reached Spruce Road. The traffic was non-existent, but about a quarter of a mile away, to the right, bright lights beckoned through the falling snow.

At last.

"Thank God," Lenora said.

Not being a frequent traveler on Spruce Road, I didn't know what sort of place lay ahead, but at this point, I wasn't going to hesitate. I was ready to take shelter in any haven that presented itself.

The closer we came to our destination, however, the more familiar it became. I knew this place. I had been here before, and only a pair of stranded travelers on a snowy night would consider it a haven. The Cauldron was a tavern with a shady reputation and a shadier clientele. Crane had once summarily dismissed it as a dive.

Now that salvation was at hand, we found the energy to walk faster, and soon we reached the crowded parking lot.

"This is why there aren't any cars on Spruce Road," Leonora said. "Everybody's here. Let's go inside."

"I've been in this tavern before," I said. "It isn't the fanciest place around, but any port in a storm will have to do."

"As long as they have heat," Leonora said, and she opened the door.

Once inside, I found the place to be wondrously warm, although dimly lit and crowded. During our long trek through the snow, I'd forgotten how it felt to be comfortable. I pushed back my hood and pulled off my snow-encrusted gloves.

The wood-cut witch, leftover from Halloween, still stood in the entrance. Given the name of the tavern, she was probably a permanent fixture. No one had thought to replace her pumpkins and lanterns with festive greens and candy canes, but then, Christmas trim wouldn't suit her. She was about as merry as the figurehead of a doomed ship.

Raucous country music blared from the jukebox, but it couldn't drown out the noise of about a hundred voices, all of them raised. The delicious smell of hamburgers frying on the grill compensated for the rowdy atmosphere, however, and reminded me how hungry I was. We had been busy rescuing puppies at lunchtime instead of eating.

"You find us a table, and I'll look for a phone," Leonora said.

She wandered toward the back, while I found an empty table in a shadowy corner. I eased myself out of my parka and hung it on a nearby coat rack. Then I pulled a chair out and sank into it. The hardwood seat couldn't have been more comfortable if it had been piled high with pillows.

I hoped that Leonora would make the call quickly and come back before someone noticed me and assumed that I was alone. The Cauldron was even more sinister than I remembered. Moreover, I didn't see a single holiday decoration, which was strange. Then, as if the walls had been listening to my thoughts, the country music gave way to "Jingle Bell Rock".

The people who frequented the Cauldron were probably ordinary enough, although the weak lighting and shadows made them appear threatening. Males with a rough and dangerous look outnumbered the few females and cast a pall over the surroundings.

I had no reason to think that drugs were being pushed with the witch's brew or that some rapist might be waiting in the shadows to drag me out to the isolated parking lot. It was only that I was tired, a condition that sets my imagination in motion. Or so I hoped. Finally, to my relief, Leonora appeared.

"I called a towing company," she said. "They'll come, but we'll have a two or three hour wait. Apparently we're not the only people who ran into trouble on the road today."

"Three hours!"

"At least we have a promise of rescue and a warm place to wait. We didn't have any specific plans. Adventure, country style, was our goal. This certainly qualifies as one."

"That's true. I'd rather be stuck in the Hunt Club Inn, but at least we can get a hamburger and hot coffee here."

"Yes, I'm famished," Leonora said. "While we eat, you can tell me more about your Christmas and the status of your romance with Crane. I've been admiring your bracelet. The stones look like diamonds. Your deputy sheriff has good taste."

Gently, I ran my hand over the glittering circlet on my left wrist. The crystals seemed to capture the heat from my body and hold it. They were warm—not sharp and cold, as they appeared. They were like Crane.

"Is he going to take you some place splashy for New Year's Eve?" Leonora asked.

"He'll be on duty. Somebody has to keep law and order in Foxglove Corners while everyone else parties."

"You can come up north skiing with me then."

"You know I'm not a good skier, Leonora. Crane invited me to go away with him to a place called Snow Lodge, but it won't be until after the first."

"That'll be fun, and much better than a date for New Year's Eve. This is more elaborate than his usual invitations. You're going, aren't you? You didn't say."

I touched my bracelet again. "Yes, I'm going."

"Well, that's good. You should go. I don't see any sign of a waiter. I guess we have to place our order at the counter. I'll do it. You look exhausted."

"If you will. A hamburger and coffee should revive me. Will you ask if they have dessert? Pie or something?"

"Hamburger, coffee and pie. Hamburger with relish, right? That's what I'll have, too."

No sooner had Leonora left the table than I noticed a man heading in my direction. I had no doubt about his destination and no place I could go to avoid the coming encounter.

He was a giant of a man, probably six feet, six inches tall, with a physique that can be best described as burly and an appearance that I considered menacing. He had a dark complexion and was in dire need of a shave. His expression was distinctly unpleasant, without the slightest hint of a smile. As he came closer, I saw that he had the cold dark eyes of a predator.

I knew I was leaping to a hasty judgement, based solely on the man's appearance, but in this case, I considered it warranted.

As he reached my table, he attempted a smile that warred with his glowering demeanor. Apparently he was a dog lover. His black shirt proudly proclaimed: I (heart) my Rottweiler.

He pushed one of the chairs aside and said in a gruff voice, "Hi. Care to join me for a drink? My name's Al Grimes."

I glanced at the Rottweiler head on his shirt. Giant and predator. I added a third image. Al Grimes had the air of an attack dog poised to strike.

His smile was gone, and he towered over me like a fairy tale giant about to pounce on his prey. "What's your name?"

"It's Jane," I said.

"Jane. That's a pretty name. How about that drink now?"

I looked over my shoulder with what I hoped was a fearful expression. "I wouldn't dare. My husband will be joining me in a minute. He'll be angry if he even sees me talking to you."

The giant seemed to comprehend this. "Okay. Later then," he said, and he lumbered off, just as Leonora arrived at the table with a hamburger plate in each hand.

"I'm sorry if I frightened your friend away," she said, setting one of the plates in front of me. "Who is that charmer?"

"Al Grimes. He loves his Rottweiler. I'm afraid it's going to be a long three hours."

"But an entertaining one, I'll bet. I hope you'll be all right if I go back for our coffee. Skip the pie, though. They only have cherry, and it looks like it came from a vending machine."

"We can have dessert at home, if we ever get there," I said. "I have two cakes from Tennessee."

When Leonora returned with the coffee and we began eating, I was almost immediately revived. While we ate, she entertained me with stories of her misadventures in Vermont and her dull plane ride home.

"It was fun, but next year, I want to have a quiet Christmas like yours with a turkey dinner, a glittering gift from an admirer, and a supernatural apparition. Did you see the phantom Christmas tree again?"

"No, but I know the story now."

I told her about Henry McCullough's Christmas Eve tragedy and what I knew about the curse and the past tenants of the white Victorian.

"I haven't had much time for ghosts lately," I said. "When I'm not rescuing dogs, I'm thinking about Crane and our trip to Snow Lodge."

I sensed that I had lost Leonora's attention. She was staring over my shoulder at something or someone. From her expression, she looked as if she were having a supernatural sighting herself.

"It's unbelievable," she said.

"What is?"

"A gorgeous man just came in. He's tall and golden-haired. Imagine a Renaissance angel in a ski sweater and blue jacket. He's over there sitting with your Rottweiler man. Talk about contrast. It's Beauty and the Beast."

I turned to see this vision who had moved Leonora to extravagant expression and recognized him instantly. He was a sometime animal rights activist and suspected doer of violent deeds for the Cause who, to my knowledge, had disillusioned at least one young girl before slithering out of town on the night of Caroline Meilland's murder.

"That's Emil Schiller," I said.

Leonora cast a surreptitious glance in Emil's direction. "I remember you mentioned him once. He was involved in Caroline Meilland's murder, wasn't he?"

"Emil was a member of her animal rights organization, but never a suspect. When Caroline was murdered, he was with her cousin. Last summer, he served time in Colorado for something he did for Caroline. Something violent, I'm sure. He doesn't know me," I added.

"That's too bad. You can't introduce us then."

What woman could resist a tall, golden-haired, gorgeous man who was mysterious and possibly dangerous? Certainly not Leonora. She rummaged in her bag and drew out a jeweled compact and a lipstick. With swift, sure strokes, she added a second layer of rosy color to her lips.

"I'm going to get another cup of coffee, Jen. Would you like one?" she asked.

"I guess so. Sure."

She rose and wove her way around the tables up to the counter, managing to capture Emil's attention for a moment as she passed his chair. He looked away from Grimes and returned her smile.

With Leonora's flair for attracting men, soon Emil would be sauntering over to our table with Grimes in his wake, a thoroughly unacceptable scenario. How many minutes of our three hours had passed? As if he could read my mind, the giant turned to give me a long, speculative stare.

While Leonora waited at the counter for our coffee, an insistent ringing cut through the din and smoke. Grimes whipped a cell phone out of his pocket. He listened intently for a second and then motioned to Emil who grabbed his jacket and slapped a bill down on the table, all in one sweeping, efficient movement.

The two men got up and hurried into the shadows at the back entrance moments before Leonora turned around, a cup of coffee in each hand. She frowned when she saw the abandoned table.

"Here's your coffee, Jen. Emil didn't leave already, did he?"

"I think so. You didn't move fast enough, but if Emil Schiller is back in town, he may turn up again."

"Alas," she said. "Not in Oakpoint."

"No. You'll have to move to Foxglove Corners. All the action is here."

"I may do that."

I took a long drink of coffee, almost burning my mouth. "Then we can take turns driving to Marston."

A blast of cold winter air engulfed me as the front door opened. Two dark-clad, grim-faced policemen came through and moved swiftly past the wood-cut witch and on into the Cauldron. Conversation dwindled to a murmur, and the air around me froze. Even the jukebox fell silent, paused between selections.

"Oh, no!" Leonora whispered. "A police raid. What are we going to do now?"

I took another swallow of coffee, grateful for its warmth. "Just sit still and drink your coffee. Think of this as another adventure."

Eleven

The presence of the police effectively squelched the raucous atmosphere of the place. I imagined that more than one person was trying not to look guilty. Leonora's customary poise seemed to have deserted her, and I soon found that my coffee cup was already empty.

Why were the officers here? At present they were engaged in an inaudible exchange with the bartender. There didn't appear to be anything urgent about their mission. In the whispered conversation that was taking place at the next table, only one word was audible: "Drugs."

The bartender led the police to the back of the tavern, in the direction taken by Al Grimes and Emil Schiller. Almost immediately the noise level rose. I breathed more easily. I couldn't imagine what Crane would think if I were taken away by the police in a raid. I couldn't imagine what he would do.

But I was overreacting. Apparently nobody was going to be led away in handcuffs. In five minutes, the police left quietly, their reason for visiting the Cauldron a matter for speculation.

"I'm glad we aren't part of a crime scene," I said. "I'll bet that call is why Grimes and Emil left. Someone warned Grimes the police were on their way."

"That call could have been about anything."

"True. I'm letting my imagination run away with me. Maybe the cops ran their patrol car into a snow bank."

"Not very likely. Well, we'll have to find something spectacular to do to end this day," Leonora said.

"I'd rather do something quiet. We've already done spectacular."

She held her wrist up to the overhead light. "The video rental place should still be open. If the roads aren't too bad, we could stop and rent some videos—if that tow truck ever gets here. We've been waiting for an hour already."

"Two more to go," I added. With Grimes, Emil, and the police gone, there was no prospect of excitement to break the monotony. Only food was left.

I said, "Watching movies is a good idea, and I have microwave popcorn at home. That reminds me, I'm getting hungry again. Let's live dangerously and try the vending machine cherry pie."

~ * ~

Our long day ended at last with a safe trip home, a quick snow shoveling session, and a trio of science-fiction movies. In the morning, Leonora left early for the drive back to Oakpoint, and I took Halley for a walk through a shower of snowflakes. Later, as I was putting the finishing touches on my makeup, a memory of the dream I'd had last night dropped into my mind with an ominous thudding sound.

Grimes had trapped me in the shadows that lived at the back of the Cauldron. I couldn't move. Even if escape were possible, I had no place to go. The back entrance, that I'd assumed was there, was only a wall.

Leonora will help me, I thought. But Leonora didn't exist in this dream version of my evening at the Cauldron.

Don't remember any more. Think about Crane. Dreams with Crane in them are always wonderful.

That was good advice. I concentrated on arranging my hair. One last swirl with the brush, one final look in the mirror, and I was ready.

~ * ~

The first thing I saw when I opened the door of The Mill House was a large poster cut in the shape of a bell and sprayed with glitter. It hung on the south wall, surrounded by framed black and white photographs of the original mill house that had given the restaurant its name.

Pushing back the hood of my parka and pulling off my gloves, I walked over to read its message:

Rock in the New Year

At the Rocking Horse Ranch

Square Dancing * Texas Barbeque *

Country Music * Live Band *

Sleigh Rides every Saturday

January through February

"Get your boyfriend to take you, young lady," said a jovial voice behind me. "It's the social event of the year."

The man who spoke so familiarly to me was short and round, with a ruddy complexion and a neatly trimmed silver beard. He wore a red jacket that matched the hue of his face, and his smile was as jovial as his voice. At his feet, a sprinkling of fallen glitter sparkled, and in his hand he held a stack of posters.

"Well..."

"Merry Christmas! Happy New Year!" he said and was gone. There should have been a puff of smoke in his wake, or a jingling of bells.

"Excuse me, Ms. Greenway," Susan Carter said. "Deputy

Sheriff Ferguson has been waiting for you. He's over there."

I smiled at her. "Thanks, Susan. I see him."

I was feeling charitable this morning. Susan was as pretty and bubbly as ever, and I didn't mind at all.

I looked toward Crane's favorite booth by the window with the view of the old mill house. All I had to do was walk into the light, for he sat in the center of an island of bright morning sunshine.

He had the Sunday Edition of the *Maple Falls Banner* open in front of him. For Crane, reading the paper was a tradition, but he also had an unopened Christmas present at his elbow. That was something new.

He got up and helped me out of my parka, and then I unwound my long scarf. Under these protective layers, I was wearing a new green knit dress. Beneath my sleeve I could feel the air-light weight of the crystal bracelet against my wrist.

Crane glanced at his watch. "You're late, Jennet. I was afraid you weren't coming."

"Not coming? If I'm ever not here, you'll know that I'm in some kind of trouble. Leonora and I stayed up past midnight, and I woke up an hour later than usual."

"I'll forgive you then—this time. Our breakfast will be here any minute. I didn't wait for you to order."

I didn't miss the twinkle in his eyes. He'd never thought that I wouldn't be here. Not for a second.

"I saw you reading that poster,' he said. "I can't take you out for New Year's Eve, honey. I'll be on duty. But we could go for a sleigh ride some time. Would you like that?"

I looked at him in alarm. "That's an outside activity, and it's way too cold."

A familiar teasing gleam was in his eyes. "I can keep you warm. Do you doubt it?"

"At five degrees? Not even you are that powerful."

"Don't be so sure," he said.

"Mmmm—okay, I won't. Do you know that man in the red jacket who just left, the one who looks like Santa Claus?"

"That's Rudy Zoller. He owns the Rocking Horse Ranch, and that's his party he's advertising. It's always a lot of fun."

I heard the regret in his voice and hastened to say, "I'd love to go on a sleigh ride, if we can wait for the weather to warm up a little. I can always find something to do on New Year's Eve, if I want to. Maybe I'll stay home."

And rest up for Snow Lodge.

"They have sleigh rides at Snow Lodge, too," Crane said.

"We'll go then."

I hadn't seen Crane since Christmas, which, I realized, was only a few days ago. I missed his company and his touch and the sparkle in his gray eyes that I was seeing now. In some deep, secret place, I kept the unspoken agreement between us that Snow Lodge would be our new beginning as lovers. Why would I care that he wasn't able to take me out on New Year's Eve?

"Do you have some place to go to celebrate?" he asked.

"Leonora asked me to go skiing with her, but I'd really rather stay home. I don't need confetti and champagne."

Crane reached for my hand across the table and squeezed it. "We'll ring in the New Year later at Snow Lodge."

"I hope you'll be safe on New Year's Eve, Crane. That can be a wild night."

"Things are usually pretty quiet around here. There'll be private parties, mostly. A lot of people will be at the Rocking Horse Ranch. Now and then, things get out of hand, but it's not like in the city, where they've been known to greet the New Year with gunfire. We concentrate our efforts on the roads."

This year was different though. A murderer had stolen the peace and security of Foxglove Corners. I wanted to discuss the case with Crane, but not just yet. Something else was on my mind.

I hadn't been able to take my eyes off Crane's present. It was wrapped in blue and white paper with a gingerbread man pattern and a matching tag that proclaimed in red ink: To Crane from: Susan.

"I see that you have a late Christmas present," I said.

"It's from Susan. They're brownies, I think. Everybody gives me baked goods around the holidays. The ladies do, I mean. They must think I'll die of starvation, sitting in my patrol car on these cold days and nights. I have about a dozen packages so far."

"So you won't go hungry," I said. "How thoughtful of them."

I knew that Camille had prepared a special box of Christmas cookies for Crane. Maybe it was true that baked goods were the way to a man's heart.

It wasn't until Susan had set a sumptuous morning feast of French toast and bacon before us that Crane mentioned Dr. Randolph's murder.

"That must have been a shock for you, Jennet. Wasn't he Halley's vet?"

"Almost. He had an emergency surgery the day I took her in, and Dr. Foster saw her instead. Do the police know who murdered him yet?"

"Not yet, but they think he let the killer in the house. That's in the paper."

Crane paused, as if considering whether or not he should say anything more. "Ordinarily I don't listen to rumors, but some strange stories have been circulating about Dr. Randolph. I've heard that he was part of a dognapping ring and his murder is somehow connected with it. That's hearsay, Jennet, not police information."

"That's ridiculous," I said. "Vets save animals from suffering. They don't hand them over to research labs."

"Those puppies he kept in the waiting room for adoption always disappeared after a few days. Supposedly they weren't adopted."

"I'll never believe that."

"Calm down, Jennet. I didn't say I did. You have to wonder how such stories got started, though. Dr. Randolph isn't even properly laid to rest yet. Now, tell me what mischief you and Leonora got into yesterday."

Crane drizzled syrup over his French toast and picked up his knife and fork. I understood that if he had some special knowledge about the case, he wasn't going to divulge it to me over breakfast or anywhere else. In any event, the Police Department was handling the case. Like everyone in Foxglove Corners, I would have to read the paper and listen to the news.

I said, "We didn't get into any trouble. We did a good deed," and described my puppy rescue and the part I'd intended Crane to play, if the last pup had still been available.

"That was good work, Jennet," he said. "Didn't I tell you once that when a way came for you to help animals, you'd do it? And what you did wasn't dangerous. I approve."

Then I told him the rest of it.

A frown crossed his face when I mentioned that we had been stranded in a snowstorm and taken refuge at the Cauldron to wait for a tow truck. He had just discovered the danger.

"That's a good place to avoid. If there are any criminals in Foxglove Corners, that's where you'll find them."

"I know, but last night we didn't have a choice."

I could still feel the bitter cold that had assailed me during the long walk to the tavern and the snow beating against my face, as well as the icy aura surrounding the specter of Al Grimes. It was a wonder that I hadn't caught a cold.

I didn't mention Grimes to Crane. "I only wish I knew who took the male pup. Not one of the dognappers, I hope."

"You can assume it was someone who really wanted a pup. I haven't heard about any dog thefts lately. Let's hope the dognappers are taking a holiday."

"I said something similar about crime, maybe at the same moment Dr. Randolph was being strangled, but I hope you're right."

Crane had finished eating his French toast, and here was Susan Carter, never very far away, at our booth, refilling his cup with hot coffee, moving on to her next customers with obvious reluctance. He sat watching me, saying nothing, his marvelous gray eyes inscrutable, the fresh coffee untouched.

He reached across the table and caressed my arm briefly, above the place where the crystal bracelet lay. Thoughts of killers and dognappers seemed to float away from me on a sea of longing. I wished I had magical powers. I'd make everyone else in the Mill House vanish. Or I'd whisk Crane back to the fireside in my farmhouse. Anything to prolong our time together.

Crane said. "We'll have a fancy dinner at the Adriatica one night, a pre-New Year's Eve celebration. Would you like that?"

I had lost track of the times Crane had mentioned New Year's Eve. Quickly I said, "Any place will be fine, Crane. It doesn't have to be fancy."

"There is something you could do for me, Jennet," he said. "You know, I would never tell you what to do, but I'd take it as a personal favor if you'd stay away from the Cauldron."

From his tone of voice I could tell that it was an obvious order, very diplomatically phrased, almost wrapped in bright Christmas paper. Was he hoping I wouldn't notice? Fortunately, I had no intention of going within fifty miles of the place again, in case it was one of Al Grimes' favorite haunts.

"Consider your favor granted," I said. "When the police raid the Cauldron, I won't be there."

He looked pleased with my response to his edict. I was rather pleased myself. Another thing I missed about Crane when we were apart was his tendency to be domineering, but I would never let him know that.

Laying a tip on the table for Susan, he said, "Well, it's time."

He picked up his Christmas present and the bill, while I reached for my parka. Deputy Sheriff Ferguson belonged to Foxglove Corners now. All I could do was wait until our next meeting.

~ * ~

That afternoon I went down to the basement to look for my largest suitcase. This was my least favorite part of the house. The furnace was there, periodically making its sinister noises, along with the hot water heater and other essential but unlovely equipment necessary to keep the house running. Stacked in no particular order were about thirty-five boxes that I had used in the move to Foxglove Corners. Many of them held items that I saw no pressing need to bring upstairs.

To conserve energy, I had closed the basement vents, with the result that it was cold and empty down here, except for the ever-present shadows. No matter how many boxes I stored in the basement, it would always be empty, except for the resident spiders and an occasional grotesquely shaped insect that had climbed up from the drains.

Dungeon, catacomb, tomb, habitat for a nightmare come to life—I had a dozen pet names for the place. Edgar Allan Poe would have been right at home in my basement. Although I certainly wasn't afraid to linger in this gloomy subterranean place, I avoided it whenever possible, always keeping the door closed. Even Halley ignored it.

I found the suitcase behind a box of college textbooks that hadn't yet found their upstairs niche, carried it to my bedroom, and laid it on the bed. Then I began pulling clothing from my closet in an attempt to assemble a romantic wardrobe for our weekend getaway.

I needed something dressy in a festive color, something casual and warm for the sleigh ride, and, of course, lingerie.

I opened my middle dresser drawer and took out a long white nightgown trimmed with layers of ivory lace. I held it up and, with a sigh, returned it to the drawer. It was too bridal. My long cotton gowns were too old fashioned, almost grandmotherly. The baby doll pajamas were too sweet, but my long sheer aqua gown with its matching floral patterned peignoir would be perfect. And I wouldn't have to worry about getting cold, not with Crane there. I laid each piece in the suitcase and decided that I was finished. All I needed to add was the green dress, perfume, and a makeup case.

A sudden sound behind me set my heart jolting out of its normal rhythm pattern. I turned around to investigate, but nothing had followed me upstairs from the basement. It was only Halley, who had been sound asleep a little while ago.

She regarded the suitcase with typical canine curiosity. It wasn't a new object to her, but she hadn't seen it since last summer. She sniffed it, apparently decided that it was harmless, and stood still, looking at me.

"Let's go downstairs, Halley," I said. "We can go outside for a long, cold winter walk or have a snack in the kitchen. Which?"

Halley had no preference. Later in the kitchen, after a short, cold walk, I contemplated baking, specifically the art of rolling out cookie dough. Inspired by Susan's brownies, I was going to bake cookies for Crane for Valentine's Day. This would be a trial batch.

I had inherited my mother's rolling pin but had never used it, as her skill at pie making eluded me. Now I opened the third cupboard drawer from the top to make sure that I hadn't left it in the basement with other rarely used implements. It was there, along with her cookie cutters.

I had red sugar in the cupboard. I'd sprinkle the cookies with messages like Heart's Desire and Truly Thine and hope the females of Foxglove Corners didn't shower Crane with baked goods on every holiday.

~ * ~

That night I dreamed about the phantom Christmas tree. Crane was there, too, and so was the fireplace. The dream was strangely disturbing, almost a nightmare.

We were sitting by the fireside, as we had been on Christmas night, he in the chair and I on his lap. The heat from the flames grew uncomfortably hot. I was about to ask Crane to move the chair away from the fire when I looked up and saw a Christmas tree in the middle of my living room. I knew it wasn't my own tree because of the multi-colored lights and the glittering tinsel.

The phantom tree was more complete now. Several presents appeared under its wide branches and a little crèche rested in a bed of artificial snow.

I turned to ask Crane if he could see the apparition, but he was gone. I was alone in the chair, trapped between the heat of the flames and the lights of the tree, and I was afraid.

Twelve

"It was only a dream. I don't know why I let it frighten me. Honestly, I don't know why I even mentioned it."

"I do," Camille said.

We were sitting in her kitchen, sharing a pot of tea, safe and comfortable in a place removed in time and space from my nightmare. Wherever I looked, I could see Camille's blue and white pottery collection, to which she was constantly adding new pieces.

Camille's kitchen was like safe harbor in a storm-tossed sea. Here she doled out good advice, along with homemade coffeecake—plum-filled this morning. If the presiding spirit of her kitchen could talk, I imagined it would say, 'Others have come through their troubles. You will, too.'

I hadn't been in her company very long this morning, but already my nightmare was fading, its lingering effects evaporating in the bright sunlight.

"Your subconscious is telling you that you're still troubled by seeing an apparition. It's perfectly normal."

"I suppose you're right. I've been trying to push the phantom tree out of my mind."

"Most dreams are only dreams," she said. "Lord knows I've had my share of nightmares. Remember the good parts of the dream and let the bad ones go, assuming there were good parts."

I didn't tell Camille about the nightmare I'd had the night before. Actually, I'd forgotten about it until a few minutes ago. The Grimes dream had no good parts.

Forget about it.

Breaking off a piece of Camille's coffeecake, I said, "You're right, Camille. I'm starting to feel better already."

"There's another interpretation. Like all of us, you've been shaken by Dr. Randolph's murder."

"Crane told me there was a rumor going around about Dr. Randolph, that he was mixed up with the dog thefts," I said.

"I know, but it's nonsense. David Randolph was the soul of kindness, and not only to animals. I remember all the times he patched up an injured animal, even if its owner couldn't pay him. People were telling good stories about David long before someone started spreading these lies."

I recalled my glimpse of him in the animal hospital, wearing his holly berry tie in honor of the season. "The one time I saw him, he looked so merry, sort of like a Christmas elf. I'd never, ever take him for a dognapper."

"He was so gentle with Twister," Camille said. "The first time I took him to the hospital for his vaccination, he was terrified, but he never minded going there again."

"That's settled then. Those stories are all lies. Why anyone would want to defame a man like Dr. Randolph is a mystery."

I reached for one of Camille's gardening catalogs that were stacked on the counter next to the coffeecake. The cover pictured an enchanting collection of spring flowers.

"Isn't it a little early to be thinking about spring and gardening?" I asked. "Winter has just started."

"It's never too early. Winter is my least favorite season. I get through these dreary months by planning additions to my garden. Since I don't have a dashing deputy sheriff to take me away to a romantic lodge for a winter getaway, these catalogs will have to suffice."

"We're going to Snow Lodge the day after New Years," I said. "Crane didn't tell me if he's made a reservation yet."

"If I know him, he has. Bring Halley over any time. Twister and I will be here."

The very thought of my weekend getaway with Crane was as warming as any dream of a sun-filled spring garden. I could hardly wait.

Returning the catalog to the stack, I said, "I don't know what I'd do without you."

This morning Camille was using the novelty Mary Quite Contrary teapot I'd given her for Christmas. The rainbow-colored garden on the china lid was a pleasant reminder that spring was the next season.

I got up and passed the last little chunk of coffeecake to Twister, who was lying in an ever-hopeful attitude at my feet. "I'm on my way into Lakeville to do some grocery shopping. Would you like me to pick up anything for you?"

"Thank you, Jennet, but I'm going into town myself later to stock up on supplies. Haven't you been listening to the weather reports?"

"Not lately. Why?"

"I heard on the news this morning that we may be getting a lot of snow by the end of the week."

"That's nothing new. It's snowed almost every day since Christmas."

"Now they're talking about a blizzard."

"Time will tell," I said. "Let's hope not."

Since I was on vacation, I could afford to be nonchalant. I didn't have to spend two hours a day driving on snow-covered roads unless I wanted to. Why worry about a little blizzard?

As I took my leave of Camille and drove into town, however, I decided that it might be prudent to add extra batteries and matches to my shopping list and maybe some food items that didn't require cooking.

~ * ~

The Inquisitor was a homegrown tabloid published in Maple Falls and zealous in its mission of exposing scandal or, in its absence, printing fiction about local personalities. While I was standing in the checkout line of Blackbourne's Grocers waiting to unload my shopping cart, I scanned the sheet's front-page headlines and saw a familiar name.

Cameron Lodge, the publisher of the ultra-respectable *Maple Falls Banner,* was *The Inquisitor's* prime target this week. One of his young female employees, a reporter, had accused him of sexual harassment. In turn, he claimed she was stalking him. It was a mess.

I had become acquainted with Cameron Lodge last summer and remembered him as a gentleman, if slightly aloof. He had recently been named one of Michigan's Top Ten Bachelors by *Michigan Life*, an honor that probably netted him a fair amount of female attention.

The Inquisitor had chosen a particularly unflattering picture of Cameron, while the photograph of his accuser suggested youth and innocence. How cleverly the tabloid communicated its position.

I recognized another familiar face on the front page and below it these incendiary words: 'Vet Stole Pets for Research'.

I added *The Inquisitor* to my groceries, along with the January issue of *Mary May* that featured an article promising to teach the reader Hot Techniques for a Cold Weather Seduction. I thought I could profit from enlightenment on both fronts.

Ten minutes later, I succumbed to temptation and sat in my car in Blackbourne's lot reading the article about Dr. Randolph.

It was sheer yellow journalism, consisting of a string of unfounded accusations, phrased in lurid language and directed toward a man who could no longer defend himself. The writer quoted anonymous sources, and the emotional passages depicting research laboratory atrocities could have been taken from any reputable source, such as an animal activist's report.

The heart of the story was a reference to a file found among Dr. Randolph's papers after his death. The circumstances surrounding its discovery were murky, but the file was now in the hands of the police. Allegedly, it contained records of the dogs Dr. Randolph had rerouted to an out-of-state supplier for use in laboratory experiments.

This attack on a dead man filled me with renewed anger. But what if the file were legitimate and incriminated Dr. Randolph in the dognappings? I hadn't known him. All I had was the testimony of others. In spite of the *Inquisitor's* reputation, not every story it printed was false. I had to learn more about Dr. Randolph's activities and try to separate truth from falsity.

Yet my intuition was telling me that he was being libeled. As soon as I drove out of the parking lot, I turned north and headed in the direction of the Foxglove Corners Animal Hospital. Whether Dr. Randolph was innocent or guilty, I felt a compelling need to offer condolences and support to someone.

~ * ~

A short time later, I pulled in front of the animal hospital, but it appeared to be closed. The building looked as if it were in mourning for the murdered vet or was keeping a low profile in the wake of the escalating scandal. A dark Dodge Intrepid at the south end of the building, indicating that at least one person was inside.

I parked near the entrance, where a large stone spaniel sat at perpetual attention, holding a basket in its mouth. Someone had tied a red ribbon around the dog's neck and filled the basket with pinecones.

I pushed open the heavy door and found Dr. Foster sweeping the floor with vigorous, angry motions. She was wearing blue jeans with a long red sweater, and her blonde hair was tied back in a ponytail.

It hardly seemed like the same waiting room I had visited with Halley only days ago. The Christmas tree, stripped of its dog bone ornaments, seemed to be dying, although I knew it was artificial. Ropes of garland lay on the chairs, wound into neat coils, and the crates were empty. The contrast from the lively place I remembered was painfully striking.

I was surprised that Dr. Foster remembered my name. She leaned her broom against the wall and walked over to the reception desk.

"Ms. Greenway," she said, with a ready, professional smile. "I didn't expect to see you today. Is there a problem with Halley?"

"No, Halley's paw is fine. Is the hospital open?"

"Yes, but we haven't been very busy lately. We—I was closed yesterday for the funeral."

I said, "I was so sorry to hear about Dr. Randolph. I didn't have a chance to know him, but my friends speak highly of him."

"Thank you," she said. "He was a very special person."

In the silence that followed, I felt uneasy and uncertain what to say or do next. Then I noticed a new display of Prime Rib Bits, Nutritional Puppy and Dog Treats and had an inspiration.

"I'd like to buy a dozen boxes of Prime Rib Bits," I said. "Three for dogs and nine for puppies."

"My goodness. Do you have a litter of puppies besides Halley?" she asked.

"No, only Halley. I'll take all but one box to the animal

shelter."

Dr. Foster took twelve boxes from the display and set them on the counter, and I reached for my wallet. My impromptu gesture would cost over thirty dollars, but as I imagined treating the canine foundlings, the warm glow I felt made the price seem like a bargain.

The silence in the hospital was unsettling. It was easy to imagine that the rooms were full of ghosts—the ghost of the falsely accused vet come back to walk the empty halls of his hospital, the specter of the strangler, and the spirits of the creatures who had died within these walls. I had only been inside the animal hospital for five minutes, and I was spooked.

"You're not all alone here, are you?" I asked. "I didn't see any other buildings nearby. It can't be safe."

"I won't stay late," she said. "I'll just finish tidying up. I don't have any more appointments today."

"Will you keep the hospital open and stay on alone?"

"I'm not sure. I've only been here since June, and I don't think I'm ready to work without a partner. David's son may move back to Foxglove Corners and take over the practice. He hasn't decided yet, so I don't know what the future will hold." ·

Her words were professional, but the grief in her voice was unmistakable. Abruptly I changed my mind about mentioning the rumors. Dr. Foster couldn't possibly be offended by a sincere offer of support.

"I'm sure no one who knew Dr. Randolph believes that vicious story in the *Inquisitor*," I said.

"Thank you, Ms. Greenway, but I'm not so sure. We've had a rash of cancellations today, all for appointments this week. I saw only two dogs today. That tells me something."

"The story came out today. Some people believe everything they read."

"David wasn't involved with dognappers," she said.

"Anyone who says so is lying. We worked together, and I knew him. Now all people will remember about him are the lies surrounding his death. All these years of taking care of animals in Foxglove Corners count for nothing."

She reached for the broom again and swept a clean area of floor.

I said, "It looks bleak now, but the police will catch Dr. Randolph's murderer any day and his name will be cleared."

"I hope so, but once a reputation is damaged, it can never be repaired. That's another form of murder."

"I agree, but most people are fair. Let's hope for the best."

I hesitated for a moment, but there was a question I wanted to ask. "Do you think Dr. Randolph's killer was someone he knew well?"

"Maybe, but people often came to his house, seeking emergency care for their pets, even on Sunday or a holiday. He never turned anyone away."

There wasn't anything more to say except goodbye. I gathered up my Prime Rib Bits. "Good luck, Dr. Foster. I hope you'll stay on at the hospital."

She set the broom aside and glanced around the plain, silent waiting room. "Thank you. I hope I can."

I pushed open the door again and glanced at the sky but couldn't see any sign of a winter storm. Still, a dark cloud of another kind had descended over the animal hospital. In a sense, it covered all of Foxglove Corners as well.

Thirteen

"Don't cook dinner tonight," Crane said. "I made reservations for us at the Adriatica for prime rib and champagne. I'll pick you up at six-thirty sharp."

I turned off the answering machine, resisting the temptation to replay the message for the pleasure of hearing his voice again. His invitation wasn't a surprise. He had mentioned a pre-New Year's Eve celebration on Sunday, and I had been expecting his call.

I didn't know when he had left the message. Halley and I had just returned from a walk in the cold. Now I had only two hours to get ready for a gala evening with Crane, but since I had nothing more challenging to do than fix Halley's dinner, I should be able to manage.

I was going to wear my black velvet jumper with a lacy white blouse, but like many a simple plan, this one went awry. First, I discovered several of Halley's long hairs adhering to the material of my jumper. They had to be removed with strips of Scotch tape. Then, my white blouse was missing a button. I lost fifteen minutes searching before I found one that matched the others and another five sewing it in place. The only accessory that was always ready was my bracelet.

I ordered myself to relax and touched the bracelet for

pleasure,

for luck, and for a measure of serenity. It made no sense to be stressed on a winter vacation day, with a man like Crane and a prime rib dinner waiting for me in the wings.

My ritual worked. When Crane knocked on the door at six-thirty, I was ready and even serene, with no trace of the last frantic hours, except for a lingering breathlessness.

"Come in out of the cold for a while, Crane," I said. "Do we have time?"

He closed the door and consulted his watch. "We have five minutes, and I intend to put them to good use. Halley, girl, step aside, while I kiss your mistress."

As he pulled me close for a kiss that surely exceeded his five-minute limit, the scent of his new cologne surrounded me.

"You're the one who smells good tonight, Crane," I said. "What are you wearing?"

"Obsession."

He moved his hands slowly down my body to my waist and up again with a sensuality that made me feel as if I were melting. "You feel very soft tonight, honey."

"It's the velvet."

"Is it?"

He kissed me again with more intensity. "We could cancel our reservations. I could build a fire."

I couldn't tell if he was serious. His gray eyes had the sparkle I knew so well, but the dinner was his idea, and he must be hungry. I couldn't always read him clearly, but I suspected he was teasing me.

"Or we could have dinner and come right back here," I said. "Then you could build the fire." I couldn't help thinking of Christmas and our long romantic interlude in front of the fireplace.

Crane appeared to be pondering the matter gravely, as if he

were weighing the advantages and disadvantages of each proposal. Finally he said, "We'll go to the Adriatica, then. I did offer you dinner."

"Yes, you did. A fancy one, as I recall."

"Is prime rib fancy enough?"

At that instant, boxes of Prime Rib Bits began to dance around in my head like sugarplums. They were in my trunk, waiting to be delivered to the shelter dogs. I hadn't thought about them since I'd left the animal hospital.

"What's funny?" Crane asked.

"I'll tell you over dinner," I said.

Later at the Adriatica, though, I forgot about the dog treats as I listened to Crane enlighten me about his inquiries into the dognappings. Our waiter had served our salads and a basket of hot rolls and bread. Crane began eating immediately, confirming my suspicion that he was hungry, and I unfolded my napkin.

"I had lunch with Jake Brown today," he said.

"Who's Jake Brown?"

"He's the deputy sheriff over in Ellentown."

I remembered then. Crane had been going to talk to him about the stolen dogs.

"Jake doesn't know anything more than he told the reporter, but since the article appeared, two more dogs were reported missing, both this week."

"Was this in Ellentown?"

"Yes. One was a German shepherd. His owner left him tied outside a hardware store for only fifteen or twenty minutes. When he came back, the dog was gone. The same day, another dog disappeared from a fenced yard."

"It looks like the dognappers are back then," I said.

"Since they were in Ellentown, I'll look for them to be moving back our way."

111

"Doesn't that exonerate Dr. Randolph? He's dead and dogs are
still disappearing. He can't be stealing them from beyond the grave."

"Not necessarily. The vet could have been working with someone else, maybe with more than one person. By the way, did you hear about the story in the *Inquisitor*? I know you don't read tabloids, but a lot of people do. It's doing a lot of damage."

"I read one today. It's all rumor." I told him about my stop at the animal hospital and Dr. Foster's fear that she might have to close her doors.

I noticed that Crane had managed to finish his salad, even as he was giving me this latest news. No matter how hungry I was, I always seemed to lag behind my dinner companions.

"The part about the file is true," Crane said.

"Can you tell me about it?"

"Sure. It's no secret. An anonymous person sent a large brown mailer to the police station yesterday before the *Inquisitor* hit the stands. Inside was a long list—descriptions of dogs, their weights, some names, and dates. There were also several newspaper clippings about lost dogs."

"Did you say the sender is anonymous?"

"So I've heard."

"Well, then."

"The list appears to be written in Dr. Randolph's hand. A handwriting expert is checking it out."

At this point, it didn't look good for Dr. Randolph, but there was only the file and not his explanation for it.

I finished my salad, reached for a roll, and broke it in two. Crane, the Romantic Hero, had returned. He smiled at me and poured champagne into two tall flutes. On cue, our waiter appeared with the main course.

I cut a small piece of prime rib. "This is a wonderful dinner, Crane."

"It's not as fine as the one you cooked for us on Christmas. Gianetta agreed to have your favorite dessert on the menu tonight."

I stopped eating for a minute to absorb this amazing fact. I knew that Crane was on a first name basis with the cook but hadn't realized that she'd fill a special request for him.

"What is my favorite dessert, Crane? I can't think of one I don't like."

He smiled again, a teasing, secret smile that I didn't often see.

"It's chocolate meringue pie. You may not know it yet, but that's your favorite."

I hadn't thought about chocolate meringue pie in a long time, much less eaten any. He was right, though. If I had to choose one favorite dessert, it would be chocolate something, and I loved pie.

"You know me too well," I said.

When we were finished with our meal, the waiter brought us two enormous pieces of chocolate pie. I sent the fork cutting through the snowy peaks of meringue down to the rich dark chocolate filling.

Crane raised his champagne flute, and the candlelight set the flecks of frost in his eyes a-glitter.

"To the happy New Year," he said softly.

"Yes, to the happy New Year."

"And a fire in the Victorian farmhouse, as soon as you finish."

I lay down my fork, leaving the last tiny bit of crust on the plate.

"I'm ready," I said.

~ * ~

The next day I visited the animal shelter to deliver the Prime Rib Bits. Winter lay on the porch with the blue merle side of his head resting against the hard wood of a post. He appeared to be waiting for someone.

As soon as I started up the walk, he rose and stretched lazily. Then he stood still, his ears laid smooth against the sides of his head. With his tail wagging and his eyes bright with anticipation, he was like a silver statue turned by sorcery into a lively dog. I couldn't believe that no one had claimed him yet.

"Winter, boy, how are you today?" I asked.

The shelter dogs in the yard, aware of my arrival, were barking their demand for equal attention. Winter discovered the Prime Rib Bits and nudged my hand with a cold nose. I set the bag down and stroked his silky head on the tri-color side.

Letty opened the front door before I could ring the bell. She was dressed for the cold weather in a long, heavy coat, with a scarf draped loosely around her neck and another one on her head. Henry stood behind her. He, too, was well bundled up. They looked as if they were about to embark on an Arctic expedition.

"Oh, Jennet," Letty said. "Hello, come in. We're on our way out, but Lila is here. So is the vet."

"Is something wrong?" I asked.

"One of the new little retrievers is sick. Dr. Foster says it's a common parasite in young dogs. She's leaving enough medicine for the pup's sisters, too."

"I know about the dognappers, Jennet." Henry said. "Has your sheriff friend found Luke yet?"

"I'm afraid not, but he'll keep looking. Did you see any ghosts this Christmas, Mr. McCullough?"

"No," he said.

I still held the bag of Prime Rib Bits. Winter, who had followed me in from the porch, nudged the bag with his nose.

"Well, we're off," Letty said. "You know the way to the kitchen, Jennet. Lila's in the yard. If we get snowed in, the animals will eat. They have plenty of dog food, but we humans can't eat that."

"It doesn't look like it's going to snow," I said. But I had detected something in the brittle air this morning, a hint of blizzard, perhaps? Maybe Letty and Henry were right.

"Snow is on the way," Henry said. "It'll be here by the end of the day."

After Letty and Henry had left, I made my way to the kitchen, with Winter trailing behind me. Lila and Dr. Foster were just coming in through the side door. The young vet wore blue jeans again and a bright pink jacket. Her long fair hair tumbled down over her shoulders.

"How's the puppy?" I asked.

"She'll be fine and ready for a new home in a few weeks," Dr. Foster said. "All the other dogs are in tip-top shape."

"We found a good home for Charcoal," Lila said. "Sit down, both of you. I'll make us some tea."

Dr. Foster joined me at the table. "I'd like a warm drink," she said.

Winter sat at my feet, his eyes fixed longingly on the brown bag that was now on the table in front of me. I relented and took out one of the boxes of dog treats.

"I didn't realize you made house calls, Dr. Foster," I said, as I fed Winter four Prime Rib Bits.

She reached into her pocket and took out a card. "Please call me Alice. If you need me for Halley, call me any time. The hospital is closing for a few weeks, but we hope to reopen on the first of February. David's son decided to move back to Foxglove Corners."

"What will you do in the meantime?" Lila asked.

"I'm going to stay here. I'll be available for house calls, but

I don't expect to be very busy."

"Do you think we could search the animal hospital for a copy of the file the police have?" I asked. "It might tell us who is trying to brand Dr. Randolph a dognapper and why."

"We could look," Alice said. "I think I know who 'Anonymous' is. Recently David had to fire a receptionist who didn't work out. She would have had access to his papers. The day she left, she was very angry. I don't have any proof, though."

"Do you think she fabricated the file?"

"I don't know if she'd go that far. David didn't confide in me, but I had a suspicion that something was troubling him."

Lila poured the tea and passed the sugar and creamer to Alice who poured a measure of cream into her cup, added a teaspoon of sugar, and stirred the tea briskly, hitting the sides of the cup with each revolution of the spoon. It was as if either the cup or the spoon had displeased her. She stirred the tea with the same angry energy with which she had swept the floor of the animal hospital.

"Maybe by the time Dr. Randolph's son comes, we'll have tracked these lies to their source," I said. "I'll be in touch with you soon."

"Thanks, Jennet. I'll take all the help I can get."

She finished her tea in two hasty gulps. "I'll be on my way now. I have a few more house calls to make. Call me if the puppy isn't much better by tomorrow morning."

When Alice had gone, Lila said, "She's a nice young woman. I hope you two can find out what's going on."

I'd been looking at the empty crate in which Crane's foundling had taken refuge. "Did something happen to Brown Dog?" I asked.

"She's found a new place to hide, upstairs in one of the empty rooms. She's eating now, and she goes outside on a leash, but only with me. I keep her crate door open all the time. Sometimes she goes inside to be alone, but she's stopped snapping at the other dogs."

"That *is* progress," I said. "And you still have Winter. I'm so glad."

I laid my hand on his head. He was sitting quietly at my side, his gaze fixed on the box of dog treats.

"We've advertised, but no one's come for him. I'm afraid we'll never find him a new home. Most people want a puppy. I thought Henry might adopt him, but he says he's too old to have another dog. Of course, Henry's waiting for Luke to come home."

"Winter is long over his puppy rowdiness," I said. "He'd be a wonderful companion for Henry."

"He would, but Henry isn't interested."

"I wish I could take Winter home with me," I said.

This wasn't a spur-of-the-moment idea. Nor was it wishful thinking. I realized that I had wanted Winter the first time I set eyes on him.

"Why can't you?" Lila asked. "Didn't you say you live on ten acres?"

"I do, but I'm away at school during the day. My neighbor is going to take care of Halley because I'm afraid to leave her outside alone. I can't ask her to take on two dogs. Besides, some day Winter's owner may show up. I don't want to get attached to him."

But if I could overcome those two rather major obstacles...

"I almost forgot to tell you," Lila said. "We're postponing our open house because of the blizzard, but we have a new idea to find homes for our animals. Henry's nephew, Fred, has a television show. It's really about raising and showing horses, but he says we can have a guest spot once a week to showcase one of our dogs."

"That's a great idea. Which one of you is going to be on television?"

"Not me," Lila said quickly. "I'm sure I'd be too nervous to utter a whole sentence. Letty is the one who has more experience with people. She's looking forward to it. Be sure to watch us at nine in the morning, a week from tomorrow."

"I'll be back in school then, but I'll tape it. I should be leaving now, too, Lila. I'm going away for the weekend, and I still have a few things to do."

Lila took a sip of her tea. "You're going away with a blizzard coming?"

"I won't be alone. I'm going with my friend."

Simultaneously, all the dogs in the yard began to bark. I started to get up, just as Lila said, "Who's out there? Letty just left. She can't be back already."

Winter ran to the window and stood with his paws on the sill. He growled. It was a low menacing sound that came from deep in his throat.

"I didn't hear anything," I said. Then I did.

A blue van had stopped in the driveway about three feet from the gate to the yard. The van door opened. A tall, burly man jumped down and dashed up to the fence. While the dogs merged into a frantic pack, leaping and pawing at the fence, he reached for the latch and started to pull the gate open.

Fourteen

Lila's voice was high pitched and fearful. "Who is he? What's he doing?"

"It's Al Grimes! Hold onto Winter, Lila."

I raced past Lila to the side door, flung it open, and demanded, "What in the hell do you think you're doing? Close that gate and get out of here!"

Grimes' hand froze on the gate. He'd only opened it a crack so that not even the smallest of the puppies could squeeze through, but I had no doubt of his intention.

I saw the flicker of recognition in his cold eyes. He still reminded me of a predator, a powerful jungle beast crouched in a place high above me, fangs bared to crunch his prey into pulp.

He was a beast with a voice. "Well, if it isn't Jane. Nice seeing you again."

Behind me, Lila uttered a cry. Winter sailed past me through the open door like a silver bullet, seventy or eighty pounds of airborne fury. He sank his fangs into Grimes' left thigh, slicing through the material of his pants.

Grimes roared in pain and sent his massive fist crashing into Winter's head. The dog's scream drowned out the barking of the shelter dogs and Grimes' curses. Winter lay where he had fallen in front of the gate. A stream of blood soaked through his

119

silvery, black-mottled fur.

I fled to Winter's side, while Grimes, holding his hand to his damaged thigh and still cursing, escaped to his van. Steering erratically, he backed out of the drive and into the street.

Gently, I touched Winter's head. When I drew my hand back, it was covered with blood. Winter had been struck in the same place that had sustained the previous injury.

Frantically I tried to apply pressure to stop the flow of blood. I needed a blanket, quickly.

See if he's still alive, I told myself. He was, for the moment.

Lila's voice was shaking, and her eyes were bright with tears. "I'm sorry; I couldn't hold Winter. He's too strong. Is he dead, Jennet?"

"No, but I don't know how badly he's hurt."

She closed the gate and leaned weakly against it. "The other dogs are all here. That man didn't get one of them."

"Call Dr. Foster back, Lila. Call Crane."

While Lila went into the house to make the calls, I stayed at the side of the big blue dog, talking softly to him and trying to quiet the excited puppies in the yard. When Lila returned, she brought a damp cloth from the kitchen and laid it on Winter's wound. As she did, I was sure that he stirred.

"Do you think that man was the one who hurt Winter before?" she asked.

"I'm sure of it. Winter remembered him. Otherwise, he wouldn't have attacked a stranger."

A few snowflakes landed on my sleeve, glittering on the purple material of my dress like tiny pieces of frozen lace. Shivering, I brushed them off, but more fell to take their place.

"I'll go back in and get our coats." Lila glanced at the sky. "That horrible man isn't going to forget that Winter attacked him. He did bite him badly, didn't he? I've never heard of a collie biting before."

"Neither have I, but I'm sure some of them do."

"Winter has made an enemy all right." Lila reached over and touched my shoulder in sympathy. "And I'm afraid that you have, too, Jennet."

~ * ~

New Year's Day brought a raging blizzard that ended my dreams of a holiday getaway with Crane. About Winter, however, I had good news. Dr. Foster had examined him and predicted that he would make a full recovery from Grimes' brutal blow.

It was four o'clock in the afternoon. Since early in the morning, the snow had been falling heavily with no sign of a lull. Crane, the Romantic Hero, had fallen by the snowy wayside, a victim of capricious fate and the stormy weather. His shiny badge reminded me that I had no claim on his time today, as he was on duty. I supposed I was an unofficial stop on his ongoing patrol of Foxglove Corners.

I hadn't had a chance to tell him about Grimes and Winter yet.

"I'm called back into action for a snow emergency," Crane said. "I'm sorry about our weekend, honey."

I tried hard to keep my deep disappointment from him. I'd been counting on this time alone with Crane for so long. I felt as if my happiness was disappearing under the layers of snow.

"I know you have to stay in Foxglove Corners, Crane. Snow Lodge will still be there when the blizzard is over," I said.

Sheets of stinging precipitation blew in from the east, and the strong wind whipped the snow that had already fallen into high drifts. This morning, one look through my bedroom window had convinced me that the forecasts were accurate.

"They have even more snow at Snow Lodge than we do here," Crane said. "The manager is keeping our reservations on hold. We need two days together. You always have weekends off, and I'll arrange to have one at the same time. We'll get there yet."

"Now we'll still have something to look forward to," I said.

The television forecasters were calling it a snow event, but it was really a major blizzard. A snow event sounded less threatening—not that people felt threatened. They were still on the move, coming and going and colliding with one another on snow-drifted roads, even though today was a holiday. Already numerous accidents had been reported, and cars were being abandoned in the snow.

"It's really bad out there," Crane said. "There must be six inches of snow on the ground already, and we're expecting six more. I'm glad you and Halley are safe and warm here."

Hearing her name, Halley wagged her tail. She had been standing next to Crane's chair, holding her dinosaur in her mouth in the hope of attracting his attention.

"Give it here, girl!" Crane took the toy from her mouth and flung it into the hallway. She scampered after it and brought it back to him in a second.

"I have to go, Jennet," Crane said.

"Do you really have to go right away?" I kissed his lips lightly and then kissed them again, more intensely. His mouth was still cold from the wintry blast, even though he'd been inside talking with me for a while.

I wanted to tell him about my adventure at the animal shelter. This was the first chance I'd had, and all we'd talked about was the weather.

Crane looked at his watch. "I can stay ten minutes. I'll consider this my coffee break."

"In that case, I'll start the coffee. Would you like fruitcake or pound cake?"

"This weather calls for bourbon pound cake and hot steamy coffee. A lot of both."

While I waited for the coffee to percolate, I told Crane about Grimes' attempt to steal the shelter dogs and how Winter had driven him off with a well-aimed bite.

"Then Lila called the police," I said.

"Did you take down the van's license plate number?" Crane asked.

"No, I didn't have time, but it was blue, nondescript, no dents or decals. I know the man. His name is Al Grimes. I'd like to get Winter away from the shelter in case Grimes comes back."

"That's unlikely," he said. "Dognappers like to operate in the shadows. Now he's been seen."

Crane had listened to my tale without surprise, with only a slight frown, but his eyes had turned a glacial shade of gray. If I didn't know him as well as I did, I would surely be cowed by now.

"I wondered when you were going to tell me about this," he said. "I saw Lila this morning."

I might have known that Crane had already heard about the incident. With contacts at every turn, there was very little he didn't know.

"This is the first time I've seen you, " I said.

"What I don't understand is why I haven't heard about this man before."

"I told you about the night Leonora and I were stranded in the snow, when we had to stop at the Cauldron to call a tow truck."

He didn't respond. He was waiting for me to elaborate. I could almost hear his thought: But you didn't mention Grimes.

"Al Grimes offered to buy me a drink. That's all."

"And how did you turn him down? You *did* turn him down?"

"I said I was waiting for my jealous husband."

"And he believed that?"

"I don't know. I really didn't care. He didn't approach me again. That's all that mattered. This is strange, though. He was sitting at a table with Emil Schiller."

"The animal activist associating with a dognapper? That's something to look into. I'll see what I can find about Schiller's recent activities. As soon as the storm is over, I'm going to bring in Al Grimes for questioning."

"Can you do that?" I asked. "I wondered if Grimes can say that he struck Winter, in self-defense, because Winter was biting him."

"He can say whatever he likes. He was trying to steal the dogs. You and Lila are witnesses."

"I'm afraid it would be his word against ours."

"I'm going to question him anyway," Crane said.

I looked out my kitchen window. Jonquil Lane was well on its way to being drifted over. If Crane lingered much longer, his patrol car would be buried. I didn't call his attention to that fact.

"Grimes may not be the man's real name," Crane said. "Can you describe him for me?"

"That's easy. He's very tall. When you look at him, you think of a giant. Both times I saw him, he was unshaven, and he has a mean look. That night at the Cauldron, he was wearing a shirt that said 'I (heart) My Rottweiler'."

"That's too vague. How tall would you say he is? What color are his eyes?"

I made another attempt. "He's approximately six feet six inches tall with a heavy build and a dark complexion. I didn't notice the color of his eyes, but have you ever been confronted by a wild animal?"

"More than once."

"Then you know the look in his eyes. I'm sorry, Crane.

That's the best I can do."

The coffee was ready, the mugs were on the table, and I didn't know why we were talking about Al Grimes. With our romantic weekend buried under six inches of snow, we could at least have a few minutes of closeness before Crane had to leave.

"Sit still, Jennet," Crane said. "I'll pour the coffee."

I got up and looked for my bread knife. "The bourbon in your aunt's pound cake will help to keep you warm."

"Lila believes you may be in some danger from this man because you interrupted his attempt to steal the dogs," Crane said. "If we can nail him for the dog thefts, we will. Maybe he thinks you live at the shelter."

"I may adopt Winter," I said. "When I told Camille what happened, she said she'd be happy to take care of both dogs."

"I think it's a good idea for you to have another dog around the house. Winter sounds like a good protector."

"It's the other way around, Crane. I want to make sure he's safe."

"You can look out for each other, then."

I watched him eat his cake and drink his coffee, unhappy that he had to go out into the blizzard again. In spite of what I'd said, I wished that we were at Snow Lodge. But no one could control the weather, and wishful thinking was futile. All too soon, he finished his coffee and got up.

"Jennet, you have a way of attracting danger even when you're doing a good deed. I don't think this man will bother you again. My ten minutes are up, honey. I'm off. Stay inside this weekend. You probably won't have a choice. I'll stop back when I can, and we'll reschedule Snow Lodge."

He pulled me up a bit more roughly than usual and kissed me with more urgency. When he moved away from me, I felt colder than I had on the night Leonora and I had been stranded in the snowstorm.

"Goodnight and Happy New Year," I said. "Take care of yourself."

I opened the door for him and watched him make his way through the snowdrifts to his patrol car.

I knew that he would be careful. He had come through New Year's Eve without incident, and, I reminded myself that he was more than a match for the elements. All the same, when I saw him drive away, I had an overwhelming desire to call him back.

The timing of the blizzard was unfortunate. If only it could have started snowing tomorrow, after our arrival at Snow Lodge.

~ * ~

That night I lay under my warm comforter and listened to the wind howling. Because I couldn't sleep, I looked through the window across the room, watched the snow falling, and thought about Crane. Once again, I decried the timing of the snowstorm.

Crane and I snowbound at our romantic getaway was a more desirable scenario than I alone, snowed in at my house, while Crane...

Here my thoughts wound down. I didn't want to picture Crane battling the snow and the wind on this terrible night. I preferred to think of him in some warm place, an all-night diner, perhaps, drinking more hot coffee. My dormant generous nature added a pretty young waitress to serve him.

After a while, I transferred the fantasy to my kitchen, dismissed the waitress, and placed Crane in my arms. It would be easier to court sleep with a vision of Crane, smiling seductively at me, than the glowering image of Grimes.

I thought I had banished the incident at the shelter and Lila's dire prediction to the back of my mind, along with the phantom

Christmas tree, but tonight there had been something in Crane's voice, some tone I recognized, that had stayed with me.

His implication that Grimes wouldn't be a threat to me had set off a loud clanging bell that I could hear clearly. Crane thought exactly the opposite. Because I sensed his true feeling, I was uneasy. In truth, I was more than uneasy, but not yet afraid.

Halley lay on her side at the foot of my bed sleeping. I was grateful for her presence and eager to add Winter to my household. Two dogs would be double protection. If only I could add one deputy sheriff, poised for a dramatic rescue, security was practically guaranteed.

I imagined that I was probably safe. Having been sighted, Grimes might well have moved on. As far as I knew, he didn't know my real name. Nor did he know where to find me. Even if he possessed this knowledge, he wouldn't be likely to track me down in the middle of a blizzard. I hoped that Winter's bite had disabled him temporarily and that Crane would find him soon.

Pushing Grimes out of my mind, I brought back Crane. I rewound our last kiss and fast-forwarded to Snow Lodge. There I lay in his arms, while the snow kept falling until it reached the roof, shutting us away from the outside world.

None of this fantasizing relaxed me. I was about to go downstairs for a cup of cocoa when I felt myself drifting off. Soon after that, between fearful imaginings and wonderful ones, I fell asleep.

~ * ~

When I woke, my first thought was to see if the blizzard had ended. My second was to see how much snow had fallen during the night. I pushed back the comforter, shivering as the cooler air beyond my bed reached me, found my slippers, and hurried to the window.

All I could see was white. Foxglove Corners was literally

buried in snow. All the familiar landmarks were obliterated, and the wind had sculpted the snow into high drifts and fantastic shapes. With a little imagination, I could almost see the form of a great hulking giant beyond the oak tree.

Jonquil Lane was drifted over, making it impassable. Beyond the lane, Camille's house resembled a great yellow cake in the shape of a mansion with white frosting drizzling down its walls. I was looking at the quintessential marshmallow world.

Halley was awake, stretching and still drowsy, although she had slept through the night, while I lay awake, alternately entertaining myself with romantic vignettes featuring Crane and frightening myself with dark thoughts of Grimes. She would have to go outside. Before I did anything, even before breakfast, I would have to shovel a small area for her to walk on.

I found a pair of wool pants in my closet, took a turtleneck out of my dresser drawer and a long, bulky sweater from the closet shelf to make up the recommended cold weather layers. Downstairs, I added my parka, gloves, and highest boots.

The shovel was in the basement. Descending those shadowy stairs to the lower level of my house was as unappealing a prospect as clearing snow before breakfast, but unless I wanted to remain snowbound indefinitely, I had no choice.

Telling Halley to stay, I switched on the light and walked slowly down, imagining that I saw Grimes in every shadow. I found the snow shovel lying against the north wall, along with the rake and a few other seldom-used tools.

Halley waited for me at the head of the stairs, peering curiously down as if wondering where I'd gone, but making no attempt to follow me. When I came back up, I closed the door. She began an impatient whining and pushed ahead of me in her haste to go outside.

When I opened the kitchen door, I saw the magnitude of the task that lay ahead of me. The snow was almost as high as the doorknob. I looked with dismay at my boots. The drifts would reach up to my hips. As for poor Halley, she would sink in a sea of white.

At the same time, I saw that I had no choice. No strong-armed Southern gentleman lingered at my door to take the shovel from my hand. With grim determination but no enthusiasm, I began the daunting task of clearing a path, one shovelful of snow at a time.

Fifteen

Ordinarily I would have been overjoyed at the prospect of staying inside for an entire day with nothing to do, but human nature is perverse. By noon of the first day after the big snow, I began to feel restless.

I stood looking through my living room window at Jonquil Lane and my own front walk. Both were impassable. Everything was as still and white as an unframed snowscape. An overpowering need to be going somewhere, anywhere, blew over me like a wind-driven drift of snow.

I had managed to clear a small space for Halley in the dog run, as well as a section of the front porch. That was the extent of my morning's accomplishment. My arms and shoulders were already aching, and I wasn't looking forward to any more shoveling. Even if I were able to clear my driveway, Jonquil Lane would remain unplowed. Because this was the biggest snowfall in twenty years, snow removal would be a formidable task in Foxglove Corners.

I was grateful that I still had power. I can face anything as long as I have heat, light, and the telephone. I called Camille first to see how she had come through the storm.

"I've never seen anything more beautiful than this snowfall!" she exclaimed. "I've been outside taking pictures before anyone makes tracks to spoil it."

"How did you manage? I've been shoveling all morning and hardly made a dent in the snow."

"I cleared part of my porch and took pictures from there. I think I have some good snapshots of your house."

"Do you think anyone will plow the lane?"

"Eventually someone will. Enjoy this enforced solitude. It'll be over soon enough. Most of southeastern Michigan is snowed in today. I'm sorry about your weekend plans."

"We'll still go," I said.

"I made a big pot of beef stew and set some aside for you, enough for about three dinners."

"That sounds wonderful. I'll come get it as soon as I can."

The thought of homemade stew was a strong lure, but I didn't think I'd be walking across the lane to the yellow Victorian any time soon, and certainly not today. At times like these I wished that I were more athletically inclined. A pair of cross-country skis and the ability to move in them would come in handy now.

Next I called Lila to tell her that I had decided to adopt Winter. "As soon as the roads are passable, I'll pick him up," I said. "If his owner ever shows up, we'll say that I was fostering him."

I could tell that Lila was pleased, but at the same time, she sounded a little sad.

"I'm going to miss Winter, but you're the one who should have him. I met Crane in the Corners yesterday. When I told him what almost happened, he insisted that we buy a lock for the gate and watch the dogs when they're in the yard. We're to call him immediately if we see that Grimes man again."

"Those are good precautions to take. Do you have a lot of snow on Park Street?"

"We sure do, but a nice young man is shoveling it for us. I

think it's exciting being snowbound. The dogs love it."

"Tell Winter that he's going to have a new home," I said. "I'll be seeing you soon, Lila."

Finally I dialed Leonora's number. Once again I suspected that I had awakened her.

"Happy New Year," I said. "I hope you were up."

"I just came downstairs for a glass of juice," she said. "After two trips, I'm exhausted. I need another vacation."

"How much snow do you have in Oakpoint?"

"Enough. I don't really know. I haven't turned on the radio or television. No one's been around to plow the street yet, so I'm going back to bed. Don't worry about driving in on Monday, Jen. Most of the schools will be closed. Coach Barrett called me. No one's been near the school parking lot."

An extra vacation day tacked on to the Christmas recess was too good to believe. "The custodians have all day and tomorrow to clear the lot," I said.

"They'll never have it finished by Monday. I'm sorry you couldn't take your trip. It's too bad you weren't safely nestled in your rustic lodge before the snows came."

"I had the same thought."

"I'll see you on Tuesday, then. Happy New Year to you, too."

I longed to call Crane, but instead, I turned on the television and listened to as much of the storm team's coverage as I could endure. The weather people were exultant. They had called the blizzard early in the week, and it had happened. Now they had an ever-expanding variety of stories to relate.

Most of the accounts centered on roads, none of which were in better shape than Jonquil Lane. I watched a series of ominous views of drifted over fire hydrants and roofs in peril of collapsing under the weight of heavy snow, suggesting possible future tragedies.

To balance the dismal picture, happier scenes and faces flashed across the screen. People emerged from their houses to dig away at the mountains of snow that surrounded them. They helped their neighbors. Children brought out their sleds and made snowmen.

Inspired by the rash of snow activity paraded before me on the screen, I sprang into action. "Let's go outside and shovel snow again, Halley."

She was instantly on her feet and at my side, wagging her tail and waiting. I supposed she thought we were going for a walk.

~ * ~

I like to think I have the personal resources to fill the hours of my day, even one when I'm snowed in. I kept busy. First I wrote two tests for the end of the semester later in the month and corrected compositions for three of my classes. Then I dismantled the Christmas tree, wrapping the ornaments in tissue paper and packing them in boxes. A few branches at the back had dried out, posing a fire hazard. I tugged it out of the stand and dragged it to the porch but left the balsam roping and red ribbons on the railing in place for a little while longer.

At four, I had an inspiration. If I were going to give Crane cookies for Valentine's Day, I wanted to be reasonably sure they would turn out well. That would require practice. Gathering ingredients, utensils, and heart-shaped cutters, I made cookie dough and rolled it out until I was satisfied with my efforts. As I did, I imagined all the messages I would write in red sugar on the hearts.

At five-thirty, I was thinking about Camille's stew and wondering what I should make for my own dinner when I heard the welcome sound of a tractor coming my way.

I rushed to the living room window and looked out. Dr. Linton, my neighbor on the western side of the lane, was clearing a path straight from his garage to my house. Snow flew in every direction, creating a way out where there had been only insurmountable snowdrifts.

Later, just before dark, someone plowed Jonquil Lane. I had no idea what the conditions of the county roads were, but even though Foxglove Corners was still technically snowbound, the immediate future looked brighter.

Being snowed in and having a holiday fall at the end of the week tends to make me lose track of time, but I hadn't forgotten that tomorrow was Sunday. Now I wouldn't have to miss meeting Crane at the Mill House. I resolved to present Dr. Linton with a token of my appreciation for his kindness as soon as I could get to a store—a spring blossoming plant, perhaps.

~ * ~

Now the way was clear for me to meet Crane for breakfast, but as it happened, he came to me instead. He was still on duty, but I reminded myself that this was the case almost every Sunday, rain, shine, or snow. He sat down at the kitchen table, leaned back in the chair, and gave Halley a welcome pat on her head.

His eyes were weary, and the fine lines that crinkled around them were more pronounced. They still retained their sparkle, though. These days, it was never far away. His warm smile sent my heartbeat racing.

"If I remember, you offered to cook breakfast for me once," he said. "How about this morning?"

"That offer is always open, Crane. You look so tired."

"I am. I didn't realize it until I sat down."

"How many hours more?"

"Four or five. Then I'm going home to get some sleep."

Halley had run to fetch her penguin and returned, holding it in her mouth and waiting. He didn't seem to notice her. I took off my cardigan sweater and started to tie on my Holiday

Humour apron, the only Christmas accessory I hadn't packed away.

"I think I can duplicate any breakfast special the Mill House has on the menu, except for one with country ham. I don't have any ham. What would you like?"

His eyes lingered on my red apron. He was reading its message.

'Come woo me, woo me, for now I am in a holiday humour and like enough to consent.'

Thank you, Rosalind, I thought, *for the invitation, so perfectly worded that Shakespeare might have written it especially for me to say to Crane.*

"What I was really hoping for was something besides food," he said.

"Tell me, what were you hoping for?"

He pulled me onto his lap. "This."

He wasn't too weary to kiss me soundly. When he had finished, I ran my fingers along the lines at his eyes, smoothing them.

"I can't do this at the Mill House," he said, moving his hands slowly down past my waist.

Some time later, I said, "Tell me what you want for breakfast so I can get started. I'm as good as the Mill House cook but not as fast."

He laughed. "Whatever you have," he said. "That'll be fine, honey."

I eased myself off his lap then, smoothed my hair, and finished tying the apron. "Scrambled eggs and bacon then? I have both." I took the frying pan out of the drawer at the bottom of the stove and put a bit of shortening in it to heat. "I have blueberry preserves and orange juice."

"That all sounds good."

He got up and reached for the percolator. Playfully, I pushed him down again.

"I'm in charge of making breakfast, Crane. While you've been working, I had a long rest. Is the worst of it over?"

"We're in better shape than they are downstate," he said. "Around here, most of the roads are passable. We came through the storm without any serious trouble. Who plowed your drive?"

"Dr. Linton. I'm fortunate to have good neighbors. Leonora thinks that school will be closed on Monday. If it's true, I'm going to pick up Winter then."

"Good. I'll be glad when he's here. I'll be off on Friday night, and I'm going to take you to the Carnival Theater. It's not Snow Lodge, but it's something."

"I'll be looking forward to it," I said.

Finally noticing Halley, Crane threw the penguin into the hall for her to retrieve, and I cooked his breakfast, giving the eggs several swirls with the fork to coax them into yellow fluff. As I added bacon, toast, and juice, I said, "I think this is as good as anything the Mill House can offer."

"Better, I'd say."

Her penguin forgotten, Halley regarded the bacon with a covetous eye. Crane slipped her a piece and then began to eat ravenously.

All too soon, he got up and set the empty mug on the counter. "You really know how to take care of me, honey. I sure wish I could stay."

That was my wish, too, but I'd learned not to long for the impossible. Sometimes the probable was sufficient.

I kissed him goodbye and sent him back outside into the bitter cold again, but the snow was finally tapering off, and his long holiday tour of duty was nearing its end.

After a false start, the new year was finally headed in the right direction, with the snow under control and an evening with Crane at the Carnival at the end of the week. All I needed for perfection now was a definite new date for our romantic weekend. Fortunately, we had three more months of winter left.

~ * ~

Even after I had seen Al Grimes at the animal shelter with his massive hand on the gate to the yard, I persisted in thinking of him as a permanent fixture at the Cauldron, rather like the wood-cut witch. I imagined him sitting with Emil Schiller or walking away from my table, blending into the shadows.

It was illogical, but the thought provided me with an illusion of security. If I never returned to the Cauldron, I wouldn't have to see Grimes again. Also, I had Halley, and soon I would have Winter, too.

I refused to listen to the warning voice that said, 'Reality has its own scenario. Grimes may be nearer than you think'.

By Monday, Foxglove Corners was almost back to normal. Plowed, blown, and shoveled from roads and driveways, the snow had no place to go but skyward. Everywhere I looked, it rose in mounds so high I couldn't see over them.

The main roads around Foxglove Corners were passable. Because all the schools in southeastern Michigan were closed, I had one more day to pursue my own interests, one of which was bringing Winter home.

On the way to the animal shelter, I stopped at Hazelton's hardware store. They were doing a brisk business in snow blowers, as well as shovels for the less affluent, but my shopping list had nothing to do with the snow. Once inside the store, I headed for the pet section. I wanted Winter to have his own new possessions when he came to live with me.

I found a leash, a chain, a large food dish bearing the inscription Dog in Gothic letters, and a frisbee that we would save for the spring. Walking past the crowd of people clustered around the snow blower display, I took my pet supplies up to the counter.

"Snow blowers must be selling like hot cakes," I said to young Tim Hazelton, as he scanned the items.

"We'll be out of them soon. I heard on the radio that we were one of the last stores with snow blowers in stock. Everybody is flocking here."

He scanned the items slowly. "That'll be fifty seven dollars even. You must be getting a new dog."

With happy thoughts of spring and Winter running across the fields to catch his frisbee, I wrote a check for my purchases. "Yes, I'm bringing him home today."

I walked briskly to the exit, balancing my package in my left arm as I checked to see that the latch on my shoulder bag was fastened. While I was looking down, a long arm reached past me to open the door.

I was about to thank the man for his courtesy when I saw that the arm belonged to the last person I wanted to see. Al Grimes towered so high above me that he could easily have touched the ceiling.

Sixteen

The words of thanks died in my throat. We were both outside the store now and alone in the parking lot. My car was parked at the end of a line of trucks and vans.

His lips arranged themselves in a sneer. "Well, if it isn't Jane again. Seems you're everywhere I go these days."

Nothing about him had changed. He hadn't gotten that shave yet, and his eyes were as cold as I remembered them. He was a predator who thought he had snared his prey. But I wasn't going to be trapped.

I started to walk away. "Excuse me. I'm in a hurry."

"Not so fast, Jane. You called the cops on me. You told them I tried to steal your dogs. You and that old lady are both crazy. You say I'm a thief? You're the thieves. You stole my dog."

With every word Grimes uttered, he seemed to grow angrier. By the time he had finished, the veins in his temple and neck were bulging, and his large fists were clenched. Next to him, I felt a foot smaller than my height, which was average. As much as I would have liked to run for the sanctuary of my car, I forced myself to look up into his furious eyes without flinching.

"No one called the police, and you *were* trying to steal the shelter dogs. Don't try to deny it."

"I was just looking for my dog. Just taking back what's mine. Why would I want those mangy mongrels when I got a good dog of my own? You set that big gray mutt on me, too. That's not very friendly. If I get rabies, I'm going to sue you."

All right, I told myself. You've stood up to the man. He's delusional. End this.

Fine. But how?

Another man came out of Hazelton's, carrying a bag of rock salt and a snow shovel. I glanced toward him with a half smile. He crossed in front of us to a black truck without looking our way.

"That dog was protecting his property," I said. "Stay away from the shelter. It's under police protection now."

In situations like this, I always like to have the last word. I left Grimes standing there and walked away as quickly as I could, without appearing to be running. I resisted the impulse to turn around, even when he shouted, "Tell that *husband* of yours to take better care of you, Jane. You're going to have some big trouble real soon."

~ * ~

As I sped away from Hazelton's, Grimes' threat and his angry voice were with me in the safety of my car. I planned to stop at the animal hospital before going on to the shelter to take possession of Winter. Driving fast seemed to calm me.

Lila was right; I had made an enemy. Grimes' rancor went back further than the day he had attempted to steal the shelter dogs. He knew I had lied to him that night at the Cauldron, and he resented it. But why was I thinking of what I'd told him as a lie?

A tale told to an unknown man in a tavern isn't a lie. The universal translation of 'My husband will be here in a minute'. is 'I'm not interested in you. Go away and leave me alone'.

Apparently, Crane had brought Grimes in for questioning, as he said he would. It was only natural that Grimes would proclaim his innocence and blame me.

I had acquitted myself well during the brief, unpleasant encounter in Hazelton's lot. Now it was over, except for the fear. On one of the many future occasions when I found myself in Crane's arms, it would be easy to tell him that I was afraid of Grimes, but I didn't want to do this. I needed to be able to take care of myself. I didn't aspire to be a damsel in distress, even though I would never send a knight in shining armor on his way.

But Crane was the most perceptive person I'd ever met. He probably already knew about my fear.

I had to stop thinking about this. I might tell Crane about Grimes' veiled threat, or put it out of my mind as the rambling of a bully. I didn't know which yet. I didn't believe Grimes' claim that the shelter had his dog—if he even had a dog. Remembering his Rottweiler shirt, though, I thought that part could be true.

I had wanted to take on the dognappers, and that's what I was doing. In fact, I might be on my way to a breakthrough right now. Alice had called late last night to tell me about some puzzling information she had come across.

"I want you to see it for yourself. Can you come to the animal hospital tomorrow?"

I said that I'd be there around noon, although I would have preferred a more hospitable meeting place, like my house or hers. Besides being depressing, the hospital was in an isolated location. While it remained closed, I didn't consider it a safe place for anyone to linger.

Neither the holidays nor the blizzard had made me forget that the strangler might still be in Foxglove Corners. Now there was also Grimes. Still, the mystery of Dr. Randolph's murder and alleged involvement in a dognapping ring had to be solved. I could hardly wait to investigate Alice's clue.

The parking lot was plowed. Toward the back, in front of the private entrance, Alice had parked her car. Except for the 'Closed' sign on the front door, anyone would think that the hospital was open. I pulled next to the Intrepid, my recent clash with Grimes temporarily forgotten in my eagerness to learn what Alice had discovered.

She must have been watching for me from the window because she opened the door before I could knock. Her eyes were bright with excitement.

"Good morning, Jennet. I'm so glad you're here. After I talked to you last night, I found something else."

I stepped inside and stamped the snow from my boots on the indoor mat. The interior of the hospital was warm but not inviting. I followed her into the hall that bisected the building. The doors to the examining rooms were closed, and only the restless spirits were in residence. When we spoke, the room threw our voices back at us. I didn't know how Alice could work here when she was alone.

"Let's go in my office. It's more comfortable," she said, as she led me to one of two small rooms at the back of the building.

Here was one place that didn't look forbidding. Alice had decorated it with personal, homey touches. In a cleared space on her desk, a large picture of a lovely Siberian husky looked down on a white bag from the Doughnut Palace. Nearby, on a small table, a coffeemaker bubbled. The air was heavy with the smell of chocolate and maple.

She handed me the box. "Help yourself, Jennet."

I took a maple-frosted doughnut and set it on a napkin, while Alice poured coffee into a mug with the image of a bloodhound on one side and a capsule description of the breed on the other.

Then she took a sheaf of papers from the top of a three-tiered white tray on her desk and handed them to me. They were ordinary wide-ruled sheets with holes, meant for use in a three-ring binder.

"This is what I found after we talked. What do you think?"

I examined the papers closely, one at a time. Names like Lucky, Bandit, and Goldie appeared on every other line, each one followed by a short descriptive phrase, a notation of the dog's weight, and a date. Goldie, for example, was a golden retriever weighing forty-two pounds. Next to her name was written November 3rd.

Anxiously I searched the list for 'Luke—brown collie—seventy pounds—December 23rd.' I didn't see it.

"This must be the list the *Inquisitor* mentioned," I said. "The one the police have. Is this the original?"

"I'm sure it is."

"And is this Dr. Randolph's handwriting?"

"I think so. There's nothing mysterious about this clue. It's a list of dogs. All of them were brought to our hospital for care during the past year. Every one is missing. I treated some of them myself. I checked through our files to be sure."

I estimated the number of names on each sheet and multiplied by four, ending with a rough estimate of fifty dogs. This was the first time I had brought all of the stolen dogs together in my mind.

"This is an incredibly large number," I said.

"There may be many more."

"Something has been troubling me. According to the *Inquisitor*, Dr. Randolph sold pets for research. These dogs must have been returned to their owners after their treatment."

"I know," Alice said. "The only way that statement makes sense is if David supplied the dognappers with addresses."

"You don't think he was one of the dognappers, do you?" I asked.

"I still believe in David. Lila gave me a description of Al Grimes. David was a refined and kind man. I can't imagine him even knowing someone like Grimes, much less working with him."

"I just came from a confrontation with Grimes at the hardware store," I said. "He blames me for turning him in to the police."

"The police found him? Oh, I'm so glad about that. But you said a confrontation? Did he hurt you?"

"He tried to convince me that he was innocent. He threatened me. That's all."

"That's serious, Jennet. You should report it to the police."

"Maybe I will." I set the list of names down on the desk. "Even if in some bizarre scenario Dr. Randolph were involved with the dognappers, he would hardly steal his own patients. That would make no sense at all. Are you going to give the list to the police?"

Hastily, Alice took the papers from me, folded them, and put them in her large handbag.

"Of course not. They have their own copy, but apparently they don't know that the dogs were our patients yet. We want to clear David's name, not blacken it further. You won't tell anybody what we're doing, will you?"

A vision of Crane in uniform flashed before my eyes. I could hear his voice take on a stern, admonishing tone as he repeated his favorite adage: "Don't meddle in police business, Jennet. Let them do the work they're trained to do."

Nothing would be gained by revealing Alice's discovery. I said, "I don't have any fondness for the police. Once I turned evidence over to an officer, and he scolded me for not doing it sooner."

I took another doughnut from the bag, broke it in two, and reached for a tissue, as raspberry filling dripped down on the desk. "This list may not be what it seems. You said you found something else?"

"Yes," she said. "This is what I mentioned on the phone."

From the second tier, she took what remained of a dog calendar, the kind that features a different dog for each day of the year, along with a quotation or snippet of pet care information. All of the sheets up to December sixteenth were gone. The December seventeenth page was covered with doodles, and the rest of the calendar pages were blank.

"I found this in David's desk drawer," Alice said. "It was pushed to the back and covered with a section of the *Banner*. I have no idea why he saved the newspaper. Maybe just to hide the calendar. Maybe there's no significance at all."

She cleared a space on the desk, and I set the calendar down. On December seventeenth, Dr. Randolph had drawn on practically every inch of the page. The finished product looked like a surrealistic depiction of Christmas. Miniature firs and houses appeared to float in space. He had sketched dogs' heads with long floppy ears and a small sleigh. In a heavier hand, he had written three dates: November twenty-sixth, December twenty-sixth and January twenty-sixth.

"David loved to doodle, especially when he talked on the phone," she said. "Sometimes he drew whatever he was talking about."

"Fir trees, houses, dogs and a sleigh. Well..."

I took a bite of doughnut and tried to make sense of the floating images. Alice poured the last of the coffee, dividing it between us.

"David invited me out to dinner for the first time in November," Alice said. "We talked about winter sports and activities we both enjoyed. He asked me if I'd like to go on a sleigh ride with him."

"Do you think the little sleigh he drew referred to this ride?"

"Maybe. He might have been checking on when the rides were offered and writing possible dates."

"I don't think we had snow in November."

"No, and not much in December. The fact that the calendar was hidden might be significant," Alice said.

"Unless he stashed it in the drawer and forgot about it. May I see the paper?"

She handed the *Banner* to me, and I set it on the desk over the calendar. I scanned the articles but didn't see anything relevant.

We were going nowhere. The clues weren't leading to any major discover, or even a minor one. Since the significance of the scribbled sheet from the dog calendar eluded me for the moment, the only telling piece of evidence was the list of stolen dogs. That might only implicate Dr. Randolph further.

"Let's give these clues time to simmer—like a stew," I said. "Let me think about this. You do the same and keep on looking. May I have copies of the calendar page and list?"

"I'll make them," Alice said, but when she returned in a few minutes with the promised copies, her earlier excitement had evaporated. "Maybe they're just meaningless scribbles on a calendar."

"But this could be a clue." Not wanting to end our meeting on an unhappy note, I added, "I wanted you to know that I'm adopting Winter."

"I'm so glad you're giving him a home." Alice handed me the picture I'd noticed earlier. "This is my Shelby. She was a rescue dog. Do you think Halley will accept Winter?"

"Halley is the gentlest, sweetest collie I've ever known. My neighbor's dog lived with us last fall, and I'm sure it'll work out with Winter." I got up and reached for my shoulder bag. "If

I have a sudden inspiration about the mystery, I'll call you."

I tucked the sheets Alice had given me into my pocket and searched for my car keys that always sink to the bottom of my bag.

"I'll keep looking through David's papers," Alice said. "Maybe I'll find something else."

I left her pulling another file out of a box on the floor and set out for my last stop of the day.

~ * ~

A man was clearing the driveway of the animal shelter, tossing heavy snow against the fence with what appeared to be great ease. He had already moved so much snow in front of the gate that it was almost completely hidden. No dogs played in the yard today, and the sisters' station wagon was parked in the street.

The man with the shovel looked up. He was young and strikingly handsome, with hair that seemed to hold the colors of the morning sun. Emil Schiller, animal rights activist, Grimes' tavern companion, and Leonora's Renaissance angel pushed the shovel into a snowdrift and smiled at me.

Seventeen

"Good morning, ma'am," he said. "Watch your step. The walk is icy."

I had no time to conceal my surprise, but Emil was already resuming his work, apparently unaware that I'd recognized him.

Gingerly, I made up way up the walk and climbed the stairs. Someone had spread a generous layer of rock salt underfoot. The empty bag lay on the porch, alongside a broom.

I rang the doorbell. From inside the shelter, the dogs were barking so loudly that I wondered if their number had doubled since my last visit.

Letty opened the door part way, allowing me just enough room to squeeze through. Six leaping, yapping young dogs surrounded her, trying to be the first to greet the company. Besides the little golden retrievers that I had rescued, the shelter had three new puppies, all of them black. Winter lay by the fireside, calmly watching their antics, but Brown Dog was nowhere in sight.

"Our new pups are unwanted Christmas presents," Letty said.

They were tumbling over one another in a race to the door. "The poor little things," I said. "Well, someone will adopt them."

"I hope so. Winter has been waiting for you. We told him he was going to his new home today. I think he understands."

"Of course he does, don't you, Winter?"

Even before I said his name or approached him, Winter was at my side, tail wagging and ears laid smooth against the sides of his head. His eyes were alert, and he looked whole and beautiful. When he grew his new coat, all traces of the double injury would be gone.

I laid the bag from Hazelton's on a table, took out Winter's new chain, and slipped it over his neck. "It's official now, Winter. You're my dog."

Lila had joined us. She was dabbing at her eyes with a white handkerchief. "I feel like crying. I go through this every time we lose one of our dogs."

"Nonsense," Letty said. "This is what we do, Lila. We'll always have another dog to take his place."

"What do you know about the man who's shoveling your driveway?" I asked.

"We only just met him," Letty said. "His name is Emil Schiller, and he's a lifesaver. He came to our door on Saturday morning and offered to shovel our snow for twenty dollars."

"He shoveled Henry's snow, too," Lila said. "He's an angel."

"Did he say if he has a regular job?"

"He's between jobs," Letty said. "He shoveled enough on Saturday so that we could get out if we had to and came back today to widen the drive."

"If you don't mind, I think I'll wait until he's finished to leave. You two go on with whatever you were doing. I'll stay here in the living room and play with the puppies."

Letty frowned. "Is anything wrong?"

"It's probably nothing."

Emil didn't know me; I was pretty sure of it. I reviewed the past times when we had been in close proximity, at the Harvest Ball in October and recently at the Cauldron. Our paths had never crossed, and I didn't think anyone had ever mentioned my name to him, not even Grimes who knew me as Jane. My knowledge of Emil came from second hand accounts, some of them biased, and from Crane's investigation.

How much of this should I tell Lila and Letty? Or should I say anything at all? Just because I had seen Emil Schiller in the company of Al Grimes, I had no reason to leap to the assumption that he had come to the shelter with sinister intent. My mind stuck at this point. It was possible that Emil knew Grimes only casually as a Cauldron regular. It was also possible that they were associates.

I said, "Emil Schiller used to be an enforcer for an animal rights organization. I saw him with Al Grimes only last week. I don't know how significant that is," I added quickly, as I saw the surprise in Letty's eyes. Beside her, Lila raised her hand to her mouth as if to cut off a gasp.

I was almost sorry that I'd said anything. If Emil was only a nice young man between jobs, I was being unfair to everybody. But I didn't really believe that, and the animals who'd already been stolen and those at risk were more important than a possible unjust accusation.

"We had no idea..." Lila began.

"We won't hire him again," Letty said. She walked over to the window. "He's almost done."

Lila said, "I told you to ask him for references, Letty. After all those dogs disappeared, after the attempted theft..."

"In a snowstorm, no one asks a young man with a shovel for references." Letty turned away from the window. "Crane suggested that we have someone shovel the snow up against the fence as a barricade."

"That'll only work until the January thaw. When the snow melts, we'll have to come up with another plan. If the dognappers are still around. Maybe they'll be caught by then. Have either one of you seen Grimes skulking around lately?"

Lila shuddered. "No, and I've been watching. I've had nightmares about him. I'm so glad I wasn't alone that day."

"Crane picked Grimes up for questioning," I said. "As soon as I see him, I'll ask how it went."

"This holiday it's been one thing after another," Lila said. "I had to give my statement to the police after Dr. Randolph's murder; then that Grimes man tried to steal our dogs. Now his friend comes right to our door."

Letty picked up one of the little retrievers and dropped her into my lap. "This is Daffodil. All of the puppies have gained weight, and each one has her own little personality. We've named the others Daisy and Dandy—short for dandelion."

I held Daffodil and let her gnaw at my fingers while her sisters chased their tails at my feet. The black puppies fell into an instant slumber. Being too old for such puppy pleasures, Winter contented himself with looking on.

Before long, Emil knocked on the door. He stood in the hallway, stamping the snow off his boots on the dark blue floral patterned rug.

"All done, ladies," he said. "I used up all the rock salt on the walk, but be careful if you go outside. Cute pups," he added, as the black puppies, now awake, discovered a potential new playmate.

Letty fumbled in her purse and pressed a twenty-dollar bill in Emil's hands. "Thank you. We could never have dug our way out alone."

Emil pocketed his money and left with a casual smile for all of us. Now positive that he didn't know me, I watched through the front window as he walked down Park Street in the direction of the library. He must have left his car in their lot.

I said, "I'm going to wait a few more minutes before I go."

"You're making me nervous, Jennet," Lila said. "Are you really afraid?"

"If there's even the remotest chance that Grimes and Emil are working together, I want to make sure that Emil doesn't know I'm taking Winter."

Letty said, "You say there's no danger, but you don't sound like it."

"It never hurts to be careful." I set Daffodil down on the rug, and she lost no time in scampering away.

"Don't forget to tape our show on Friday," Letty added.

I fastened Winter's new leash to his chain and reached for the bag containing the dish and Frisbee. "I won't."

After a few minutes, I looked outside again. No one was in sight. I decided that it was safe to leave. Probably it had been safe all along, and I was becoming paranoid.

"Good luck with your television debut, Letty," I said. "Winter, we're going home."

~ * ~

Camille was the first person to welcome Winter. She had driven the short distance from the yellow Victorian to my house to deliver the stew.

"There's too much snow on the lane for walking," she said. "Now, you won't have to cook until Friday. This is the best stew I've made in a long time. I've had some every day."

"Thanks, Camille. This is my lucky week. Crane is taking me out to dinner on Friday. Come in and see Winter."

I took the containers and her coat and called the dogs, which proved unnecessary. They were already in the kitchen, forming a canine welcoming committee of two. Halley, wildly excited at seeing Camille again, pranced around her, nipping at the air, while Winter, more reserved, as befitting his mature years and his new status in the house, stood quietly waiting to be introduced.

I stooped to pick up Halley's stuffed penguin. It had lain on the floor since yesterday when Crane had thrown it for her. Both dogs had been playing with it in a mild tug-of-war game. My two collies wouldn't need a period of adjustment. Halley had accepted Winter on sight, and they had bonded instantly.

Camille was suitably impressed. "Oh, he's so beautiful! I've never seen such gorgeous markings. His head is half blue merle and half tri-color, just as you said."

"Winter, come closer and meet Camille," I said.

He came to her then, and Halley seized her opportunity to toss her penguin into the air. It landed at Camille's feet. I thought for a moment that the two dogs might overwhelm Camille, who was delicately built, but she understood canine behavior. Especially, she knew collies. Once she'd had a collie of her own.

She held out her hand for Winter to sniff. "You poor dog. I hope that cruel man is somewhere nursing a painfully throbbing leg. Did they ever find him, Jennet?"

"Yes, and I saw Grimes again today at Hazelton's. He denies doing anything wrong and blames me for calling the police, which I didn't do, not exactly. I mean, I told Crane. That's not the same thing. Grimes sort of threatened me."

"There's no 'sort of' about a threat. You have to tell Crane."

"I will, but I'm going to turn the tables on Grimes. I don't know how yet. We wanted to catch the dognappers. Now we have a real person to target."

"I know, but I don't want you to get hurt," she said.

"I'll try to be careful."

"Tomorrow when you're in school, I'll come over between ten and eleven to let the dogs out, and again around two."

"I don't know how I can ever thank you," I said.

"I'm glad to do it, and I'm so happy you adopted Winter. What will you do if his owner ever shows up?" she asked.

"I'll return him. It may never happen, though. I hope it doesn't."

Blithely, I had welcomed uncertainty with open arms. Because I now considered Winter mine, I didn't want to think about his previous owner. As for Grimes, I had no doubt that we would meet again. Now there was Emil Schiller as well, an unknown equation.

I didn't know why I had invited so many new complications into my life. Keeping one step ahead of my English classes and trying to steer Crane toward a state of greater permanence were sufficiently difficult tasks without adding grim possibilities lurking in the shadows.

~ * ~

On Tuesday I discovered that many of Marston's students were still on vacation, some of them literally. It was a relatively easy day, which was fortunate, as I was finding it difficult to make the transition from holiday to ordinary school day.

Looking limp and less energetic than usual, Leonora carried her tray into my room at lunchtime. "I've been used to having a leisurely lunch whenever I'm hungry. I guess it's back to twenty minutes and school food."

"Since our adventure in the snow, I've been busy," I said and filled her in on my activities. "And you're going to be interested in this. I saw your Renaissance angel shoveling snow at the shelter for twenty dollars."

"He's a handyman? He's too gorgeous to be doing odd jobs."

"He's too young for you, Leonora. Besides, he's a suspicious character."

"You don't know that, and I can appreciate masculine beauty. Speaking of which, I've been going out with Coach

Barrett lately, but this is a secret from the kids," she added. "The last thing I want is for them to catch on."

"Adam Barrett! Well, that's a surprise."

Having confided this fascinating bit of news about herself, Leonora promptly changed the subject. "Did Henry McCullough ever find his dog?"

"Not yet, and I'm almost certain that Grimes stole him. I can't bear to think about Luke ending up in a research lab. He would never survive that."

"Unfortunately, research dogs aren't meant to survive," Leonora said.

"I asked Crane to keep a lookout for Luke, but he hasn't seen him. Lila says that Henry is going to stay on in the Park Street house indefinitely, in case Luke comes back to the last place they stayed together. It's all so sad. I wish I could find him."

"Why don't you use your computer?" she asked.

"That's a good idea. I could search for collies, lost dogs, rescue collies, whatever I can think of, and dognapping, too. Maybe I'll learn something that will help me."

"Don't forget research labs," Leonora added.

I glanced at the clock. The bell would ring in five minutes, but the afternoon classes always went by quickly. Today, as soon as I fed the dogs and walked them, I was going to begin my search on the Internet. What had seemed hopeless not twenty minutes ago was now possible.

If only I could find a way to delete Al Grimes from the picture.

Eighteen

When I came downstairs on Friday evening, Halley was busy chewing her rawhide bone, Winter was asleep by the fireside, and Crane was sitting in a chair by the window reading my issue of *Mary May*, the one with the hot techniques article. The title was splashed gaudily across the cover in orange letters.

Crane looked up. With a devilish smile, he set the magazine down on the end table.

I was annoyed at myself for the warmth I felt spreading over my face. I hoped that, if he noticed, Crane would attribute my heightened color to my new rosemist blush.

He said, "You're the prettiest thing I've seen all day, honey. Are you ready for a night at the Carnival?"

The appreciation in his eyes warmed me more thoroughly than the cup of hot tea I'd had after school. In my red dress with the crystal bracelet sparkling against its sleeve, I felt that I was as pretty as he thought.

"I'm more than ready," I said. "It's been a long four-day week."

"That's the downside of having a two-week vacation. I see that Winter is making himself at home. Isn't it a sign of acceptance when a dog sleeps on his side?"

"I think so. Winter has acted as if he's at home since his first day here."

Even as Crane said his name, Winter was awake, lying in an upright position and alert, as if he were aware of a coming change. Halley, too, had abandoned her bone and was at attention. The dogs sensed that they would soon have the house to themselves.

Crane held my long black coat and bent to kiss the back of my neck. "The police brought Grimes in for questioning, Jennet," he said. "He had his story all ready. Unfortunately they can't hold him."

"What did he say?"

"That he heard someone had taken his dog to the animal shelter by mistake. He claims he was just trying to take back his property."

"Does he really have a dog?"

"He says he has a Rottweiler named Snapper."

"Oh, yes. He loves his Rottweiler. Grimes told me the same story and let me know that it was my fault he was questioned."

The change in Crane's voice was sudden, and his eyes seemed sharper. "When was this?"

"I ran into him at Hazelton's." I might as well tell Crane everything now. "Grimes threatened me. I don't know if he was serious."

"What exactly did he say?"

"Something about telling my husband to take better care of me, that I was going to be in trouble soon. I just walked away."

"What husband is this?"

"The one I invented to get rid of him that night at the Cauldron."

I could tell by Crane's grim expression that he was worried. That pushed my own anxiety a little higher up the scale.

He said, "I don't like this, but leave Al Grimes to me. I'm

going to take care of him."

Those were wonderful words to hear, but I didn't really believe that Crane could erase the threat of Grimes from my life. I would have to do that myself. Nonetheless, I was glad that he wanted to help me.

"I always knew there were advantages to dating the law," I said, borrowing one of Leonora's phrases.

Crane looked inordinately pleased. "We'd better get moving, or we'll miss the beginning of the movie. Afterward, how about hamburgers at the Lakeside Grill? We haven't been there yet this year."

"It's fine, and can we set aside a few minutes to discuss an idea I have for dealing with the dognappers?"

"Sure. Later at the Grill. I have two pieces of information for you, too, but it's nothing that can't wait."

I told Halley and Winter to watch the house, Crane locked the door behind us, and we walked the short distance to his Jeep. Snow flurries sparkled in mid-air, hardly seeming to touch the ground, and the night air was cold but not bitter.

Once we were inside the Jeep, Crane reached over, took off my glove, and moved his fingers slowly up to my wrist, where the crystal bracelet lay. He didn't say a word. He didn't have to.

I was definitely with Crane, the Romantic Hero tonight. Whenever he arrived in his Jeep, I knew there was a good chance that he had left his stern deputy sheriff persona at home.

Besides being romantic, Crane was in a rare teasing mood. When we turned onto Spruce Road and neared the Rocking Horse Ranch, he pointed out how ideal the snowy weather was for an outside activity.

"Would you like to skip the movie and dinner and go for a sleigh ride instead? We could stop for hot chocolate afterwards."

"I think I'd rather see *Somewhere in Time* and have a

hamburger."

His warm laugh held a thousand promises. "Okay, that's what we'll do. We'll save the sleigh ride for Snow Lodge."

Reassured and basking in a warm glow of anticipation, I glanced out the window as we passed the Rocking Horse Ranch. Ropes of garland and blue lights decorated the rambling gray brick house and the barns clustered nearby. People boarded their horses here and took riding lessons. Sleigh rides originated at the ranch, and one of the barns had probably been the scene of the rocking New Year's Eve party.

The rest of countryside was buried in deep, glistening snow. Vast expanses of white remained untouched by plow or shovel, and on either side of the road, towering spruce trees shadowed the road, lending an air of desolation to the scene.

A few miles beyond the ranch, we passed a ramshackle barn that had weathered to an unattractive no-color. Part of one side was caved in. Perhaps someone had driven a tractor into it, or it might have simply succumbed to rot. The barn was a good distance from the road and surrounded by snow.

In Foxglove Corners, where the emphasis was on building pricey new houses and maintaining existing ones in style, a standing structure in such a state of disrepair was a rare sight. If an inanimate object were capable of communication, this old barn, situated in an area of affluence, would tell of want and loss. Farther back from the road, I glimpsed a larger structure, probably a house that appeared to be as run down as the barn and equally inaccessible.

I mentioned some of this to Crane, who was not usually attuned to vague feelings and inanimate communications.

"The barn has been in that condition ever since I can remember," he said.

"I wonder why the owner doesn't tear it down."

"I don't know. Maybe this snowy winter will be the death of

it."

We were now driving through a dark, wild stretch, and I put the place and its sad atmosphere out of my mind to concentrate on the prospect of being with Crane for the entire evening. Soon afterward, we were sitting close together in the dark theater, sharing popcorn and impressions of time travel and romance. Although *Somewhere in Time* wasn't a vintage holiday movie, it seemed a perfect escape for this particular season.

With Crane's arm resting firmly on my shoulder, I felt well protected. I could almost believe that I had never walked slowly down my basement stairs, waiting for a vengeful giant to leap out and grab me. Tonight Grimes' parting threat seemed as remote as the time of the movie.

As the film drew to an end, I said, "I'd love to go to Mackinac Island someday. In the wintertime maybe."

Crane kissed me lightly. "We will—someday."

All around us, people were getting up and moving. Crane reached for my coat. He took the empty popcorn box, threw it into a trash container, and we joined the crowd that was streaming out of the theater.

"They're showing classic romance movies for Valentine's Day," he said.

When were inside the Jeep that Crane had parked on a secluded side street, he pulled me across the seat and kissed me thoroughly and for a long time. We were just like kids parked in a lover's lane—but not quite. Willow Street wasn't lover's lane, and we were both past our youth. Come to think of it, we had our own houses and plans for a weekend at Snow Lodge. My teen years had never been this exciting.

But somewhere between Willow Street and the Lakeside Grill, Crane turned into the sheriff's deputy who loved to talk about the more graphic aspects of his life and considered the dinner table to be the perfect setting for this kind of narration. After a grim recital of expressway spinouts and frostbitten members, he began telling an anecdote about a man who had found himself trapped in a barn with a hungry coyote.

"Stop, please," I said. "I don't want to know how that story comes out. Wild animals make me think about Grimes."

"All right, I'll stop, but I told you not to worry about him," Crane said. "Now, Jennet, tell me that you're not going to launch a private investigation into the murder of Dr. Randolph."

"I never even thought about doing that."

"I don't know if I can believe you. I remember how determined you were to find out who killed Caroline Meilland."

"That was different. Caroline was my friend. I never even met Dr. Randolph. His partner, Dr. Foster is the one playing detective. Her main interest is to clear his name."

"That's a relief," Crane said.

I thought he looked more disappointed than relieved, though. Possibly he had been looking forward to a rousing debate over hamburgers. I decided to offer him a few crumbs.

"I've been playing detective myself, but it has nothing to do with Dr. Randolph's murder. I'm searching the Internet to see if I can find Luke."

"Did you have any success?"

"Not yet. I saw dozens of pictures of lost collies, all colors and ages. Some are pet quality, but others look as if they came from championship lines."

"I'm afraid Luke is gone," he said. "Is McCullough still holding out hope for his return?"

"Lila says he's going to stay in Foxglove Corners until that happens."

"It's sad to think about an old man waiting for something that will never come."

"It's heartbreaking, but I'm trying to stay optimistic. I looked up pet theft, too. Research labs buy animals for their experiments from Class B dealers. Men like Grimes collect dogs and cats from people who don't want them or steal them for the dealers. They're called bunchers."

"Like any business, it's all about money," Crane said.

"The dealers are supposed to be regulated by the government, but there aren't enough regulators, so men like Grimes can operate with little fear of prosecution."

"Unless they're caught taking a pet," Crane said.

"Exactly. I think I've come up with a way to trap them, but it's a little sketchy."

"Tell me."

He listened without comment as I described the highlights of my plan. "When I say dognappers, I'm thinking about Grimes. Suppose someone were to offer him a lure—something he wouldn't be able to pass up. I'm thinking about an offer of free puppies."

"All right," Crane said. "You put a 'Free Puppies' sign in a prominent place in town. Grimes sees it. That's assuming he's in our town to begin with. What then?"

"We'll catch him in the act. Maybe we'll take pictures for proof. A video camera would be even better…" I trailed off as my sketchy plan skidded to a halt.

"And then what happens?"

"We call the police."

"You're hoping that Grimes won't notice he's being set up, which is high risk. By the way, what hapless pups are you intending to use as bait?"

"I'm not sure. We'll arrange it so that the puppies will never be in any danger. I don't know how yet."

"Who is this 'we' you refer to?" he asked.

"I haven't worked out the details. Maybe Henry, Lila, Letty, and Alice."

Was any one of us a match for Grimes? I was, and Alice certainly. Maybe Letty...

"I see. I thought you were afraid of Grimes," Crane said.

"Did I say that?"

His voice took on a familiar lecturing tone. "Well, if you aren't, you should be. Al Grimes is a dangerous man. I found out that he's been involved in dog fighting in Detroit for years. He trained fighting dogs and organized fights. Last year, he dropped out of sight."

I could guess what Grimes had been doing since then. Stealing dogs, hanging out at the Cauldron, harassing me... I came back to the present. "That I (heart) My Rottweiler shirt he wears. It makes perfect sense."

"Dog fighting is a bloody business, and it's illegal in Michigan," Crane said. "Dogs are trained to fight each other to the death, with kittens and puppies used as live bait. One way or the other, Grimes is making his living on animals."

A puppy trembling in a cage, a tiny kitten thrown into the path of a killer dog in training. The images Crane described were burned in my mind. No longer hungry, I put the rest of my hamburger down.

"Grimes is an evil man," I said.

"This is the man you want to trap when you get everything worked out?"

I knew when to surrender graciously. "I don't relish the prospect of confronting Grimes again, and I won't take him on alone. But the only way our dogs will be safe is if someone stops him."

"Agreed. Someone. But not you."

Then I remembered. Crane had two pieces of information. "What else were you going to tell me?"

"It's about Emil Schiller. I didn't find anything to implicate

163

him in the dog thefts. Since October, he's been seen with two known members of the Michigan Militia. That isn't illegal. He doesn't have a job, except for odd ones here and there. He hasn't joined any other animal rights organization."

"I wondered how dedicated to animal welfare he was."

I looked across the table at Crane. He had finished eating and looked as if he was in an unusually good mood in spite of the dark territory we'd been traversing.

"You don't think my idea is a good one, do you? As I described it to you, I thought it was a little farfetched myself."

"The word entrapment comes to mind," he said.

"And another word—protection. Protection for the dogs."

"Here's still another one, honey. Foolhardy. I'd rather see you on a trail of another mystery."

"You're condoning my sleuthing activities when I'm not even practicing them. How unlike you, Crane." I softened the words with a smile.

Crane could afford to make that extravagant statement since I'd assured him that Alice was the one investigating Dr. Randolph's murder. I had no intentions of enlightening him further.

"If you're finished eating, we should be getting home," he said. "It's late, and I have a plan of my own for us. It isn't sketchy either."

I was happy to see that Crane, the Romantic Hero, had returned. I needed a brief respite from criminal talk.

"What would you say to a nice warm fire and some quiet time together?" he asked. "We'll lock the dogs in the sunroom."

"I'd say it has more appeal than anything else we talked about tonight."

"I think so, too." He picked up the bill and reached for my coat. "Let's go."

I slipped my hand in his as we went through the door into a wall of blowing snow flurries. Anticipating an evening of romance, I felt safe and warm. But afterward, when Crane went home, what then?

My only plan had been derailed before I'd even implemented it, and rightly so. In its present form, it was bound to fail. Emil's place in the dognapping ring was still a mystery, and as for Grimes, he was even worse than I'd imagined.

The images flared up. Living puppies and kittens bought as bait... Blood... I (heart) my Rottweiler... I moved closer to Crane, and he tightened his arm around me.

Having a knight-to-the-rescue in my corner would be a valuable asset, although I hoped that I would be able to defeat Grimes on my own.

Nineteen

A few days passed, and the temperatures moderated. All around Foxglove Corners, the high mounds of snow drew closer to the earth. Snowmen lost their carrot noses and branch arms, turned into puddles, and disappeared into the ground. Wreaths dried and drooped, and the wood-cut Santa Claus in Dr. Linton's yard leaned sideways.

Christmas became a distant memory. I took down the wreath and the balsam roping and dragged the tree out to the front of the house, where I strung its branches with popcorn for the birds.

I didn't see Grimes. Since he stayed out of sight, I shoved him back to the farthermost corner of my mind and ordered him to stay there.

One day I realized that the last of the big snow was gone. Then it snowed again, just enough to give the ground a fresh white cover. Because it was cold, the snow stayed. The January thaw hadn't happened yet.

I was warming up in the kitchen of the yellow Victorian on a Saturday morning. Camille and I were sipping hot chocolate. At our feet, the tired canines lay lapping water from a large bowl. We had just returned from a long walk. Navigating the lane was easier now that it wasn't drifted over in snow, and with the three dogs, I felt safe again—three times as safe.

"Will there really be jonquils on Jonquil Lane in the spring?" I asked Camille.

"Yes, and daffodils," she said, "along with every kind of spring plant you can think of. The developer had a passion for spring flowers. He planted the first bulbs and named the lane. I've planted dozens more, on your side and mine."

"I'm going to plant flowers as soon as the ground thaws," I said. "I can't wait until spring."

Camille laughed. "I know the feeling, but we're only in dreary January. Besides, you and Crane haven't had your winter getaway yet."

"Maybe we're destined not to go. We were going to take a color tour in October, but I came down with the flu; and then all the leaves were down. We may end up spending all of our time together in Foxglove Corners."

"Would you mind that?" Camille asked.

"No, but I'd rather go away with Crane for two whole days."

Apparently Crane had been thinking about our winter getaway, too. I met him later that afternoon at a diner on Spruce Road. He was drinking coffee. I ordered another cup of hot chocolate.

"Snow Lodge is far enough north to have snow well into spring," he said. "We'll get there, honey. Never fear."

"I don't need to go to Snow Lodge to have a romantic time with you," I said.

Slivers of frost appeared in Crane's eyes, and he grew quiet.

"What's the matter?" I asked.

"Are you saying that you don't want to go away with me?"

"I don't think so. Did I say that?"

He trained his eyes on me and didn't answer right away. At last, he said, "No, you didn't."

He couldn't possibly think that I'd changed my mind about going away with him. Or could he? I'd better reassure him. "I'm ready to go any time, except for next weekend. That's the end of the semester. It's the busiest time of the school year. Any weekend but that one."

"I'll pick a date then and let the manager know. Are you going shopping today?"

"No, but I might buy a spring plant. I'm meeting Alice Foster at the animal hospital. She says she found a few more clues."

I was deliberately downplaying my meeting with Alice. She had also come across a name.

"Those rumors about Dr. Randolph have died down," Crane said. "Alice doesn't have some idea of trying to catch his killer, I hope."

"Not that I know of, unless her plans have changed. I'll know when I talk to her. I should be going. I told Alice I'd be there at one."

I came around to his side of the booth, laid my hand against the side of his face, and kissed him. I hoped he would notice that I was wearing the crystal bracelet.

"I'll see you tomorrow for breakfast," I said.

He smiled then, a smile that traveled up to his eyes, making them several degrees warmer.

"At the Mill House," he said.

I wasn't happy about leaving Crane, but Alice was expecting me, and his coffee break must be over anyway.

"I'll see you soon—in twenty hours, to be exact," I said.

He smiled again. "I didn't know you were counting the time, honey."

~ * ~

I stopped at a bakery to buy a dozen doughnuts, taking time to make a leisurely selection, and drove on to the animal hospital. Alice's Intrepid was parked in the lot. As I locked my car, I noticed that the snow made the place seem even more isolated than I remembered it being on my last visit.

I knocked loudly and waited. When Alice didn't come to the door and I found myself growing uncomfortably aware of the extreme cold, I knocked again with more emphasis. Finally, overcome by impatience, I turned the knob and pushed on the door. To my surprise, it opened.

As I stepped inside and closed the door behind me, the unrelenting cold seemed to follow me. Still shivering, I stood in the vestibule, set the doughnut bag down on the ledge above the coat rack, and took off my parka and gloves. It was so cold inside the building that I almost felt like putting them on again, but I hung the parka on the coat rack next to Alice's brown suede jacket.

I raised my voice several notches and picked up the doughnut bag. "Alice, I let myself in. I guess you didn't hear me knocking."

There was no answer. The building was soundless, and the deep quiet enveloped me as the frigid air outside had done.

"Alice?"

I turned, took a few steps into the waiting room, and recoiled in horror at the sight of the neat little room systematically torn apart. Chairs lay on their sides, the Nutritional Treats display had been overturned, and boxes of Prime Rib Bits had tumbled to the floor where they lay in an untidy heap.

In the office behind the reception desk, file drawers hung open, and manila folders and paper were strewn around. It looked as if a winter tornado had touched down inside the hospital.

My God! Where was Alice?

I called her name again and walked warily past the reception desk into the hall. The doors of the examining rooms were open. The greatest concentration of mess was beyond the back exit, where Alice's office was located.

I had to find her and call the police. In what order?

I heard the low menacing growl a fraction of a second before a great black dog bounded out of the room opposite the back door. Instinctively, I stepped back, and the bag fell out of my hand. Doughnuts spilled out in a nutty and powdery mix of custard, lemon, and chocolate. I stepped on them and slid in a puddle of custard as I tried to flatten myself against the wall.

This was no friendly, fawning canine to be distracted by food. He was a massive and powerful Rottweiler with muscles that rippled under his sleek black fur. More to the point, he was all bared fangs and blazing eyes, a living weapon of mass destruction, and I was his target. For one brief, horrifying moment, the dog waited.

I froze, all of my considerable knowledge about canines gone in a blur. I forced myself to think, to remember. Should I speak softly and soothingly to him? Stand still and meet his stare or look away? Or run for my life?

He can run faster.

I remembered. When facing an impending dog attack, you were supposed to lie down and pretend to be dead. And cover your face.

Yes, that was it; that's what I had to do. Cover my face. I couldn't die in the powerful jaws of a Rottweiler, not when I had loved dogs all my life.

He was going to spring...

I ran. My destination was the nearest examining room, but I knew I'd never reach it. There was no time for last thoughts of my loved ones, and my life didn't flash in front of me. All I saw was a huge black body in motion and a face that held all the fury of hell.

A whistle shrilled through the silence. Now it was the dog who froze. Instead of lunging at my throat, he turned and ran down the hall and out through the exit. In that instant, I managed to move, and I ran myself—after him, straight to the same door. I pulled it shut and listened for the click of the locking mechanism as it snapped into place.

It's over. I didn't die. It wasn't my time.

I leaned on the hard wood surface. My heart was racing, and I was colder than I had been all day. The deadly chill reached all the way through to my soul. I was shaking violently, and my mouth was so dry I felt as if I was going to choke. But I was alive.

Thanks to a whistle, I had been spared a horrible death. Someone outside had called the killer dog off, undoubtedly the same person who had brought him here in the first place.

And if it wasn't too late, I could open the door, just a crack, and maybe catch a glimpse of him or even his car... But what if the dog was waiting on the other side?

A low, muffled moan from the other end of the hall broke into my thoughts.

"Alice!"

There was no answer, but I knew that I had to get control of my runaway symptoms and focus on Alice. I followed the sound to her office.

Like the rest of the animal hospital, it had been ravaged, its contents scattered in every direction. Even the picture of Alice's dog lay on the floor, the glass shattered into pieces. I found Alice there, leaning on her desk and holding her hand to her head.

I hurried to her side. "Are you hurt? Here, let me see."

She moved her hand. The flesh around her temple was red and angry.

"I guess I was unconscious for a few minutes. Is he still

here?"

"No, he's gone, thank God. Someone called him off with a whistle, and I locked him outside. It was a close call, though. I've never been so scared, not in all my life."

"Who are you talking about, Jennet?"

"The dog," I said. "The Rottweiler. I thought the hospital was closed."

"I meant the man. Is he still here? Or maybe there were two of them." She glanced fearfully at the door. "Is anyone else in the hospital?"

"There's no one but me now. Here, sit down. When you can talk, tell me what happened."

I picked up her desk chair and gently guided her to it. The coffeemaker had miraculously escaped damage, and the strong, rich aroma of coffee bounced me back into normalcy. I found Alice's cup on the floor, chipped but unbroken, filled it, and brought it to her.

"Drink this," I said.

"That man—he said his name was Ben Grayson—claimed that his dog was refusing his food. He saw the 'Closed' sign but took a chance when he noticed the car in the lot. It was a damned lie, and I fell for it."

"He must have been here when I let myself in, but I didn't see any other car outside," I said.

"He must have parked on the other side of the hospital."

"Was his dog a Rottweiler?"

"He didn't mention the breed. He wanted to know if I would look at him first. People often leave their dogs in the car until they're seen, especially if the dogs are aggressive."

"Was this man unusually tall, dark, and unshaven?" I asked.

"You're thinking about Al Grimes. No, he was about my height. He had fair hair and was very well groomed. His hair was more stylish than mine."

Alice had just described Emil Schiller. I knew I was leaping to a hasty conclusion, but we didn't have time for the leisurely approach.

"Did you notice the color of his eyes?" I asked.

"They were blue. Ben Grayson was blond with blue eyes. He was a very attractive man and a damned liar."

"That sounds like Emil Schiller," I said. "I saw him with Al Grimes one night, and I suspect they might be connected."

"I heard that name before," Alice said. "Last summer, David's daughter, Dawn, was dating a man named Emil Schiller. David mentioned that he didn't approve of him. They could be the same man. That isn't exactly a common name."

"Do you know why David didn't approve of Emil?"

"I'm not sure, but I can call Dawn and ask her."

Alice was holding onto her cup tightly, as if it were a lifeline, but she had yet to lift it to her mouth.

"After you drink some of your coffee, I'll drive you to Emergency," I said. "The doughnuts fell on the floor, and I stepped on them."

"No, I don't want to go to the hospital. I think I'll be all right. Somebody hit me, and I never saw it coming. I was talking to Mr. Grayson or Schiller, whoever he is. I was looking right at him. There had to be two of them. I have to call the police."

"Sit still, Alice. I'll do it."

"Okay. Tell them the hospital's been burglarized and a man assaulted me. No, make that two men." Alice took a sip of her coffee and slumped against the back of her chair. "And, Jennet, there's a little refrigerator in David's office and ice cubes in the freezer. Could you bring me some, and one of the towels? A little ice might help."

I made the call to the police and assembled a handmade ice compress. In taking care of Alice, I had almost gotten over my fright, but not entirely.

When I came back, she was holding the picture of her dog, carefully removing the sharp shards and throwing them into the wastebasket.

"The police say they'll be here as soon as they can, but I told them I was going to take you to Emergency," I said. "You need to have someone look at that injury. That's more important than making a police report."

She smiled wryly and pressed the ice compress to her temple. "I'm a doctor, Jennet. I feel better now, or as good as I'm going to for a while. Why did you think my intruder was a dog?"

I told her about the Rottweiler and the whistle that had spared me from a gruesome death.

"The dog must have been part of the team. The idea was to get me out of the way so they could search the hospital. I'm glad I took the list and the calendar home." She patted the pocket of the long purple sweater she wore over her violet dress. "What I found is in here. I had them in the one place they didn't look. I'm so glad I wore this sweater today."

She took a handful of photographs out of her pocket and handed them to me. "They were in the Z folder."

I laid the eight pictures down on Alice's desk and stood back to study them.

The photography was mediocre at best, but I could still see the crates crammed close together in a large, dark room and the dogs packed tightly inside them, as if they were no more than insentient objects or stuffed toys. Their expressions ranged from anxious to frantic.

I felt ill, almost as if I were the one who had been struck on the head. The caged captives reminded me of the laboratory dogs in Caroline's pictures. The difference was that these were the 'Before' pictures.

"This is some kind of temporary kennel where dogs are kept until they can be moved or sold or whatever is planned for them," I said. "Where do you think this place is located?"

"I wish I knew."

"We have to find out where these pictures were taken. I've been thinking. It's possible that Dr. Randolph was conducting an investigation, the same as we're doing."

"Oh, Jennet, yes, of course. That would explain so much."

"From what I've heard about him, it's what he would do."

"I tracked down Lisa, the girl who used to work for us," Alice said. "She wouldn't admit to anything, but I feel certain she was the one who contacted the *Inquisitor*. Now she's afraid of being sued or prosecuted."

"Lisa should have kept looking," I said. "These pictures make a much more powerful statement than a list."

"I found another calendar sheet for December sixteenth with the name Mike written in David's hand."

"I wonder if Mike is one of the good guys or the bad guys. Maybe he's the one who took the pictures."

"I don't think David did. He wouldn't have taken such poor photographs."

"Unless he had to take them quickly and secretly," I said. "Can you recognize any of the dogs?"

"I'm afraid not, but our dogs represent only a handful of the ones that were stolen."

The list, David's drawings, the eight photographs and a name. We had four strong clues now. I saw each one of them as a possibility, an individual box in a collection that we were unable to open at the present time. But that would change.

"Remember the third date," I said. "Maybe something is going to happen on January twenty-sixth. But what? And how will we know when it happens? It's unfortunate that Dr. Randolph didn't leave a more detailed account of his investigation. Or maybe he did, and our burglar found it first."

"I don't know what they could have found. I made an extensive search. And David didn't expect to be murdered. At first I thought it was a random killing in a robbery. Now I think you're right. His murder had to do with his investigation."

"Where do we go from here?"

"I'm not sure. I can't think now." Alice put the ice pack down on her desk and touched her temple lightly. The bruise was already beginning to discolor the damaged flesh. The burst of enthusiasm that had lent strength to her voice slipped slowly away. "The ice is starting to feel unpleasant. It makes my head hurt more. Maybe I'm not all right, after all."

She looked around herself in dismay. "And my office is such a mess. Is the whole hospital like this?"

"They did a pretty thorough job. I don't know what I was thinking about to let you sit here and discuss clues. I'll take you to Emergency now and come back tomorrow to help you clean up."

Alice got up slowly, almost as if she were reluctant to take the first step.

"Thanks, Jennet. I'll take you up on your offer of a ride, but I think I'll hire my neighbor's daughter to put the hospital back in order. Kids can always use extra money, and she wants to be a vet when she grows up."

"All right, and on the way I'll tell you everything I know about Emil Schiller," I said.

Twenty

As I walked up to the Caroline Meilland Animal Shelter in a swirl of blowing snow, I saw a Christmas tree in the bay window of the old white Victorian house next door. It was a massive balsam, whose branches filled the entire window, and the multi-colored lights wound around them shone like individual jeweled beacons, still and brilliant.

I knew the tree was only an enchanting apparition, but it frightened me.

My dream ended before I could put my grocery bags down and ring the shelter doorbell. Wrenched back to a waking state, I knew that I was in my familiar brass bed in my own house.

It was too warm under the comforter. My chest and neck were wet with perspiration, and my arms ached. I felt as if I had been carrying a heavy load over a long distance. Then I remembered the killer dog, my grounded-in-reality reason to be afraid. If a dream world were logical, a Rottweiler should have been poised to attack.

I tried to fall asleep again, but I couldn't. Pushing the comforter down to my waist, I lay still, concentrated on breathing, and tried to return to a relaxed state that would induce sleep. Instead, I kept reliving the dream and my experience in the animal hospital.

The Christmas tree apparition was a one-time-only event, and someone had prevented the dog from savaging me. That's what I told myself, but I knew that at some time in the future, I might encounter the Rottweiler again and, when I least expected it, I could see the tree in my waking hours. As far as I knew, tree and attack dog were unrelated.

My own dogs were asleep. Halley lay in her favorite place at the foot of the bed, close to Winter, who was blocking the doorway. If I didn't remember that he was there, I would fall over him in the dark. Neither dog stirred. Their dreams, if dreams they had, must be peaceful ones of good food, long walks, loving words, and pats. I envied them.

I reached over to the wicker table and switched on the lamp. Forty watts of electric light were sufficient to reveal the view from the window and the new snow falling. I closed my eyes and thought about driving to the Mill House in the morning where Crane would be waiting for me.

Eventually, I fell asleep. The next time I woke up, the phantom tree dream didn't seem so frightening. I was able to pack it away in my mind, as I had the Christmas ornaments. But I couldn't pack away the Rottweiler.

~ * ~

I didn't have to tell Crane about my latest misadventure. As usual, he'd already heard about it.

He said, "I drove past your house at seven-thirty last night, but your lights were out so I didn't disturb you. Are you sure you're all right, honey?"

The concern in his voice and his eyes were warm enough to banish the sub zero temperature. I slid into the chair opposite him and began to remove my many snow-fighting layers.

"I'm fine, Crane. I only have a lingering fear of being mauled to death by a savage dog. Alice is the one who was injured, but she's going to be all right. She's staying home today to rest. The next time she goes to the animal hospital, she'll take her dog with her."

Along with the concern in Crane's eyes, I saw exasperation and admiration—a curious combination that he reserves for me.

"A country animal hospital should be one of the safest places you could go, but if there's danger, you'll find it, Jennet," he said. "The FCPD tracked down Ben Grayson. He's middle aged and bald. He owns a German shepherd, but he hasn't taken him to the hospital since last spring."

"My, he's clever."

"Who's clever?"

"Emil Schiller, AKA Ben Grayson. He used the name of a real person."

"We don't know that Schiller was one of the burglars," Crane said.

"From Alice's description, it's a good guess. She remembered hearing his name before, too. Emil used to date Dawn Randolph. Her father didn't approve of him."

"That's not exactly a motive for murder."

"I know, but if it's true, it might be relevant. Alice is going to check on it."

I leaned back in the chair and slowly unfolded my napkin, setting the knife, fork, and spoon in their proper order. Over place settings I had complete control.

"Are you really all right, Jennet?" Crane asked.

I knew I could share my greatest fear with Crane, even though I'd hardly admitted it to myself yet. "I'm fine, but I've never been afraid of a dog before. After yesterday, I thought I might look at Halley and Winter in a different way, but it didn't happen. They're my dogs. That Rottweiler is a product of his breeding and training."

"Do you think it was Grimes' Rottweiler that almost attacked you?"

"It's possible. That's a good choice of breed for a trainer of fighting dogs."

"I see a lot of Rottweilers," Crane said. "They're popular dogs. Your idea isn't farfetched, though. I'm going to give you a can of mace—just in case. Now, about this other matter." He handed me the *Banner*, turned to the Editorial Page and folded lengthwise. "You've done it again," he said, with that same admiration-exasperation mix.

"What have I done?"

"Signed your name to a letter that's sure to rile up the wrong people, especially now."

At the top of the page was my letter to the editor, in print at last. I had written it in December, before the murder of Dr. Randolph and the murky charge of dognapping, before I'd met Grimes at the Cauldron, before I thwarted his attempt to add the shelter dogs to his collection.

"It's a good letter, Jennet. You have a way with words, even if you tend to get a little carried away, but I wish you'd have used another name."

"I had to sign the letter," I protested. "The *Banner* wouldn't print it if I didn't. Anyway, I never take anonymous letters seriously."

I scanned the letter to see if the editor had omitted anything or changed my words. It was all there, exactly as I'd written it, warning people about the dognappers and describing several commonsense precautions to take.

I couldn't find anything inflammatory in my letter, except for my liberal use of melodramatic words like vile and despicable. No one could possibly be offended, except a dognapper or a research scientist.

"You may be opening yourself up for some trouble down the road," Crane said.

I'd heard almost the same words from Grimes the day he

threatened me in Hazelton's lot. How different they sounded when Crane spoke them.

"Are you talking about more trouble than walking into a burglary and almost getting ripped to shreds by a killer dog?" I asked. "Has something happened?"

He turned the paper over and pointed to a news story. "Nothing new. The dognappers are still around. They hit Ellentown again and took five more dogs. None of them were collies."

"That's no surprise. They already stole all the Ellentown collies."

By now, I had taken off my gloves and scarf and eased out of my parka. All three items lay in a damp heap over the back of the extra chair.

"Let me hang that coat up for you," he said.

He brushed the last of the snow from the hood and hung the parka on a peg, where it proceeded to drip onto the floor. When he sat down again, I saw only a look of admiration on his face.

"That's better now. How do you manage to look prettier every time I see you?"

"Maybe it's the secret spell," I said. "Did you order breakfast for us yet?"

"I sure did. We're having French toast this morning for a change. Here's Susan with it now."

"And bacon, too. That smells so good!"

"Good morning, Ms. Greenway," Susan said. "I read your letter. Imagine having your writing published in a paper."

Quickly and efficiently, she transferred our breakfast from the tray to the table, setting the French toast, the bacon, and the grapefruit juice in their proper places and the pitcher of syrup close to Crane.

Susan and the syrup pitcher placement were predictable. They were almost symbolic. Crane was the important one at the table. In some subtle way, Susan always let this be known.

"Anyone can send a letter to the editor and have it printed, Susan," I said. "You just have to write about a subject that really matters to you."

She poured more coffee in Crane's cup. "Maybe I will."

I looked at her a little more closely than usual. She seemed a bit downcast today. For a second, I wondered why, and then Crane was thanking Susan and saying something to me. I had to ask him to repeat it.

"I asked you what kind of clues Alice Foster found."

"Pictures of dogs crammed into crates and the name of someone Dr. Randolph may have contacted. After what happened yesterday, she's moving everything to her safety deposit box. We think Dr. Randolph was investigating the dognapping ring when he was killed."

"That makes more sense than anything else I've heard about him," Crane said.

He looked up from his French toast and held me fast with his steely gaze. I could have anticipated his next comment.

"You ladies don't intend to draw Grimes out into the open with an offer of free puppies, do you?"

I recognized his words as a command, masquerading as a question. He was alluding to my sketchy plan. I'd almost forgotten about it. Now that he had mentioned it, I thought it was worth taking out of storage and dusting off. Maybe it had hidden merits.

I said, "We're at the searching and thinking stage. I promise I'll let you know before we do anything more ambitious. This may well be one of those matters for the police."

"Good. That's exactly what it is."

He returned to his breakfast, and soon both of his plates were empty. As usual, I was lagging behind. I should have had a half order.

Susan refilled Crane's cup again, and he sat back to drink his coffee and watch me. He was silent, as he often is. Sometimes, this bodes ill for the one being watched, but this wasn't always true. I knew that I hadn't done anything he would consider risky lately.

I concentrated on finishing my bacon. Finally, he said, "I made our reservations at Snow Lodge. We're going the last weekend of January."

"Finally. I hope we don't have another snow emergency."

"I know your semester is ending, but will you be too busy to go to the Carnival with me on Friday? They're showing old westerns this week. There's one I especially want to see."

"I'm never too busy for old westerns and you. I'll try to finish all my schoolwork by Friday. Then I can relax and enjoy the weekend."

"And next weekend, we can relax together and enjoy Snow Lodge," Crane said. "We'll finally go on that sleigh ride." He talked as if he had ordered the snow and reserved the sleigh as well. "They have fireplaces, too," he added.

I smiled at him, remembering the pictures in the *Michigan Traveler*. "It's going to be wonderful."

All the same, I felt a trifle uneasy. All of this talk about Snow Lodge might jinx our romantic weekend once again. Was it possible to have two storms of the century?

I didn't say anything about this, though. Crane was a little touchy about Snow Lodge, and I realized that I was ambivalent, as well as uneasy. It was understandable. I knew that we both had high hopes for the weekend. On our first weekend together as lovers, I hoped that I would be able to please him.

Now how could any woman find pressure in a situation like that?

There, I'd said it. Well, to myself, I'd said it.

Crane was setting dollar bills on the table for Susan, gulping the last of his coffee, picking up the check, holding my parka for me. Breakfast was over. Soon he'd be back to patrolling Foxglove Corners, but the rest of the day stretched before me, filled with possibilities.

"Try to stay out of trouble, honey," he said. "Especially stay away from Rottweilers until I give you that mace."

~ * ~

After parting with Crane, I went home, walked the dogs, and became unaccountably restless. I was in the mood for a solitary Sunday drive and perhaps a visit to the animal shelter. As soon as I settled the dogs with fresh water and biscuits, I set out again.

Since it was Sunday, Foxglove Corners was more deserted than usual, with everything steeped in snow and silence. I passed the library and the post office, both of which were closed. Sometimes I thought that the little hamlet slept through the winter and napped all summer.

Hoping to find some puppy entertainment and conversation at the shelter, I turned down Park Street, but the sisters' station wagon was gone, and the yard was empty. All of the dogs must be safe inside. Henry's house looked quiet, too. Apparently everyone had found something to do today. I reminded myself that I had all my semester's end schoolwork waiting for me at home.

What should I do now? Usually I kept busy, sometimes doing two or three tasks at once to carve out time for what mattered the most to me. Today, with the luxury of an entire afternoon and evening, hours of unfilled time, I was driving aimlessly around

'Closed for the Season.' I read the sign as I passed the ice cream parlor. This had been a favorite place for Crane and me during the summer. I had first seen Lucy Hazen there.

"Stop in any time," she had often said. "I write all day,

every day, so I'm always happy to take a break."

I'd planned to visit her to talk about Henry McCullough's Victorian but had never done so. Now was the perfect time. Newly energized by a sense of purpose, I charted a course for Dark Gables, Lucy's house on Spruce Road.

En route to my new destination, I passed the Cauldron, acres of dark spruce trees on either side of the road, the Rocking Horse Ranch, and, ultimately, the derelict barn—where something was wrong. On second thought, it wasn't exactly wrong, only different. I slowed down and pulled off to the side of the road.

When I'd last seen the barn, it had been snowbound and inaccessible. Now, someone had cleared a way straight to the front door. I could drive up to the barn and investigate.

Slow down, Jennet, I told myself.

There wasn't one chance in a hundred that the cleared path was significant. Still, I sat in my car with the engine idling and let my imagination roam free.

With its apparent status as a ruin and location far from the road, what an ideal place this would be to hide something. A stolen car or goods, perhaps? How about a cache of abducted dogs bound for research labs?

All I had to do was drive my car up to the barn and look inside. It might be locked, but there was a good chance that it wasn't. Why would anyone lock a barn that was on the verge of falling down? A section of the north wall was already broken. Maybe I could see through the opening.

Do it, I told myself. Probably all I'd see were hay and mice. Then I wouldn't have to keep wondering.

I looked around but couldn't see anyone else in the vicinity to catch me trespassing and demand that I state my business. No 'Private Property—No Trespassing' signs were posted.

I didn't move. Inside my head, I could hear Crane's voice.

He wasn't lecturing me about foolhardy behavior or meddling in police affairs. He was telling a story about a man who had found himself trapped in a barn with a hungry coyote. I'd begged him to stop, so I had no idea what happened next. How the man happened to get trapped in a barn with a coyote remained a mystery, along with pertinent details, such as whether the coyote was weak or rabid, and the outcome.

Never would I interrupt Crane in mid-anecdote again. I assumed that the man had fared worse than the coyote. My imagination, often working against me, created an especially grisly finale, with Grimes' black Rottweiler, Snapper, replacing the coyote.

I imagined myself stepping inside the barn, whereupon the door would slam shut, or be slammed shut by an unseen hand, trapping me inside. Even without the coyote, this would be a deadly dilemma.

You're a coward, I told myself. *You have no courage, not a bit. Only a child is afraid of what isn't there. I can't imagine why Crane admires you.*

That last thought convinced me. I started the car and turned down the narrow, cleared path. If the old barn held a secret, I intended to discover it.

Twenty-one

The barn door was locked, but I wasn't going to let that discourage me. The wood looked so old and weak that I thought I could easily pull the door open with one or two tugs. I was wrong. Someone had done a good job of securing the ancient structure. That indicated the presence of something worth locking up inside.

I didn't hear any sounds. If stolen dogs were being kept here, they would be making their presence known, unless they were drugged. Most likely, something entirely different was inside the barn. Maybe nothing at all. But if I stood here without acting much longer, I would be in danger of freezing.

The broken panel was a logical place to start my investigation. Pulling my hood closer around my neck, I walked around to the back of the structure. No one had cleared a path around the barn for a curious passerby. I stepped in high snow that came up to the tops of my boots. Walking became a chore. I had to force my way down through the snow to the hard surface beneath and drag my feet out again. I made it by taking one slow step at a time.

The sides of the barn that couldn't be seen from Spruce Road were in an even greater state of deterioration. Someone had closed the fissures in the walls clumsily, using scraps of mismatched wood nailed haphazardly in place.

The entire area at the back that had been pushed in was repaired in the same careless fashion. The barn was nothing more than a dilapidated ruin and a collection of scrap wood. A high wind would easily blow it down, but for me, at this time, it was impenetrable.

I turned to go back to my car at the precise moment I heard the ominous rumble of a tractor. As I rounded the corner of the barn, I saw the driver coming down the path, following the tracks made by my car.

Not more than ten minutes could have passed since I'd made my impetuous decision to investigate the barn. He couldn't have been very far away; but how could I have been so focused on my discovery that I had failed to hear the tractor? And how was I going to explain my presence on his land, assuming this was his land? I'd have to come up with a convincing story in the next minute.

The man stopped the tractor and jumped down to the ground, where he stood in front of me, regarding me with an expression that I couldn't read.

I recognized him. Although I had only seen him once, his appearance was distinctive. Short, round, and ruddy, with a silver beard, the man to whom I had to explain my intrusion had posted an advertisement for the Rocking New Year's Eve party at the Mill House. He wore the same bright Christmas-red jacket today. Crane had told me his name, but I couldn't remember it.

The man's eyes were shrewd, but I didn't think he was angry. Apparently he had recognized me, too.

"Don't I know you from somewhere, young lady?" he demanded.

Stalling for time, I said, "I don't think we've ever met."

"You're on private property. What are you doing out here, snooping around my barn?"

My car is making a noise, and I thought there might be a piece of lead pipe or something I could use to... I could do better than that.

"I'm sorry. I couldn't resist taking a look at this wonderful old barn. I'm looking for one that isn't too expensive to renovate and live in. Something exactly like this. Is it for sale?"

He looked at me as if I had just proposed something preposterous or illegal.

"You want to buy this old relic? It's too rundown to be renovated. You could build a fancy new barn for a fraction of what it would cost to make this place livable."

"I can't afford to build, and I don't have the land. I want a barn that's already standing, like this one, and a little piece of property of my own. I know I can turn it into a handsome, rustic residence."

"Impossible," he said. "It can't be done." He took a few steps toward me and frowned, but not in an unfriendly manner. "You look familiar, young lady. Do you ever come to the barn or maybe to our Saturday night shindigs?"

"Sometimes. That New Year's Eve party was a real blast, wasn't it? Now, you sound like you don't want the barn, and I do. I know I could make this work. I'm a good carpenter. What price are you asking?"

"I said it can't be done. I know about these things. I'm Rudy Zoller, ma'am. That's my ranch over there. And who might you be?"

"My name is Jane—Green," I said. "Are you sure you won't reconsider?"

"Find yourself a nice little apartment in Lapeer, young lady. Carpentry is man's work, and besides, it's dangerous for a girl living out here alone."

Just this one time, I let these sexist remarks pass by unchallenged. "Dangerous? How?"

"There's wild animals," he said. "And wild men with guns. You'd be eaten up alive and be squandering your money to boot."

I had taken my little fantasy as far as possible, and it had extricated me from a potentially embarrassing dilemma. I touched the weathered barn with what I intended to be a fond gesture.

"I guess I'll have to look elsewhere then. Thank you anyway, Mr. Zoller. I'm sorry for trespassing on your property."

"Well, that's okay, sweetheart," he said. "No harm done. Come around next Saturday night. We always have a rocking good time here, New Year's Eve or not."

"I might just do that."

He stood beside the tractor and watched as I got in my car, started it, and drove away. I waved to him, but after that, I didn't look back.

Surely Rudy Zoller didn't believe my wild tale, even though he acted as if he had. Could he have some mysterious agenda of his own? Well, no matter. I was back on Spruce Road, driving away, heading for Dark Gables. I still didn't know what was in the barn, and I suspected that Zoller had something to hide. He had been very emphatic about steering me away from his property. If I wanted to return, I would have to come up with a credible plan.

~ * ~

The slender paperback had a garish cover with lime green and bright red colors bleeding into black. I gazed at the sketch of a skeleton standing over an empty coffin with a black bell in its hand and tried to find a connection to Henry McCullough's house.

"I wrote *The Devil's Bell* when I first heard about the haunted Victorian on Park Street," Lucy said. "This is an extra copy, Jennet. You're welcome to keep it."

"Is there a Christmas tree apparition in the story?" I asked.

"At first, but it got lost in revision. I'm disappointed that you haven't seen the phantom tree again."

"I don't want to see it. I dreamed about it twice. That's enough."

Lucy made no attempt to conceal her excitement. "Do you remember the dreams?"

"I don't want to be a character in one of your books, Lucy," I said. "I don't want my apparition turned into a skeleton tree that moves of its own accord."

"Don't worry. You're too old to be one of my protagonists. I write for teenagers. But that description was wonderful. Maybe you should try your hand at writing a horror novel."

We were in the sunroom of Dark Gables, the one room in Lucy's Gothic mansion that was filled with light. Here, summer lasted all year around with white wicker furniture, botanical prints, green plants, and delicate wind chimes. We were drinking hot tea and feasting on gingerbread while the cold and snow kept their distance, along with the mystery and danger that swirled around me.

"All right," I said. "I'll tell you what I remember. In my first dream, Crane and I were sitting in front of the fireplace in my house. I looked away for a moment and saw the phantom Christmas tree. When I turned around, Crane wasn't there."

"Ah," Lucy said. "That's significant."

"That Crane was gone? How?"

"Let me think about it," she said.

Gathering the folds of her enormous black shawl around her, she leaned back in the wicker loveseat and picked up her teacup.

I said, "Last night, my dream was a recreation of the first time I saw the tree in Henry's bay window. Both times, I was afraid."

"Dreams are strange," Lucy said, "but they're not glimpses into the other world. They reflect your fears. Will you let me know if you see the phantom tree again, while you're awake, that is?"

"I will, but I'm hoping it won't happen."

If it did, Lucy would probably be the first one I would contact, since she was very knowledgeable in otherworldly lore. I reached across the table and helped myself to another gingerbread square.

"I've been admiring your bracelet," Lucy said. "The stones are crystals, aren't they?"

"Yes, this was my Christmas present from Crane."

"My, how lovely it is! He has good taste, and he chose wisely. Crystals have magic. Speaking of magic, Jennet, would you like to know what the tea leaves will reveal of your future?"

I picked up my teacup and took a sip instead of the great swallow I had intended.

Lucy told fortunes by interpreting the patterns formed in the teacup by the leaves. She called them symbols. On Halloween night, she had looked into my cup and foreseen my future with Crane in bright and rosy colors. If my fortune had changed since then, I didn't want to know about it. Sometimes, a little bit at a time to experience and savor is the better way.

But how could I decline her offer without offending her? I decided to fall back on the truth.

"Crane and I are going to go to Snow Lodge on the last weekend of January," I said. "I don't want to know how it will turn out in advance. I'm hoping for the best."

"I understand. There's really no need for a second reading. You're going to find true happiness with Crane. I saw it before. You may have to wait a while, though."

"I can do that," I said. "The idea of interpreting symbols has always fascinated me. In my English classes, I fight a constant battle to convince my students that they're exciting."

"You can tell them it's like a parlor game. For example, let's say the leaves form a shape that reminds you of two hearts joined together. How would you interpret that?"

"As two lovers together."

"I agree. Let's try another one. A basket overflowing."

"Happiness. Everything you've always wanted."

"Yes. Both joined hearts and an overflowing basket suggest a very happy fortune indeed. Now, how about a long, horizontal line?"

"Flat line or death, a long life, a trip? I don't know. That one is confusing."

"I'd say a long life. To me, the confusing symbol is the Christmas tree in your apparition," Lucy said. "It should symbolize joy, but to Henry McCullough, it's associated with bereavement. In your fireside dream, there's also loss. Crane was gone."

"Interpreting symbols isn't all fun. Sometimes it's frightening," I said.

"When you're reading tea leaves, you have to rely on your intuition, or maybe your connection with a person," Lucy said. "Studying people is a hobby of mine. That's how I build my characters."

"But most of your story people are vampires and zombies."

"Ah, yes, but they were once people."

"Speaking about studying people, do you know a man named Rudy Zoller?" I asked.

"Mr. Zoller and I aren't friends, but I know a little about him, mostly from stories in the paper. Why do you ask?"

"I saw him around Christmas at the Mill House, and I just came from an awkward encounter with him. He caught me trespassing on his land." I told her about my discovery at the old barn and my suspicion that it was being used as a holding place for stolen dogs.

"Zoller used to live on that property, but he grew too rich and fancy for it," she said. "He built a new house and turned the ranch into riding and boarding stables."

"How did he make his money?"

"In real estate. Selling land to developers. He owns a restaurant and a motel, too. His main interests are hospitality, entertainment, and running for mayor. He uses one of the barns for weekend parties and sleigh rides in the winter. In the summer, there's line dancing. I often wondered why he never had the old buildings demolished."

"You know a lot about him," I said.

"Remember, Jennet. People are my hobby. Do you really think Rudy Zoller is mixed up with the dognappers?"

"I don't know. Anything is possible. People didn't have trouble believing that Dr. Randolph was a dognapper."

Lucy sighed. "That's true, but I hope David's name is cleared one day. Rudy Zoller considers himself a public figure. He wouldn't like to see his image tarnished."

She had a point. Involvement in any crime would put an end to Rudy Zoller's political hopes. If he were branded a dognapper, he would lose all the goodwill he'd gained through hosting Saturday night parties at the ranch.

"I can think of two more possible suspects," I said. "One of them, Al Grimes, tried to rob the animal shelter. He's a giant of a man and more terrifying than one of your villains. Henry McCullough's old collie, Luke, may have been one of his victims."

"Oh, no, not Luke! Henry was so attached to him. Do you remember those pictures Caroline Meilland had of the research dogs?"

"I've never forgotten them. I would do anything to put an end to Grimes and his vile operation."

"If Caroline were alive, she'd find the dognappers and run them out of town on a rail."

"Since she isn't, we'll have to carry on her tradition," I said.

I finished the last of my tea and the last of the gingerbread square and set my napkin, neatly refolded, beside the cup. I could happily stay in Lucy's sunroom longer, enjoying good company and the illusion of summer, but I knew that Lucy worked on her writing every day of the week.

"I have to go home and take my dogs for their afternoon walk," I said. "Thanks for everything, Lucy. Besides having fun, every time I visit you, I learn something."

Lucy rose and drew her black shawl closer to her body. "Keep in touch and be careful, Jennet. Sometimes, I think there's more horror in everyday life than in my books."

"Sometimes that's true," I said.

~ * ~

"You can't be serious, Jennet. What reason would I have for trespassing on someone's personal property?"

Crane was the Deputy Sheriff tonight, very official and commanding in his uniform. His eyes were almost as cold as his gleaming badge.

I had asked him to stop by the derelict barn to see what, if anything, was inside.

"It would be a perfect place to hide something," I said. "Several crates filled with dogs, for example."

"Foxglove Corners has many places like that."

"Like the barn? That's the only one I've ever seen."

"Out-of-the-way places, I meant. Secluded, secret places. They're all over."

I tried a different approach. "Your job is to keep the peace. You're here at my house tonight. Maybe you thought something was wrong, and you stopped to investigate. Now, let's say you're driving by the barn and notice something suspicious. Naturally, you'd have to stop and see what was going on. You're an officer of the law. No one would challenge you."

"I'm here tonight because I saw your lights on. Usually you're in bed when I drive by."

It was late Wednesday night, around ten. I had been working overtime. The semester was winding down, and I had a stack of research papers to read and a deadline. I wanted to finish them before my Friday date with Crane.

I couldn't think of any other way to convince Crane to join my investigation. "If there's a chance the old barn is being used to hide stolen property, I thought you'd want to know it," I said. "Well, now I've told you. I know you'll do what's right. You always do."

I suspected that Crane didn't approve of my latest adventure, but I had turned the matter over to him now. He should be grateful.

"I baked a banana pecan bread," I said. "Would you like to try some with a cup of coffee? You look awfully cold."

"That'd be good. I *am* cold. When did you find the time to bake?"

"After school."

I filled the percolator and cut him a thick slice of Southern banana pecan bread, one of my own few specialties.

"Crane, what happened to the man in the barn?" I asked.

"Who?"

"The man who was trapped in the barn with the coyote."

"He survived. Luckily, he had a knife, but he got chewed up some. I thought you didn't want to hear that story."

"I changed my mind. You almost need a weapon of some kind living out here in the country, don't you? I've been thinking about getting a gun and learning how to shoot."

"That isn't a good idea," he said. "Why have a weapon that someone could take away from you and use against you?"

"Why do you assume that's what would happen?"

"Because I know you. I don't think you could hurt any living creature, not even an attacker. I don't think you'll even use the mace I brought you."

It wasn't mace but a drastically watered down equivalent called Go-Away. Crane was right. I hadn't used it yet and didn't intend to do so.

"I could almost have shot Grimes that day at the shelter," I said. "I wished I'd had a gun then."

His frown and his grim expression betrayed his disapproval. "My point exactly. You'd be too quick to shoot."

"That doesn't make any sense, Crane. It's contradictory."

"The coffee's ready," he said. "This banana bread tastes great, honey. The best I've ever had."

I poured his coffee, set the cup in front of him, and cut him another slice.

"You have me to protect you, Jennet," he said.

"You're sweet, Crane, but in the real world, you won't always be there. I need to know that I can take care of myself."

"I gave you my private cell phone number," he reminded me.

"And I memorized it."

"Then I'll always be on hand."

I smiled at him. He was indeed sweet—and strong and gallant and maybe that knight to the rescue, if I were lucky. Soon, he would be my lover, perhaps forever. Still, with or without a gun, and even though I was afraid, I was ultimately responsible for my own safety. It had always been that way. Nothing had changed.

Twenty-two

While I couldn't very well return to the old barn, I could certainly visit the Rocking Horse Ranch. If Rudy Zoller belonged to the dognapping ring, I might find some indication of this dark association on the premises. All I needed was a believable reason for being there. I intended to say that I was looking for a place to board my horse.

I was unlikely to see Rudy Zoller again, since the ranch was only one of his many business interests. Even if I did run into him, this time my excuse for being on his property was credible.

The Rocking Horse Ranch was on my way home, if I took a short detour. On Friday after school, I drove past the derelict barn and turned into a wide drive that led to the main house. At this time of day, activity at the stables was practically non-existent. Four brown horses wearing green blankets braved the cold in their corral, while one lone figure, dressed in riding apparel, looked on. I parked next to a horse van and went into the nearest of the four barns.

As it turned out, I didn't have to tell my story to anyone because very few people were inside. I stood in the dim, cool interior, inhaling the sweet smell of hay and the unmistakable odor of horse, and looked around.

The barn was quiet, except for occasional whinnying and a distant barking. Two young girls were grooming a pretty brown and white pony tethered to poles between the stalls. While one of the girls ran a brush over his back, the other braided his mane. They worked silently, and neither girl took any notice of me. The pony flicked his tail and turned his head.

As I walked down the length of the barn, admiring the horses, they followed my progress with dark inquisitive eyes. All of them looked pretty much alike to me, except for one mahogany horse that was larger than any domesticated animal I had ever seen. He had a shining coat with white markings, a massive head, and formidable teeth.

I stopped to have a closer look at him. According to the name plaque attached to the stall, his name was Folly. He appeared to be approachable, but I knew enough about his species not to extend my hand in friendship.

One of the horses whinnied. Around the corner, a small, shaggy dog raced toward me, barking as ferociously as if he had come upon an intruder stealing the barn's supply of oats. Behind him came a young woman clad in jeans and carrying an enormous bucket. She shooed the dog away and asked, "Can I help you find somebody?"

"I'd like to see Mr. Zoller," I said. "Is he around?"

"Ordinarily he'd be up at the house this time of day, but he left for Kentucky yesterday."

"I'm sorry I missed him," I said. "When will he be back?"

"Not until early next week. I'm Shelley. Maybe I can help you."

I told her that I was looking for a good place to board my horse. "Is there anything else going on at the ranch, besides the Saturday night social activities and the sleigh rides?" I asked.

"We offer riding lessons for people of all ages and a grooming class. If you're interested, check on days and times in

Winter's Tale   Dorothy Bodoin

the office at the main barn."

The shaggy dog had wandered back and was sniffing the contents of the bucket.

"Do you board dogs, too?" I asked.

"No, only horses. Tag is one of the barn dogs. We're a stable. I'd say we're the best around, and not just because I work here."

"That's what I'm looking for."

"I'm sure we have room, but you'll have to see Mr. Zoller. Come back on Tuesday. When you do, go around to the house."

"I'll do that. Do you mind if I have a look around?"

"Go right ahead," she said. "I have to get back to work."

For the next fifteen minutes, I wandered up and down, peering into the stalls and corners. Then I investigated the other barns, one of which was used for the ranch's social activities. On my tour, I encountered Tag again, and a slinky black cat that watched me with unfriendly green eyes. Mostly, all I saw were horses in surroundings that were relatively clean, except for the ever-present cobwebs.

If Rudy Zoller had any secrets, they weren't in this place. Perhaps my next stop should be one of the Saturday night shindigs. Well, why not? In a social setting, I might find someone willing to gossip.

I was ready to leave the ranch. This had been a good idea, but it was going nowhere. Everything around the place looked open and legitimate. I should have remembered that dognappers like secrecy. They would hardly leave traces of their nefarious activities lying around with the tack boxes.

I went outside through a door on the western side. Here the snow-covered land sloped gradually downward to the old barn and the deserted house in the distance. From where I stood, they looked as attractive as the ranch house and the new structures I had just visited. The scene reminded me of a

Currier and Ives print, complete with a sleigh, set against the white background of a three-plank board fence.

I stopped to read the poster that was tied with red rope to one side of the sleigh.

Sleigh Rides

Every Saturday Night

January through February

(Weather Permitting)

Apres Ride Party at the Main Barn

The sleigh was an antique model, still in fair condition, but obviously intended for display rather than use. I ran my hand along the fancy scrollwork on its side. The evocative piece seemed to tell of old-fashioned fun and romance in the snow. I could almost hear sleigh bells and laughter and feel the wind as it blew snow against my face.

But a strong breeze had set wind chimes in motion, the laughter originated from the barn I'd just left, and as for the snow... I looked up. That was real. Large, cold flakes drifted down from the gray sky, giving the area a fresh new cover.

For the first time, I began to understand the lure of a sleigh ride in the arms of the man you love. I could hardly wait to tell Crane about my change of heart.

~ * ~

As I turned right on Spruce Road, my destination the nearest byroad that would take me to Jonquil Lane, I glanced back for one last look at the ranch. Two words came crashing together in my mind: Doodles and symbols.

I must have driven by the Rocking Horse Ranch several times in the past days without noticing the similarity between the area and the drawings on the calendar sheet. Like many an

201

elusive clue, it had been literally in front of my eyes.

Dr. Randolph had drawn Christmas trees and houses. Spruces lined the road, and on the Zoller property were two houses and four barns. I had just seen the sleigh. Instead of dogs, there should be horses, but that was a minor point. The rest of the analogy fit. I wished I'd paid more attention to the barn dog, Tag. I couldn't remember if he had floppy ears.

Little details were irrelevant. To his other drawings Dr. Randolph might as well have added an arrow aimed straight at the Rocking Horse Ranch.

As soon as I reached my house, I took out my copy of the calendar sheet and studied it carefully. I didn't find anything to contradict my theory. Thanks to Lucy and her tea leaves-symbols talk, I'd made the connection. I was going to have to thank her once again.

~ * ~

Nothing is more frustrating to an amateur sleuth than to realize that she can't share a brilliant discovery immediately. Now that I had stumbled onto the significance of Dr. Randolph's artwork, I wanted to tell someone. Alice was my obvious first choice, but she wasn't at home. I left a message on her answering machine and then called Camille, who had gone out as well. That left Crane, the person I wanted most of all to tell.

While I waited for him to arrive, I kept going to the mirror to reassure myself that I looked all right. I'd had my hair trimmed yesterday and thought it was a little too short, but I had confidence in my new dress. The brilliant blue color and modest scattering of beads at the bodice matched my present mood.

I had just fastened the clasp on my crystal bracelet when I heard the dogs barking and Crane pounding on the door. Ordering the dogs to Stay, I hurried to let him in. Light snow dusted his sheepskin jacket, and he held a bag from the Steak Place in his hand. I took the coat and laid it over the chair. The bag I set on the counter.

"Hi, honey," he said. "Come here and let me kiss you."

I came and moved my hands slowly through his hair, feeling the snow that had mixed with the silver strands. He kissed me soundly. His lips were icy, and his face was rough and cold, but as I breathed in the scent of Obsession, I felt as warm as the summer.

He held me away from him, looking at me with an intensity that made me feel weak.

"Your hair—did you do something new to it?" he asked. "I like it."

He reached out and touched an errant strand, one I'd failed to secure in its proper place. He didn't seem inclined to let it go.

"I had my hair trimmed a little," I said.

"You look mighty fine tonight, pretty fancy for a movie date with a simple deputy sheriff."

"There's nothing simple about you, Crane."

He ran his hand slowly along the beads at the bodice, letting them wander up to my neck. The blue dress had passed the test. Now, on with the mystery.

"I feel like celebrating," I said. "All my schoolwork is done, we have a date, and I made a discovery today. I'm sure now that the dognappers are keeping stolen dogs in the Zoller barn until they can move them to the next location."

"Make that were."

Behind me, Halley gave a pathetic little whimper. Both of the dogs had discovered the bag from the Steak Place. Just this once, dogs and bones could wait a little while longer.

"What do you mean by were?"

"The barn was packed with empty crates, but the dogs were

gone.

All we found were some rusty old tools and a wheelbarrow without handles."

"But there were empty crates?"

"Yes, and dog food spilled on the floor and mice. It was so crowded you could hardly move. Your intuition was right."

I closed my hand over his. He had acted in typical official fashion, doing as I'd asked after seeming to dismiss my request.

"I thought you weren't going to investigate the barn," I said.

"I changed my mind, but it was done by the book, with a search warrant. Your dogs are hungry, honey. Did you forget to feed them again?"

Yielding to Crane's teasing and canine begging, I took two steak bones out of the bag. When I spread them on newspapers on the sunroom floor, the dogs fell upon them.

"That should keep them busy while we talk. Here's what I found out today." I told him about Dr. Randolph's doodles and my theory that someone must have called him with information about the dognappings. "The tip came from the Rocking Horse Ranch. I'm sure of it."

"It could have happened like that, but don't you think he would have drawn a rocking horse?"

"Yes, if he was writing a message, or he would have used words. He wasn't leaving clues; he was just doodling. Alice thought he was inquiring about a sleigh ride."

"He might have been doing that," Crane said. "Do you think you might be manipulating the facts to fit your theory?"

I considered this possibility, but in my view, the facts pointed to the conclusion I'd drawn. "I think Dr. Randolph was implicating Rudy Zoller," I said.

"Not necessarily. Not according to Zoller. I talked to him yesterday. He claims that he doesn't know anything about dognappers, only what he read in the paper. He had no idea that anyone was using his barn for illegal purposes. He says he'll have everything cleared out and the barn torn down."

"Do you believe him?"

"There's no proof that he's lying," Crane said. "He says that he's only at the ranch one or two days a week."

Something was wrong with Crane's account. How could he have talked to Rudy Zoller?

"I was at the stables yesterday looking at the horses, but I didn't see anything suspicious there," I said. "A girl named Shelley told me that Zoller was in Kentucky."

"I made contact with him just before he left."

"Here's something else then," I said. "Dr. Randolph wrote three dates on his calendar. Two of them have passed, but the third one is January twenty-sixth."

"That's next week."

"Maybe they're planning to move the dogs out of the state on that date. They already moved them from the old barn. Where do you think they took them?"

"It could be any place, maybe to another barn somewhere. Didn't I tell you that Foxglove Corners has many secret places where you can hide anything and never worry about someone finding it? They'll want some secluded location where no one will notice people coming or going."

"If something is going to happen on the twenty-sixth, that gives us a little time, but not much. What can we do?"

"You can't do anything but keep on watching. So far, you've been very observant, and it's paid off. I watch all the time. This isn't just the place where I keep the peace. It's my home. If there's trouble, then I take care of it. As for you..."

He captured my runaway strand of hair in his hand again. "I don't want you to do anything except take care of Halley and Winter. The law will deal with the dognappers."

"Mmm, maybe," I murmured.

Crane's desire to protect me was gratifying, but I had no intention of sitting at home with my dogs while he waited until something happened to take action. I had Al Grimes, Emil Schiller, and Rudy Zoller, three very likely suspects, a few good clues, and a strong feeling that I might come across the key to the mystery soon.

For tonight, though, I was willing to call a temporary halt to the sleuthing game and explore the western movie scene with Crane, along with whatever would follow. In this, I knew definitely where I was headed.

Twenty-three

When we came out of the theater, Susan Carter was standing in line at the ticket counter with her escort, Emil Schiller. To the casual observer, they were a perfectly matched young couple, both of them golden-haired and attractive, but from what I knew of Emil, I hoped that Susan would be able to hold her own with him.

Emil greeted me with a bright smile. Anyone would think that our acquaintance went farther back than those few minutes at the animal shelter in the aftermath of the big snow. As usual, Susan's first greeting was for Crane. When she introduced Emil to us, she sounded almost shy.

Emil shook Crane's hand. To me he said, "I saw you at the shelter, ma'am, but we've never been introduced."

Quickly I said, "Call me Jennet."

"You two, enjoy the movie," Crane said. "It's a classic. Goodnight, Susan—Emil." Then, without further conversation, he took my arm and hurried me past the line out to the sidewalk.

"Really, Crane," I protested, "you don't have to drag me away. I'm willing to come."

"Sorry, honey."

He freed my arm and held my hand instead. As we walked slowly back to Willow Street where he had parked the Jeep, he said, "Susan's new boyfriend is Emil Schiller. There's a coincidence. She hasn't been very happy with him."

"I'm surprised she'd tell you something like that."

"Susan looks on me like a big brother. She said something about it last week, not much, though. She didn't mention his name, just described him."

Like a big brother? I stole a glance at Crane in the dark. Did he really believe that? "Women always focus on Emil's appearance first," I said.

"I wish I knew more about Schiller, but Susan is a smart girl. If he's mixed up in anything shady, she'll drop him."

"That's if she knows about it. I'm surprised to find them going to an old western movie like *She Wore a Yellow Ribbon*."

"Susan is a nice old-fashioned girl. Besides, everyone likes John Wayne."

"Somehow I don't think that Emil is a nice old-fashioned boy," I said.

"Maybe I should have a little talk with Susan about Schiller."

"Do it. I'll bet she'll listen to you."

The winter night was beautiful, calm and perceptibly warmer in spite of the light snowfall. The mood that had inspired me to wear the blue beaded dress was still alive. I felt as if I could walk hand in hand with Crane all the way to Jonquil Lane.

"They say it's going to warm up for a day or two," Crane said.

"A two-day January thaw. I'll take it." But let it snow again for our weekend at Snow Lodge, I thought.

A thin layer of snow covered the Jeep, and the trees that lined the street shimmered in the light of the lamps. Ours were the only tracks on the sidewalk.

Crane said, "You sit inside and keep warm, honey, while I clear the windows."

I started to protest that it wasn't that cold and I could use a brush as well as he could but remembered just in time that Crane was at heart a Southern gentleman who took his heritage seriously. I let him hold open the door of the Jeep for me and help me inside. Leaning back in the seat, I watched him as he sent the snow flying back into the street. For the hundredth time, I told myself how fortunate I was to have Crane in my life.

Still, a puzzling contradiction insisted on threading its way through my relationship with him. As much as I enjoyed letting him shower me with old-fashioned gallantry and make all the decisions, some part of me wanted to be independent, to pursue my own mystery to the end, and slay the dragon or giant, whichever appeared first.

How could I reconcile these two warring parts? Or was it even possible? At present, I didn't know, but I suspected that I would soon find out.

When the windows were free of snow and Crane was in the Jeep beside me, he said, "We're going to have dinner tonight at a new place."

"Where is it?" I asked.

He smiled that slow smile that could turn an icicle to water on the coldest day of the year or melt a heart.

"It's a surprise," he said. "I found a place where that pretty blue dress will feel right at home."

~ * ~

The January thaw arrived in the early hours of the morning while I was still sleeping. When I came downstairs to fix breakfast, I saw that the last of the snow had melted away. I opened the kitchen window and breathed deeply. The morning air that rushed in was almost balmy.

As I ate my cereal, I noticed how bare my windowsill looked. I needed daffodils or tulips to celebrate the improvement in the weather. Spring was on my mind. Like an invasive plant in an untended garden, I imagined the fever would soon spread to everyone in Foxglove Corners.

Along with the temperatures, my spirits soared. Memories of last evening with Crane and our rapidly approaching trip to Snow Lodge mixed with spring-induced euphoria to make me feel almost airborne. Everything seemed new and exciting, and I planned to make the most of this first day of the weekend.

Last night we had gone to a picturesque country inn for a dinner of roasted chicken, which was their specialty. The Briar House was as Victorian and country as could be, and the food was delicious. I looked on our cozy, intimate, romantic time as a prelude to Snow Lodge, but it wasn't, not quite. At the end of the evening, Crane took me home.

Although I hadn't fallen asleep until after midnight, I wasn't the slightest bit tired. After I finished breakfast, I would walk the dogs, and then set off for town, leaving them to recuperate in the sunroom while the mud dried on their long, thick coats and drifted down to the floor. I'd brush their coats and deal with the clean up when I returned.

~ * ~

My first stop was the animal hospital. Alice was expecting me. I'd called her early this morning to tell her about my discovery.

The building was as isolated as ever, with only Alice's car in the parking lot. With the snow gone, however, the place seemed less sinister. Still, when I heard a dog barking inside, my heart skipped a beat.

This time Alice opened the door immediately. At her feet stood a Siberian husky whose dark eyes sparkled with delight at the prospect of company. This was Alice's guard dog, as staunch a protector as my gentle Halley.

"Hi, Jennet," Alice said. "Come in and meet Shelby."

Unlike my exuberant collies, Shelby sat quietly at Alice's side waiting for me to make the first overture. As I offered her my palm to sniff and told her how pretty she was, she wagged her tail.

"When I adopted Shelby, she was a little timid," Alice said. "She's more outgoing now, but not with everyone. Come on back to my office where we can talk."

Inside the hospital, all traces of the burglary had vanished. A faint smell of paint lingered in the air. On the reception desk, a terra cotta dish garden of hyacinths and daffodils added a touch of color and welcome.

Spring must be on Alice's mind, too. She was wearing a bright yellow sweater, her hair was a few inches shorter, and her lipstick several shades pinker. Spiky bangs hid the place on her forehead where the assailant had struck her.

"We're going to reopen the hospital on the first of February," she said. "It's going to be a fresh, new start. Best of all, we're closing in on the dognappers. I have a new clue."

With Shelby at my heels, I followed Alice down the empty hall. In spite of the hospital's new look, memories of my traumatic experience lingered. No one could scrub or paint them away. This was where I had stood, immobilized by fear, waiting for the Rottweiler to attack me. This spot, right here, was where I had dropped the bag of doughnuts.

Alice and her helper had done their best to erase the burglary from the hospital's history. Her office was neat and tidy again. Shelby's picture had a new frame, and the coffeemaker was bubbling away.

"Tell me about your clue," I said.

"First, the news isn't all good. One of my patients disappeared from her yard yesterday. She was a chocolate lab named Lily. Mrs. Gorman, Lily's owner, was outside with her, raking fallen branches, but left her alone to answer the phone. When she came back, Lily was gone."

"What's the good news?" I asked.

"A real lead. Have you ever seen a silver van with a large winged brush painted on both sides? It's called the Flying Brush."

"No. I think I'd notice a van with an unusual name like that."

"It's a mobile dog grooming service. I saw it the other day on my street. Last week, a man came to Mrs. Gorman's door to give her his card. He said he was a groomer for the Silver Brush. She wasn't interested but took the card anyway. Now she thinks that he came back later to snatch Lily."

"I've never known groomers to solicit business that way," I said. "Usually, they're so busy you have to make an appointment in advance. Was he a mean looking giant of a man with a limp?"

"On the contrary. She described him as young, of medium height, and somewhere in his twenties with blond hair and blue eyes. In her words, he was cute and friendly."

"That sounds like Emil Schiller."

"I thought so, too. Yesterday I called Dawn Randolph to ask her about Emil. She said they didn't go out very long. Her father disapproved of him because he wasn't going to college and didn't have a steady job. Dawn wasn't pleased about his lack of ambition either. Then Emil just stopped calling her. She hasn't seen him in months."

"Could Emil have dated Dawn to get close to her father and then dumped her when he had the information he needed?" I asked.

"I suppose it's possible."

"There's Emil's connection to Grimes," I said.

"Yes; I'm sure they're working together. The number on the card has been disconnected, and the Information Operator doesn't have a listing for a grooming service with that name."

"Because it's one van, not a business," I said. "That's a diabolical way to case the neighborhoods for unattended dogs. Who would suspect a dog grooming van? By the time anyone did, it would be too late. I'll make it a point to watch for it."

"You suspected that Al Grimes and Emil Schiller might be working together from the start, didn't you?" Alice asked.

"I thought it was a possibility. They're such an ill-matched pair, but they do make a good team. Emil can masquerade as an affable dog groomer and gain people's trust, more so than Grimes with his size and rough, intimidating appearance."

"I'm think you're right about the Rocking Horse Ranch, Jennet, and let's not forget January twenty-sixth. We don't want to be taken unaware.

"I'll be in school on that day," I said, "but I'll remind Crane to be extra vigilant. Whoever the dognappers are, we're going to be ready for them."

"We hope," Alice added.

~ * ~

My next stop was the animal shelter. Instead of dog treats, today I was delivering a tape. Letty had confessed that neither she nor Lila knew how to set their VCR to record programs. I'd promised to tape her television spots for them.

The shelter dogs were in the yard, running in the mud and barking their usual raucous welcome. I recognized only one of the unwanted Christmas puppies. The others must be new.

"You and the pups look good on television, Letty," I said.

"Thanks, Jennet. We found new owners for all three of your little retrievers."

"Are you sure they're in good homes?" I asked.

"Very sure. Lila created an application for adoption and an interview form, and we investigated them thoroughly."

"We have four new puppies," Lila said.

Henry was visiting today, sitting in a rocker. At first, I thought he had a brown sweater or a throw on his lap. Looking more closely, I saw that it was a dog.

"Is this one of them?" I asked.

As the small creature burrowed deeper into Henry's arms, I recognized her. She was Crane's brown stray, who had spent most of her time until now keeping out of sight. She looked at home on Henry's lap.

"This is Brown Dog, but I renamed her," Henry said. "She's Brownie now."

"Well, you said you'd bring her into the fold, and you did, Lila. I'm impressed. Are you going to adopt her, Henry?"

"I already have," he said. "When Luke comes home, she'll be good company for him."

~ * ~

A touch of spring in the dead of winter can work magic. Wherever I'd gone today, everything looked a little brighter. My good mood carried me through a quick lunch at the Sandwich Shop in Lakeville and a stop at Warrington's for a new frosted lipstick.

I went on to Enchanted Flowers, where I bought a deep pink tulip plant. The flowers were at the beginning of their life, with buds on the verge of opening. Then I couldn't resist buying six pumpkin muffins at Almond's Bakery next door.

Someone once said that a feeling of well being is a fragile thing that can vanish in an instant like spring in January.

As I came out of the bakery with a plant in one hand, my packages in the other, and my mind on tomorrow's breakfast with Crane, I almost collided with a tall, dark man who was passing in front of me.

It was Grimes.

Twenty-four

Grimes turned and held out his hand to keep me from crashing into his body. He towered over me like a menacing refugee from a child's nightmare. His eyes were as cold as I remembered them, and he wore his I (heart) My Rottweiler shirt.

I gave myself a quick order. Whatever you do, don't let him know you're afraid of him.

"I'm sorry," I said. "Excuse me."

Holding tightly to my plant and my packages, I moved well out of his reach. I was thankful that I had them, or Grimes might see that my hands were shaking.

"Not so fast, Jane," he said. "I keep running into you. Why is that?"

Don't answer. Just walk away.

"I don't know. I have to go."

He fell into step alongside me. I thought he was favoring his left leg, but I wasn't sure.

I'd never known a man so tall. Beside him, I felt small and vulnerable, almost miniaturized. It was as if the black Rottweiler from the animal hospital had assumed a human shape and was walking beside me on the sidewalk. Familiar symptoms gripped me. My heart began to race, and I was afraid that if I tried to speak again, my voice would tremble.

"You're not very friendly, are you?" he asked.

I walked a little faster. We were on Willow Street now, only three blocks from the heart of town. All of the people who had come out of hibernation to enjoy the warm weather and the shops had vanished. The few other pedestrians were some distance from us and rapidly moving farther away.

I could cross at the light, retrace my steps, blend into the Saturday afternoon crowd on Grove Street, and wait until Grimes tired of his little game. That's what I'd do.

"I thought we were old friends, Jane," he said. "You must save all your nice words for your *husband*."

"Leave me alone," I said. My weak voice and my words sounded pathetic to me. It would be better if I didn't speak to him again.

We reached the corner, just as the light turned red. My car was parked across the street, but I didn't dare go near it. I didn't want to do anything that would enable Grimes to trace me. It would be safer to follow my original plan. Once I made it to Warrington's, I could take refuge in the crowd. He wouldn't dare harm me then, if that were his intent. Maybe he only wanted to harass me again.

Crane had told me more than once, "Never hesitate to ask a policeman to help you. That's what he's there for."

Needless to say, there wasn't a policeman in sight today, and Warrington's was a long block away. It was up to me to protect myself. I had confronted Grimes once before in Hazelton's lot and acquitted myself well. I could do it again. I took a deep breath and turned to face him.

"Like I say, Jennet," Grimes said, "you should be friendlier to me. It'll be better for you if you are."

Jennet?

"Get the hell away from me! Now!"

"If that's what you want, sure thing, darling. Later," he said. And then he smiled at me.

I turned and walked briskly away, wanting to look back and knowing that I shouldn't. I had to keep moving or risk being caught forever in the giant's grasp.

He knew my real name.

I sensed that Grimes wasn't following me. When I reached Warrington's, I glanced quickly behind me, but I didn't see him. Still, I kept walking. At the new Coffee House, next to Warrington's, I ordered a latte and drank it slowly, all the while wanting desperately to be home.

What else did Grimes know about me?

Eventually my courage returned. I left the Coffee House and stood in front of Warrington's display window, looking in both directions, but I saw no sign of Grimes. Since he was so much taller than the average man, he couldn't hide his presence, unless he was lurking in one of the store entrances.

I walked back to Willow Street, made it safely to my car, and drove home. From time to time, I glanced in the rear view mirror, although I was reasonably sure that he wasn't following me. My hands were steady on the wheel, but inside I felt as if I were spinning in a Drinkmaster.

Damn the man! Paranoia didn't become me. Was I still the woman who wanted to slay her own giant, or some weak ineffective imitation of her?

But what was the purpose behind that incongruous smile?

Forget him. He's a twisted, rejected male who thinks he's making a point.

Grimes couldn't possibly be trailing me. This country road was mine alone today, and soon I would be safe inside my own house, where my dogs were. I'd brush them, take them out walking, and try not to see Grimes' giant shadow beyond every stand of trees. Tomorrow, I'd mention the incident to Crane over breakfast at the Mill House, taking care to present it as no more than an unpleasant encounter.

~ * ~

I knew that I was dreaming. I separated myself from the unfolding events to wonder if it was normal for a person to have the same dream more than once. I would have to ask Lucy Hazen, the one person among my friends who was most likely to know this.

Time had reversed itself, traveling back through the decades to another century. Still, it kept moving. The thunder of cannon fire brought the jarring backward motion to a shattering halt. It was 1863.

I was in my log cabin home, looking out the window at the misty mountains in the distance where the battle was raging. Only what I was seeing wasn't mist but smoke.

My clothes were too heavy. When I moved, it seemed as though my legs were incased in multiple layers of warm fabric. The lace on my collar scratched my neck. I tried to push the long sleeves of my dress up away from my wrists, but they were too tight.

I heard the pounding hoof beats before I saw the lone rider coming out of the west. Even though I couldn't see his features clearly yet, I knew who he was and why he had come. I ran to the door to let him in. His tattered gray uniform was dusty, and his gray eyes were weary, but they burned with the intensity and brilliance of stars. Before I could say a word, he swept me up off the floor in an embrace so desperate that I sensed it might be the last. His face was rough against my skin.

"I thought I would never see you again," I said, trying to hold back my tears. "Come see what I've been doing."

I took him by the hand and led him to the sparsely furnished candlelit parlor where the only thing of beauty was the tall fir tree bedecked with bright bits of ribbon and fabric.

Even as I watched, the tree underwent a startling transformation. Ribbon and fabric turned into delicate ornaments

218

and impossible lights of blue and red and green and yellow. The phantom tree glittered with tinsel, and a little creche and presents appeared around its trunk.

The Confederate rider was still there at my side, and I wasn't afraid. I felt his strong body pressed close to mine and thought, This is one dream I don't want to end, not ever.

Of course, by that time I was awake.

~ * ~

The next morning I said to Crane, "I'm thinking about buying a gun."

He stopped eating and laid down his fork, with a large piece of syrup-drenched French toast still attached to it, giving me his full attention. That is to say, he trained his gray eyes on me as if he were trying to discern my true motive.

He didn't say a word. I began to feel like a suspect.

Unlike the rider in my dream, Crane was clean-shaven, but his sideburns were a shade too long to be considered fashionable in the modern world. Their eyes were alike, though, holding me with their intensity and brilliance.

Finally, he said, "That's a bad idea, Jennet, possibly the worst idea you've ever had."

The ensuing pause lasted too long to be comfortable. He said one word. "Why?"

"For protection. I'm a woman living alone in an isolated place. I have the collies, but no one would ever mistake them for guard dogs."

"That's been true since you first came to Foxglove Corners, give or take a dog."

I said, "I ran into Grimes in town yesterday."

Concern replaced the ice in Crane's eyes. "Tell me what happened. Did he hurt you?"

"No. He commented on my unfriendliness and told me that I should be nicer to him. I told him to get the hell away from me.

Then he smiled at me."

There. That didn't sound so bad when I said it aloud, except that...

"He called me Jennet, not Jane."

Crane's voice was soft, his words tinged with steel. "So he found out your real name. I'm going to have another talk with him."

"The smile was worse than anything he said. Hundreds of people must have been shopping in Lakeville yesterday. What were the chances I'd run into Grimes?"

"Slim, unless he was looking for you. Grimes has been keeping a low profile since the FCPD hauled him in for questioning."

"I still think that he and Emil Schillar burglarized the animal hospital. Now, about the gun..."

"I already told you, Jennet," he said. "I have the gun, and you have my cell phone number."

And I had his protection. I knew that.

"That's sufficient." He ate the piece of French toast and speared another on his fork.

Nothing in life was that simple. So many things could go wrong. Crane didn't live with me, and if I dialed his number, he might not always be in a position to respond. I had to be able to protect myself.

When I didn't react to Crane's edict, he said, "I still don't like the idea. There has to be another way, but let me think about it. If I decide it's all right, I'll go with you to buy a gun. I'll teach you how to shoot it."

That said, he drained his cup of coffee.

I stopped eating and looked at him. In a few minutes, he noticed and asked, "What's wrong, honey? Is something the matter with your breakfast?"

"I can't believe you'd speak so—so condescendingly to me," I said.

His expression betrayed his confusion. "How am I condescending? I know about guns, and you admit that you don't. I offered to help you. I want you to be safe."

"I know." Suddenly I felt miserable. I didn't want to quarrel with Crane. That was the last thing I'd ever want to do.

It's counterproductive, whispered a voice inside my head.

I let the escalating argument die and said, "Seeing Grimes must have affected me more than I thought."

"Put him out of your mind now. Like I said, I'll have a talk with him."

To this tempting offer, I could only add, "He'll probably say that all he did was smile at me."

I had to change the subject. The talk of Grimes and the disagreement with Crane were ruining my appetite. "Where do you suppose Susan is this morning?" I asked.

She wasn't waiting on us. Perversely, I missed her sunny nature. I even missed seeing her hovering over Crane.

"I don't know," Crane said. "She must have the day off."

"Did you talk to her about Emil Schiller yet?"

"Not yet," he said. "I haven't seen her."

"I hope that Emil hasn't done away with her," I stopped, appalled at the image that had formed in my mind—Susan lying dead, strangled by a fallen angel.

Crane said, "Stop imagining such gruesome scenes. I told you, I'm in charge." He let his hand stray to his belt and rest briefly on the handle of his gun. "If you can stay up late tomorrow night, I'll stop in to see you."

"I can. I will."

Even though the prospect of a late night visit from Crane was a delight to anticipate, I finished my breakfast silently. I felt that I had left some important matter between us unresolved—which, of course, I had.

~ * ~

221

"I adore him," I told Camille. "But Crane can be so domineering sometimes. I thought I liked that about him, and I guess I still do. The problem is that I want to buy a gun, and I want the decision to be mine."

Safe and warm in the kitchen of the yellow Victorian where we were having turkey sandwiches for lunch, I'd told Camille about my latest encounter with Grimes. Inevitably, the talk had turned to Crane.

"Of course you do, Jennet," she said. "Crane's dictatorial nature is part of his charm, but I agree with him about the gun. Now, when I was unhappily married, Richard Vesper had guns all over the house. When I was trying to think of an effective way to kill him…"

She trailed off. These days she rarely talked about her abusive late husband and that dark chapter in her life. "It's finally over," she'd said more than once. "It's in the past."

I was surprised that she mentioned it now.

"I thought about using a gun," Camille said. "You may remember that from my journal. But I decided that Richard might overpower me and take the gun away. Then he might use it on me. The same principle applies to your situation.

"You've told me that Grimes is six feet, six inches, tall and burly. You refer to him as a giant. When I think of you trying to hold off a man like that with a gun… I can't see it happening, that's all. You'd have to ambush him. That isn't your intent, is it?"

"No, I only want to be able to protect myself. I want to feel safe in my own home."

"You have Winter now. He attacked Grimes before. He's capable of defending you, if need be, unlike gentle little Halley. I know I'm glad that I have Twister." She laid her hand fondly on the head of the big black dog and slipped him a piece of turkey from her sandwich.

"There's nothing like a powerful dog and a devoted deputy

sheriff to make a woman feel safe," she said. "You're lucky, Jennet. You have both. Of course, if Grimes is trying to attract your attention, if he's becoming obsessed with you, that's another matter."

"What an appalling idea."

Her words brought back a vision of Grimes on that snowy night in the Cauldron, his offer to buy me a drink, my fabrication, and his retreat. What had he said? Oh, yes. "Later." He'd said it twice now. The man had a limited vocabulary.

"Think about the gun a little longer before you decide," Camille said. "I'm sure nothing is going to happen tonight. If you don't mind listening to the advice of a woman whose own relationship turned deadly, don't give a man total control of your life, not even our deputy sheriff. I'm fond of Crane too, but sometimes he acts like he's living in another century."

"Before women's rights," I added, "when women were helpless or pretended to be. I don't want to be like that. It's not my nature. It's only that Grimes is the scariest enemy I could imagine."

"You've convinced me," Camille said. "I hope I never see him. Now, Jennet, if it's true that you and Crane are finally going to have your romantic weekend, I'm going to bring all the dogs here together under one roof. Have you learned to roll out cookie dough yet?"

For the rest of our visit, we fell back easily on purely domestic subjects. I had taken out the specter of Grimes and dealt with it. I was sure that he was still out there somewhere, skulking in the shadows, stalking me, but against the background of Camille's blue and white country kitchen, his power had diminished to manageable size.

Twenty-five

At the end of a long and tiring Monday at Marston, my own kitchen was a cozy haven. Halley and Winter munched their biscuits in canine content, the cocoa in the saucepan bubbled and steamed, and the scent of pumpkin drifting out from the basket on the counter dared me to grab a muffin and spoil my dinner.

I picked one up but managed to resist temptation. Instead, I poured the cocoa into a mug. I'd take it into the dining room and sit at the table, sipping it slowly, forcing myself to steal a few minutes of rest before plunging into my customary evening activities.

As I crossed the threshold, a graceful shape shimmered into life in the shadows beyond the table. I held my breath as it gained form and color. Amid green branches, lights of blue, red, green, and yellow glowed like jeweled beacons.

In the kitchen, the dogs were barking. Drawn to the brightness, I moved forward on shaky legs and reached out to touch a branch.

My hand closed on air as the shimmer faded.

Shivering in sudden chill, I grasped the back of a chair to steady myself. I was looking through the bay window at a rolling expanse of brown winter grass and bare trees. Nothing else.

Nothing was there.

I sank into the chair, surprised to see the mug still in my hand, conscious of a burning sensation on my palm and the rich cocoa scent.

The phantom Christmas tree had followed me from the haunted Victorian to my own house.

One dog was whining. Halley.

I could breathe again.

My thoughts tumbled over one another, clamoring for my attention. I should call Lucy. I wanted to tell Crane what I'd seen and find out why Halley was crying. But before I did anything, I had to stop shaking.

A few swallows of cocoa helped. The liquid seared my throat but at the same time broke the spell. I kept breathing and drinking, kept my hands wrapped around the mug, and waited for the warmth to take the cold away.

Only it never did. Not entirely.

Dear God, what had just happened here in my dining room? And what did it mean?

~ * ~

I couldn't imagine why the phantom Christmas tree had appeared in my house on a mild afternoon in late January. Nor was I able to reach Lucy or Crane, and Camille's house was dark. Probably it was better if I dealt with the apparition's visit on my own at first.

The best way to do that was to continue my plan for the evening, which included making dinner and correcting papers. Then, I'd take a hot bath, set out my clothes for tomorrow, and go to bed.

But I didn't want to dream. Not tonight.

I began by returning to the kitchen, my safe, warm room. Halley was still whining, her gaze riveted on the muffin that lay outside the basket, just beyond her reach.

I gave one half to her and the other to Winter, emptied the last of Camille's beef stew into a casserole dish, and shoved it in the microwave. These familiar chores brought me back to a normal sphere. And as soon as I could talk to someone about the phantom tree, I was certain that my rising panic would vanish.

~ * ~

As I walked to my car in the bright sunshine and crisp air the next morning, my fear began to dissipate. Another long day at school coping with unruly students drove it a little farther away. When I told Leonora about the apparition at lunch, she admitted that she envied me.

"You're still having all the adventures," she said. "I'm going to have to move to Foxglove Corners."

Camille's reaction was different from the one she'd had before Christmas when I first told her about the ghost tree. She turned pale and said, "The dogs knew something was wrong. I am so afraid for you, Jennet." Lucy, gleefully anticipating a new plot, demanded that I keep her informed of future developments. Crane listened gravely and held me.

"I don't know what to say, honey. Maybe this Christmas tree is a sign of something good."

I pulled him closer. "When I woke up the this morning, I wondered if I'd imagined it. Just for a moment. Then I knew that I hadn't."

"I can't fight a ghost for you," he said. "I sure wish I could."

"A ghost tree, Crane. I want to understand it. I guess I'll wait for the next thing to happen."

He didn't say another word, but he kissed me in a gentle yet firm way that told me I wasn't alone. For the moment, it was enough.

~ * ~

After a brief flirtation with spring, the weather turned on us like
a great white dog with bared fangs. Deep winter returned to Foxglove Corners. I looked at my tulip plant in the kitchen window and longed for spring. It was the twenty-fifth day of January.

The snow fell heavily, and high winds had set all of the wind chimes in the neighborhood in wild motion. Their jingling and clanging carried across the acres and mixed with the tinkling of the chimes on my porch. My own delicate moon, stars, and sun were too fragile to survive the powerful gusts much longer. Every day, I came home expecting to find them blown away, but I never remembered to take them down.

I was waiting for Crane. The mugs were on the kitchen table and a box of cocoa on the counter. On this bitterly cold night, I was certain that he would appreciate a hot drink. He was going to stop by late this evening. I didn't know the exact time, but I hoped it would be before midnight, as tomorrow was a school day.

The dogs weren't waiting up with me, but they would both come to life when he arrived. They usually did and stayed that way, even if he didn't have a bag of steak bones for them. I supposed they adored him, too.

At nine-thirty, I noticed bright headlights on Jonquil Lane. Standing at the window, I tried to make out the shape of Crane's patrol car through the falling snow, but I couldn't do it. The vehicle didn't appear to be moving. Some unfortunate motorist was probably stranded on the lane in a snowstorm.

I left the window and looked around for something to do. I didn't like waiting. I preferred it when Crane materialized unannounced at my kitchen door. Of course, on a typical night, at this time I would be in bed with the lights out, in which case, he would only drive by, assuming that all was well. He'd told me often that he did this.

The headlights were still there fifteen minutes later when I went to the window again to see if Crane was coming, but the next time I looked, they were gone. The only lights were those in a second story window of Camille's house.

Because I was restless and had nothing pressing to do, I took out one of my happy thoughts to keep me company: Snow falling at Snow Lodge, where, by the end of the week, Crane and I would begin our long-delayed romantic weekend. I entertained myself with warm thoughts of sleigh rides, blazing fires, and falling asleep in Crane's arms. Time passed, and I felt myself growing drowsy.

He arrived at last at ten o'clock, pounding loudly on the kitchen door and breaking apart my reverie and the night stillness with his powerful presence. In through the door he came, with the wind-driven snow behind him. Melting flakes mingled with the silver strands in his fair hair, and his eyes were a glittering blend of frost and silver.

I closed the door behind him, shutting the winter out.

"I'm so glad you're here," I said.

He enveloped me in his arms the way his dream counterpart had done, and his badge pressed sharply against my chest.

"Now that's a real welcome for a cold man on a winter night," he said.

Until now, I hadn't realized how afraid I'd been. No matter how much I tried to convince myself otherwise, time hadn't dimmed the memory of Grimes or the ghostly shimmer in the dining room. All evening I had been waiting to feel Crane's strong arms around me.

"I've never felt so safe in all my life," I said.

So much for my balking at Crane's domineering ways. So much for women's rights and my impatience with helpless females. I would decide later where I stood on these issues. For now, I wanted nothing more than to be held.

"Did anything happen, Jennet?" Crane asked. "Is it Grimes? Or did you see the tree again?"

"No, I just want to feel the strong arms of the law around me."

"It's not like you to be so clingy, honey, but I like it fine."

"I'm just tired and vulnerable," I said.

"Those are two good feelings for you to have when you're with me. Is that real cocoa you have out?"

"Yes, I'll make us some in a minute. I really admire you, Crane. If you're tired, you keep on going, and if you're in any way vulnerable, I haven't discovered it yet."

With a mischievous smile, he said, "That's because I'm invulnerable. I'm the law. Where are the dogs tonight?"

They were in the room with us, awake from their winter naps and ready for play. We just hadn't noticed them. Halley had her stuffed penguin in her mouth, and Winter was wagging his tail, as if to say that he was too old for young-dog play but would still like to be admired and petted.

"I see them," Crane said. "You're good dogs, you two. How did you know I wanted cocoa, honey?"

"It's cocoa weather. Sit down, Crane. Is it bad outside?"

"Not too bad yet. The wind is blowing around the snow that already fell. We had enough warming. Your expressway should be cleared by morning."

"Did you see a car stuck on Jonquil Lane?" I asked.

"No. There's no one on this stretch of the road."

"Good. He must have gotten his car started."

I concentrated on making the hot chocolate drink the old-fashioned way, with cocoa, water, sugar, and salt. It was bound to taste better than those instant mixes I'd been using.

Crane came up behind me and captured my free hand, the one that wasn't holding the wooden spoon. "Are you really okay, Jennet? Your hand is like ice. Anyone would think you were the one who just came in from outside."

"It's just a touch of residual terror from my encounter with Grimes," I said. "It'll go away. Did you talk to him?"

"Not yet. He checked out of his motel, but there's been an arrest in the Randolph murder. I wanted to tell you about it myself. An itinerant named Vince pawned the vet's missing watch yesterday. He claims that he found it."

"That *is* good news. Alice will be glad to hear it. Don't forget that tomorrow is the twenty-sixth, Crane."

"I won't."

I gave the cocoa one last stir and poured it into the mugs. Then I added a few miniature marshmallows and a dollop of whipped cream to each drink for a festive touch.

I tasted the cocoa and kept both of my hands on the mug, letting the heat warm them. "This is really good."

"It'll keep me warm all night," Crane said.

"Well, it's not that powerful. I'll make you some to take with you in a thermos."

"Nobody takes care of me like you do, honey."

"Well, good. I aim to keep on doing it."

With each sip of the hot chocolate drink, my feeling of well-being seemed to draw closer and closer. By the time Crane kissed me goodnight and left to resume his patrol of Foxglove Corners, thermos in hand, I felt much better. I'd left the fear-filled part of me behind, and I was Jennet again. Jennet, the giant slayer.

Crane and the cocoa had a very special effect on me, almost as satisfying as having a gun.

~ * ~

The twenty-sixth of January was a long, cold day with intermittent snow flurries falling from a dark sky. I was in Oakpoint, Michigan, teaching my classes, following my lesson plans, or diverting from them. I was flexible.

I dealt with minor problems, commiserated with one of my Journalism students whose movie review had disappeared into the inner workings of the computer, and finally lost my patience with two boys who almost came to blows over a missing homework paper.

The morning was typical, and the hours flew by. I was so busy that I didn't think about Grimes until Leonora mentioned him at lunch.

"Have you seen the Rottweiler man lately?" she asked.

"Not since that day I ran into him at the hardware store."

"I don't want to alarm you unnecessarily, but do you think he's still interested in you?" she asked. "Romantically, I mean?"

I couldn't suppress a shudder at the thought. Not since that night at the Cauldron had I considered this and then only fleetingly. But hadn't Camille said something similar?

"Why would you say that?" I asked.

"I don't know. No special reason. It was just a thought."

"I hope you're wrong. He doesn't believe in the jealous husband any more, if he ever did. Remember, he called me Jennet."

"That isn't good."

"Not at all. Grimes blames me for turning him in to the police and for Winter biting him, too, I guess. These are hardly friendly overtures."

"You aren't very friendly, are you?" he had asked.

"You said that he smiled at you. Or was it a sneer?"

I sighed. Leonora was determined to bring it all back to me. The chilling smile, the predator eyes, and the fear that I hadn't been able to banish were again insinuating their way into my thoughts. My imagination was happy to have new material to work with.

"The word smile doesn't begin to convey what I saw in Grimes' expression and in his eyes. I thought I was looking at some malevolent being bent on my destruction. Let's end this discussion. It's making me nervous. I already have a class in rebellion determined to do that."

"Aren't you exaggerating about Grimes?" Leonora asked. "He's dangerous and loathsome, but he can't be evil incarnate."

"Maybe not, but that's how I see him. I'm afraid of him. I don't want to be, but that's the way it is."

"You're lucky to have Crane, then. I always knew that dating the law would be an advantage for you some day."

"Yes, thank heavens for Crane." I remembered how safe he had made me feel last night simply by holding me. "Now, I wonder what else is going to happen to disrupt the rest of the day? At school, I mean."

Fortunately, nothing did. My worst class was surprisingly subdued, and the afternoon went along smoothly. As the last bell rang, I finally had time to wonder what was going on in Foxglove Corners.

~ * ~

When I drove past the Cauldron on the way home, Emil Schiller was unlocking the door of a silver van. It didn't resemble a death wagon for dogs. On the contrary. With the picture of a large winged brush hovering over a small spotted dog, it looked a little silly. Maybe that was the idea.

I didn't hesitate. This heaven-sent opportunity might be my last chance to learn something about the dognapping ring. Almost immediately, Emil pulled out of the lot and passed me, speeding off down Spruce Road, heading north. I accelerated and followed him.

At four-thirty in the afternoon, southbound traffic was light. The Flying Brush and my car were the only vehicles going north. I hoped I could keep the van in view, because beyond the

Cauldron, Spruce Road turned into a series of curves and then grew increasingly hilly.

This was a scenic route with dark woods and charming rural landscapes. Moreover, it was always cleared after a snowfall. From Spruce, I could turn onto any one of several byroads, all of which led to Jonquil Lane.

As could Emil. At any time, he might decide to take one of them, and I might lose him. But there was a limit to how fast I dared drive. Even though the road was cleared, I might hit a patch of ice.

I could only surmise that Emil Schiller was going about his dognapping business. Maybe he was heading home or on his way to meet Susan. He might be soliciting business for his non-existent dog grooming service in a new area. He could have any number of destinations, legitimate or otherwise. Still, as long as the possibility existed that he would lead me to a fresh clue or even to the stolen dogs, I had to follow him.

He passed the Rocking Horse Ranch, where I suspected he might stop, but he kept going. We were no longer the only travelers on the road, which was good. In my silver Taurus, I felt safe and anonymous. The last thing I wanted was to have Emil realize that I was trailing him.

I lost him for a few minutes and then drove up a slight incline and spied the van in the distance. I had been driving for at least twenty minutes, and by now had traveled farther north on Spruce Road than I'd ever gone before.

Ahead was a charming old Victorian house. Painted light green with rose trim, it was as pretty as an illustration in a fairy tale book. Several yards beyond the house, to my left, I saw a narrow trail that didn't bisect Spruce. Here the van slowed down and made a turn.

I drove slowly past the green house, certain that I would recognize it again, stopped at the trail, and made my own turn.

By this time, the van was well ahead of me, a mere speck in the distance. The area was desolate and vaguely threatening with dark, bare branches that almost met above the uneven surface. I slowed my speed and glanced from right to left, hoping to find a distinguishing landmark.

Whatever you do, don't get lost, I thought.

Taking a second to orient myself, I realized that I was unlikely to lose my way unless I made a turn. No matter how far I drove down this unfamiliar trail, I should eventually come to a road that ran parallel to Spruce.

At last I came to a crossroad, beyond which the woods grew thinner. On my left, I saw a sign of habitation in this wilderness, an establishment called the Royal Pheasant. It appeared to be a private club, but it wasn't open at present.

I looked back to the road, only to discover that the van had vanished from my sight. During the second when I'd turned my head, Emil must have left the trail. I drove on more slowly now. Before long, the woods gave way to open farmland. Another few minutes brought me to a red barn. Parked at the far side of the structure with only its rear section visible was the van.

Coming to a complete stop, I looked around, imprinting the location on my memory. The barn was built in an A-line style, like a Swiss chalet. Its dark red color was a splash of brightness against the black and white landscape. Snow had drifted up high around the foundation and lay heavily on the roof.

Three horses, one of them a colt, stood in front of the barn. They turned their faces toward the road as I approached but didn't make a sound. I couldn't see Emil Schiller, which was just as well. I wasn't rash enough to risk an encounter with him in this deserted place. I only hoped that he didn't know I was there.

The barn doesn't have any windows, I told myself. Emil is inside, and you're in your car. You should be safe.

Nevertheless, I'd better not linger. I kept driving, increasing my speed a little, until I came to another crossroad. Here I turned around. When I passed the barn on my way back, Emil's van was still there. I suspected that the stolen dogs were hidden inside the barn, probably drugged or they would have alerted Emil to the presence of another vehicle passing by. If I was right about the significance of January twenty-sixth, they might not be here long.

I didn't stop until I was back on Spruce Road, safely moving with the traffic. Then I pulled over to the side of the road and called Crane on my cell phone, leaving a message with his answering machine that included detailed directions to the barn.

As I resumed my interrupted ride home, I felt pleased with myself, and I knew that Crane would be happy with me, too. I had made another discovery, all the while letting the police do the work they were paid to do—after I had provided them with an essential clue, of course.

It had all been so simple and had taken no more than an hour of my time. I was so satisfied with my accomplishment that I didn't listen to the pesky inner voice that asked, "Don't you think that was too easy?"

Twenty-six

Winter sprang from the rocker where he had been sleeping and rushed to the living room window. He stood frozen in a menacing stance with his paws on the mahogany deacon's bench, perilously close to my crystal lamp.

His bark had an angry sound. Unwilling to be left out of the fun, Halley started barking, too.

I came up behind them and looked out the window but couldn't see anything that shouldn't be there. "What's the matter, Winter?" I asked. "Halley?"

Their answer was more and louder barking.

The late afternoon was turning into twilight, and everything was still on Jonquil Lane, except for my dogs. Dr. Linton's house was dark, but in Camille's yellow Victorian, a single lamp burned in a second floor window. No cars were moving on the lane. All was well.

Snow covered the ground and clung to the branches of trees. Across the lane, the woods were dark and silent until, like a burst of brightness in motion, a deer leaped out from the trees and crossed the lane. He skirted the house and headed toward the acreage in the back. Wild with excitement, the dogs raced to the sunroom to find another viewing window. I stayed in the living room, no longer concerned now that I knew what had prompted their outburst.

Although the deer were protected from hunters and roamed freely in Foxglove Corners, I seldom caught a glimpse of one. This unexpected sighting was something I wanted to savor, and I suspected that it might prove to be the most momentous event of the evening.

The dogs had grown quiet. Reluctantly, I moved away from the window. Gazing at the winter wonderland was more fun than working in the kitchen, but I was getting hungry. I fed the dogs, made an omelet for my own dinner, and sliced a loaf of French bread that I'd brought home from the bakery, all ordinary activities that didn't rival the brief excitement of the deer sighting.

At six, Crane called to tell me that he'd received my message and was going to check it out.

"But I can't do it until later," he said. "Something is going on, and I'm right in the middle of it. I'll take care of it, though."

"What's going on?" I asked.

"You know I can't talk about it, honey. I'll see you tomorrow evening, but it'll be late again. Don't follow any more suspects. Do you know how dangerous that could have been?"

"It was a little risky, I'll admit. From now on, I'll leave the matter of trailing suspects in the capable hands of the law. Anyway, with Dr. Randolph's alleged killer in custody and a map to the dognappers' lair in the hands of the authorities, this mystery is winding down."

"I won't worry about you then," he said. "Goodnight."

"Goodnight to you, too. Be careful, Crane."

With a sigh, I hung up the receiver. Hearing Crane's voice was insufficient tonight. I wanted to see him.

After six months in Foxglove Corners, I still grew a little uneasy when darkness fell. Now it was wintertime and snowing as well. The house was warm enough, but I felt cold and isolated, even with my two dogs for company. These feelings were a byproduct of the winter and the snowy weather. I knew that they would vanish in the spring or with a familiar pounding on my kitchen door. Or when the activities of Grimes and Emil Schiller were stopped.

After dinner, I turned on the television to hear what was left of the local news. The weather report turned out to be almost as alarming as the day's assortment of accidents and fires.

Foxglove Corners was in for a mixture of the worst winter weather in years, all coming together on a single night. The weathercasters were predicting snow, turning to freezing rain, then back to snow, and finally to rain. The severity of the wintry mix depended on whether the temperature dipped below freezing.

Wondering which of these calamities would actually appear, I turned off the television and was about to go upstairs when I happened to look out the living room window. Headlights were shining out on Jonquil Lane again. A vehicle moved slowly past Dr. Linton's house and then came to a stop a little beyond where I'd seen mysterious headlights last night.

It didn't seem likely that another car had broken down in the same place. Nor did I think that last night's motorist had made a return appearance. I squinted, wishing I could see through the darkness and across the acres, wondering if the lights belonged to a silver van.

Had I been naïve to assume that Emil hadn't seen me from the red barn?

And what if he had? Didn't I have as much right to travel on the nameless trail as he did? Of course that wasn't the point. Grimes might have mentioned my name to Emil or described me, in which case I had another enemy who knew about my interest in the stolen dogs. And Emil was definitely part of the dognapping ring. I was sure of it now.

All the same, I couldn't rule out Grimes. Maybe he knew where I lived. He could be the driver sitting in an idling car on the lane, watching my house.

All I knew for certain was that these headlights didn't belong to Crane's cruiser. If the car hadn't moved the next time I looked outside, I would call Crane again.

The yellow Victorian was dark now, but the lights were on in almost every room of the Linton house. They gleamed softly through the falling snow. I was glad that I was inside my own house and hoped Crane was in some dry and cozy place as he pursued his official sheriff's business.

Turning off the lamp, I called the dogs to let them out one last time for the night.

~ * ~

Winter was annoying me. His behavior was almost as unusual as the weather forecast. I was trying to take a bath, but so far hadn't had any success because he refused to settle down.

Both dogs had been outside for fifteen minutes, which should have been ample time. They came bounding in, with clumps of wet snow clinging to their coats, two large, rowdy bundles of energy ready for before-bedtime play.

I threw a beach towel over each of them, hoping that the material would absorb the bulk of the snow before it reached the floor; but they shook themselves vigorously and sent the towels flying.

Halley dashed after her towel and played with it for a while. Then she lay down with her head resting on one of the damp edges, and I went upstairs to take a towel for myself out of the linen closet. I stopped in my bedroom for a long, warm nightgown.

Downstairs Winter was whining. When he refused to calm down, I relented and let him out again. And in again. Within minutes of being let in, he was standing in front of the door, barking sharply. We repeated this performance two more times. Finally, my infinite patience with fussy canines neared the breaking point.

"Winter, stop!" I said in a firm tone. "Settle. It's bedtime." I added, "Bad dog!" and locked the kitchen door. He looked sufficiently cowed, and I started up the stairs again.

Somewhere to the right, a crash of thunder split the silence apart. I froze on the top step. How could there be thunder when we were in the midst of a January snowstorm? I had scarcely completed the thought when the lights went out.

A bath and bed tumbled to the bottom of my nighttime activities list. Standing on the landing, I reached out into the darkness, trying to find the railing. When my hands closed around the cool wood, I stood still for a moment, listening to nothing at all.

The entire house was dead. Nothing that depended on electricity had survived the probable death hit to a transformer. The hum of the refrigerator, the various furnace noises in the basement, and dozens of other sounds I usually never noticed had disappeared.

Ever since moving to the country, I had collected dozens of candlesticks and candles, as well as assorted survival supplies in anticipation of a power failure. Quickly I reviewed the contents of the emergency basket I kept in the kitchen. Lantern flashlight, regular flashlights, spare candles, matches, bottled water, dry cereal, and crackers. I should be all right.

The first thing I needed was illumination. Every room in the house had at least one candle, but I kept the matches in the kitchen. I had to make my way to the kitchen then.

I couldn't take the chance of stumbling over one of the dogs in the dark. "Halley! Winter!" I called. "Where are you?"

Halley's answering yelp came from the general direction of

the side door. Near her, Winter was still whining.

Slowly I walked down the stairs, never taking my hands off the banister. When I reached the first floor, I made my way to the kitchen, moving my hands along the walls, letting them tell me where the doorways and familiar household landmarks were.

When I reached the kitchen, I moved to where I knew the cupboards would be, touching cold metal knobs, opening the top drawer where I kept the matches, finding the matchbox. There.

A brush of warm fur pressed against my legs. Halley had found me in the darkness, but Winter was still crying at the door.

"There you are, Halley. Good. Winter, be quiet!"

Once I had the matches, the rest was easy. I lit the kitchen candle and brought my emergency basket out from under the sink. With one candle burning and a wide pool of light surrounding me, I saw my collies. They were standing close together now, my companions in adversity, my protectors. I had an overwhelming urge to protect them.

"Come on upstairs, you two," I said. "We'll all stay together."

Carrying my candle and the lantern, I went back to my bedroom. Only Halley followed me. Winter stayed at the back door. He was still fussing, but I decided to ignore him.

Tomorrow was a school day. I would need a battery-operated clock to be sure I didn't oversleep. I found one in the guestroom and set it on the wicker table in my bedroom. Then I moved all the candles in the room to the table and added the lantern.

That took care of illumination. As for the refrigerator, I'd leave the door closed. Tomorrow, I'd have dry cereal for breakfast. The house should retain heat throughout the night, so

I wasn't in imminent danger of freezing.

I decided to skip the bath. In fact, I wouldn't even get undressed. I'd be warmer in my clothes. If the power wasn't back on by tomorrow morning, I'd take the dogs and stay with Leonora in Oakpoint. Everything would be all right. Thanks to months of preparation, I had managed my first country power outage capably.

Winter had finally come upstairs, but he showed no signs of settling down. He took the edge of my skirt in his mouth and gently tugged at it. Then he released it and ran to the door of the bedroom.

"No, Winter," I said. "You don't want to go out again."

I moved the lantern closer to my bed, blew out the candles, and lay down, hoping the dogs would follow my example. As I pulled the heavy comforter up to my chin, I wondered how the house could have cooled off so quickly. My hands were as cold as if I'd been walking outside without gloves. I tucked them under my pillow and tried to relax.

This wasn't so bad. I tried not to think about the darkness. Instead, I centered my thoughts on Crane. He was the essence of brightness. Soon I would fall asleep, and in the morning, perhaps the power would be back on. Or the forecasters might predict a return to sunshine. It was best to stay positive.

~ * ~

Another crash of thunder jolted me awake. A second thunderclap and an explosion of loud, frightening sounds followed. I heard a shattering of glass. Winter and Halley were barking in fury. All of the noise originated on the first floor.

The dogs were barking downstairs. They weren't in the bedroom with me!

A tree must have fallen on the roof... No, that had happened last June during the tornado. No trees grew near this house. A downed plane, then, or a lightning strike?

242

I reached for the lantern, switched it on, and lit one of the candles. Faint light swirled to life around me, leaving the rest of the room in shadows. I slipped on my shoes, took the candle and rushed to the door.

"Halley! Winter!" My voice sounded shrill and unnatural in the sudden stillness.

As I started downstairs, a canine scream of rage and pain tore through the silence. It was the cry of a dog in distress; but was I hearing the voice of Halley or Winter? For the first time since I'd added Winter to my household, I couldn't tell. I called them again and heard another cry, followed by the sound of a body falling, and the slamming of a door.

I froze on the landing and gripped the candlestick tighter. Dogs couldn't close doors behind themselves. I wasn't alone in the house. My defense mechanism whirred into motion, and I gave myself a series of orders: Try to stay calm. Don't give your position away. Think.

The light from my candle would reveal my location to the intruder, but I couldn't take the risk of blowing it out. That would leave me helpless in the dark.

Someone must have broken down one of the doors. It would have to be the kitchen door, for that was where the sounds had been. The house was quiet now, but the frigid air blowing freely through first floor insinuated its way up the stairs. Shivering, I moved the candle closer to my face. My shaking hand set the shadows around me into motion.

I would give anything to have my dogs with me. I didn't want to face whatever waited for me downstairs all alone.

Winter had sensed that an intruder was on my property. He had tried to warn me, and I'd repaid him by ignoring his signals and scolding him. What had happened to him? And to my little Halley?

I called her name softly, but she heard me. Desperate

scratching at the door and renewed whimpering told me that the intruder must have thrown her down the basement stairs or into the half bathroom downstairs. She was alive. But what about Winter?

The situation was clear and desperate. I was alone in the house with someone who had come after me in a snowstorm. And my canine protectors had been neutralized.

Emil Schiller had seen me at the red barn after all. He had come to silence me. Or Grimes...

Or someone else...

I couldn't hear anything now, but it was an ominous kind of quiet. Knowing that in a matter of seconds I would have to act, I tried to think what I had in the house to use as a weapon and how I could locate it.

At this point, I didn't waste time lamenting the fact that I hadn't followed my instincts and bought a gun instead of just talking about it with Crane.

Twenty-seven

As I came downstairs, walking within the path of light cast by my candle, I sensed rather than heard the alien presence somewhere on the first floor.

Halley was crying behind the locked basement door. Although her distress tore at my heart, I decided to leave her there where she would be safe, while I dealt with the intruder. I was afraid to think about Winter.

Wishing for a swallow of water to soothe the dryness in my throat, I began my slow descent. My knees felt weak, but I could do this. One step at a time.

When I reached the foot of the staircase, I stopped for a fraction of a moment to formulate my plan. The only object in the house that could double as a weapon was the carving knife. I'd been slicing bread for dinner and didn't remember putting the knife away. It must still be on the kitchen counter, but not necessarily out of my reach, if I acted quickly.

Speed was the essential element. I had to go through the hall to the kitchen, make my way around the table and chairs, and run my hand along the counter. The knife should be to the left of the sink. Then, with a weapon, even a makeshift one, I wouldn't be helpless. If I left the candle behind on the stair, the intruder might not detect my movements.

Do it, I told myself. *Act now.*

Setting the candlestick down, I crossed the circle of light, moving in the darkness quickly and quietly. I found my way around the furniture to the counter and touched the hard, cold surface of the sink. There! Moving from stainless steel to granite, I found the knife and closed my hand around its handle.

A flicker of light stole out of the darkness, throwing the reflection of a grotesque, grinning apparition at the window over the sink. It carried a candle in its hand. I heard heavy breathing and felt the first waves of heat, most likely from the candle I'd left behind.

Not Emil, but Grimes. His burly form rose high above me. He was a good twelve inches taller than I was and at least a hundred and fifty pounds heavier.

Grimes banged the candlestick down on the counter and reached around me to grasp the knife. He flung it through the hall into the dining room beyond. I heard a dull thud as it landed on the hardwood floor. Grabbing my shoulders, he spun me around until I was facing him. All the while, he leered down at me.

"You're out of time, Jennet," he said.

I drew away from him, only to find myself backed up against the counter. He shoved the candlestick down toward the breadbox. Framed in light, I saw the broken kitchen door. It had given me no more protection that a sheet of cardboard. I felt like a paper doll, fragile and easy to crumple.

How was it possible that I had only one large carving knife in the house? Now I had nothing, but I wasn't going to let Grimes think that he had won. There were traditional, time-honored ways to deal with a giant. If only I could remember one.

"What did you do to my dogs?" I demanded.

He laughed. It was a winter-cold laugh, more frigid than the night air pouring in through the broken door.

"The big one's dead, and if that other one keeps yipping, I'll kill her, too."

"I don't believe you," I said. "You tried to kill Winter twice before, and you couldn't do it."

Three times is a charm. I needed a charm.

"Yeah, well, where is he then?"

A charm... a charm... a charm...

"I'm sure you know all about dead dogs, Grimes. You're the lowest, most disgusting form of life on the planet. I wish I had my knife. I'd drive it through your black heart!"

He laughed again, as if my words had amused him. "But you don't have your knife, do you, Jennet?"

"This is home invasion," I said. "You'll pay for it."

"You're the one who's going to pay. You should have been nicer to me. I was nice to you. I could've let my dog kill you, but I called him off. That was my mistake. Now it's time for me to even the score."

His laughter was gone, replaced by a new determination. "You and that gray cur. You set him on me. Then you set the cops on me. Don't lie to me again."

One of his hands strayed absently to his thigh, and a look of pain crossed his face. His hands were massive. I could see them strangling Dr. Randolph, and I imagined them closing around my throat, even while I fervently hoped I was wrong about his intention.

Stay calm. Keep your fear hidden. Speak rationally.

"Did I do all that?" I asked. "Strange, I don't remember."

"Think again," he said.

"You're wrong. All I did was lie to you that first night. One harmless little lie. None of the rest of it was my doing. I don't regret anything that happened to you. You brought it on yourself. Even Winter's attack."

I knew that I had gone too far, but it didn't matter now.

He reached for my throat. I tried to push his massive hands back. I might as well have tried to move a gigantic block of ice. Trapped as I was by the counter, with Winter removed from my side, I was out of options.

I could hear Halley's cries behind the basement door. Strangely, they seemed farther away than they should be. What would happen to her when Grimes killed me? This was the moment when the cavalry should arrive with music, but the only sounds in the world were the giant breathing and Halley crying.

I felt his hands on my neck. They rested lightly there, almost in a caress. Then they tightened. Somewhere beyond my panic and pain, I gasped for breath.

"I could do it quickly, but I'm not going to," he said. "I'm going to enjoy this."

I had one last sliver of a chance to get away, even if it would probably end in my recapture and killing. At this point, Grimes wouldn't be expecting any resistance from me. If I caught him off guard and broke away from him... If he was too heavy and awkward to catch me...

I could run through the broken door out into the night and from there... Dr. Linton was home. He would help me. But I had to move quickly and take Grimes unaware.

Now!

I wrenched out of his grasp and darted around him, a move he hadn't anticipated. In the second before he reacted, the lights came back on in the dining room—which was impossible because they had been off when the power failed.

Impossible, but I understood. These multi-colored lights had nothing do with the electricity being restored. At first they were only a blur, like pale, fuzzy images on a malfunctioning television screen. Like a shimmer. Then, slowly they sharpened into clarity.

The phantom Christmas tree returned. The ornaments took shape, the glittering tinsel appeared; and, under the tree, the presents and the little crèche formed. Now the apparition was whole, impossibly and brilliantly there, its reality undeniable.

I had been right then. The supernatural manifestation was an ill omen meant for me, a forewarning of my death. It brought something else, though. A fragment of a memory tugged desperately at me, struggling to search the surface.

The presents and the little crèche under the Christmas tree and something else.

His massive arm frozen in mid-air, Grimes stared beyond me. "What are you looking at? Trying to trick me, are you? It won't work."

If only I could pull the memory all the way up.

From the darkness beyond the broken door there came a deadly stirring and a low growl, at the precise moment my mind found the memory.

My mother and I were making Christmas cookie ornaments. I could see her and hear her voice as clearly as if she were in the room with me. "Keep rolling out the dough, Jennet. Lightly. You need a light touch. Keep practicing, honey. You'll get the hang of it."

As Winter, eighty pounds of fury, sprang through the air and buried his fangs in Grimes' shoulder, I whirled around. Pulling open the cupboard drawer, I seized my mother's rolling pin and turned again.

Winter had his enemy pinned to the floor. Grimes was yanking at Winter's fur, trying to sit up, while Winter's jaws tore into his shoulder as if it were a prime cut of meat. Ignoring Grimes' screams of pain, I brought the rolling pin down on his head with as much force as I could muster. A loud, sickening sound like that of a pumpkin smashed on concrete echoed through the silent house.

When I saw that Grimes wasn't moving, I called Winter off.

"Good, *good* dog," I said. "Good, Winter. Come."

Because of him, I was alive. At that moment, I almost believed that Winter was invincible, but I wanted to check to see that he wasn't mortally wounded and make a fuss over him.

Although the big blue dog usually obeyed me, he was reluctant to leave his captive. Growling, he lay down close to Grimes' motionless body. Watching them, I began to realize what I had done. Maybe I had used too much force. I hoped I hadn't killed Grimes.

"My good dog," I said again, laying my hand on Winter's head, touching something warm and wet.

Please don't let Grimes be dead, I thought.

But it was Winter's blood on my fingers.

I looked for the phantom Christmas tree, but it was gone. I didn't know exactly when the apparition left, having been preoccupied with braining Grimes, but there was nothing in the living room now except darkness and the terrible cold.

My entire confrontation with Grimes had unfolded by the light of a single candle and the reflection of the bright snow outside. The tree had appeared for a moment only, but it had been long enough.

~ * ~

I wished that I could afford the luxury of tears, but since I was alive and had bested the giant, I had things to do.

First, I let Halley out of the basement. In her eagerness to be reunited with me, she almost knocked me to the floor. She licked my face fervently, and I ran my hand over her body until I was sure that she wasn't hurt. Touching her warm fur gave me strength.

While she joined Winter at Grimes' side, I found the matches in my emergency basket and lit more candles. That helped a little. I saw that Winter's head again bore witness to a brutal blow. Otherwise, he seemed to be all right, and the bleeding had stopped

The telephone in the living room was working. I called the police and Crane, in that order. Then armed with the lantern, I steeled myself to go down to the basement for a length of rope.

If I hadn't killed Grimes, he might regain consciousness and follow me downstairs. "Watch him, Winter," I said. "Keep him there."

Although I knew I could trust Winter with my life, I kept looking over my shoulder as I searched frantically for the rope. Finally I found it in a box of assorted tools. Only about two yards were left, but I had enough to tie Grimes' hands and feet, which I did as tightly as I could. Every now and then, I glanced at the rolling pin on the counter to make sure that it hadn't disappeared along with the phantom Christmas tree.

If Grimes did come to, I would hit him again.

~ * ~

In the movies, the cavalry always arrives in time to save the damsel in distress. In life, it never happens that way. My favorite cavalryman, Crane, arrived on the scene late, but he brought the police with him. The officers dealt with Grimes, who had come to a groggy consciousness at last, while Crane dealt with me.

He assessed the situation with brisk, professional efficiency and touched my throat with a gentleness that made me feel like crying. I suspected that the marks left by Grimes' hands were still there.

"Are you all right, honey?" Crane asked. "He didn't hurt you, did he?"

"No, but he wanted to."

Crane was Deputy Sheriff Ferguson tonight, in my house on official business, accompanied by the police, but I decided that the situation was unique enough to make personal contact allowable.

I was in his arms again. Everything was all right, although it had been a close call. When it mattered, I'd been resourceful and courageous, not to mention effective. Now I was entitled to a little time for clinging.

I had lit several more candles and placed them around the kitchen. I wanted to tell Crane about the phantom Christmas tree, but we weren't alone. It was just as well. I needed time to think about what had happened.

"Grimes broke in on some sort of twisted revenge mission," I said. "He hurt Winter again and threw Halley down the basement stairs."

Under the watchful eyes of Winter, the two officers lifted Grimes up from the floor. He was holding one of his large hands to his head and cursing. Although I'd put a dent in his head, apparently I hadn't done any lasting damage. But now he was even angrier than he had been before. His voice was almost a growl.

"This isn't over, Jennet. We still got a score to settle, you and me."

"That's enough," Crane snapped. "Get him out of here." To me he said, "We think Grimes is the one who strangled Dr. Randolph. The man they arrested earlier talked."

I turned to one of the officers. "Will you take this person out of my house, please? Now? And Crane, will you look at Winter and tell me what you think?"

At the sound of his name, Winter looked up at Crane and thumped his tail once. His dark eyes were clear and alert. He didn't act like a dog who had been seriously hurt, but I wanted to be sure.

Crane rubbed the fur on his neck and head and ran his hands gently along his rib cage. Finally he said, "I think he'll do, but

Doctor Foster should have a look at him. Good dog, Winter. You're a canine hero."

"I'll kill that mongrel the next time I see him," Grimes vowed, as the officers dragged him out of the house. "And I'll get you, too, Jennet."

Then he was gone, but his voice and his words echoed in my mind. I longed for Crane to hold me again. He was still standing at Winter's side.

"Did you say that you hit Grimes with the rolling pin?" Crane asked. "You're amazing, Jennet."

"Yes, while Winter held him down. That was after he took my carving knife."

"You keep surprising me, honey."

I wanted to hold fast to the approval I heard in Crane's voice. I wanted him to elaborate on it, but he had launched into one of his gruesome anecdotes.

"There's a tale told about one of my female ancestors during the War. When a Yankee tried to force her door open, she took a knife and chopped off all the fingers on his right hand. You remind me of her, Jennet."

His words had created the scene for me in full Technicolor. I found it a bit too gory. "Good Lord, Crane. How ghastly! I wouldn't have gone that far. I was aiming for Grimes' heart."

"That was a long way above you, honey," he said. "It's like the inside of a freezer in here. Let's get you some place warm."

It really was cold. With the arctic air flowing in through the broken door, the temperature inside the . house must have dropped forty degrees since the power had gone out.

"Camille called the police before you did," Crane said. "She heard a crashing sound. It must have been Grimes breaking through the door."

"I thought Camille would be asleep by now."

He took me by the hand and led me to the kitchen window.

"Come look."

The yellow Victorian was ablaze with lights on both floors. Now it was Dr. Linton's house that was dark.

The snow had stopped. Once again it was a marshmallow world in Foxglove Corners. The freezing rain hadn't yet materialized, and I hoped the regular rain would stay away, too.

"You can't spend the night here," Crane said.

"There can't be much of the night left, and I can't leave. I have school tomorrow."

Crane showed me the time by his watch. How could it be only eleven? So much had happened that I thought it was long after midnight.

"The door is broken," he said. "Grimes is gone, but anyone or anything else could get in. You're going to spend the night at my house, and the dogs, too. I'll be on duty, but the power is on there, and you can make yourself warm and comfortable."

"But I have to go to school tomorrow."

"Just take what you need for school. I think I can find someone to fix the door before you get home. I'll put up a temporary barrier tonight. I know you have some leftover paneling in the garage."

Crane had it all arranged, and I was happy to have him take charge.

"You go get your clothes then and whatever else you need," he said. "Tomorrow is Friday. After that, you'll have the whole weekend to recuperate."

He smiled and gave me a quick kiss, and I went upstairs to gather my clothes and makeup in an overnight case. I added the dogs' leashes and my book bag. Although this couldn't have taken me more than ten minutes, Crane had a large piece of pine paneling hammered in place by the time I rejoined him in the kitchen.

Suddenly I remembered. This was the weekend of our trip to

Snow Lodge. We were leaving tomorrow after school. The confrontation with Grimes had driven it temporarily out of my mind.

Together, Crane and I extinguished every candle in the kitchen. Then I gathered everything I was taking and followed him through the makeshift door he had put in place.

He had backed my car out of the garage and parked it next to his cruiser. The dogs were already inside, Halley in her crate and Winter in the passenger's seat. Both of them were subdued and undoubtedly waiting to see what fresh adventures this unusual night would bring.

I said, "With only one more day to go, I hope nothing else is going to happen to keep us from going to Snow Lodge."

Crane smiled again. The familiar gleam was back in his eyes. "Nothing's going to happen, honey. I won't let it."

Twenty-eight

Even when Crane wasn't in his house, his strong presence filled every room. I delayed going to sleep as long as possible so that I could sit in the leather chair near his vast collection of Civil War memorabilia and think about him.

He kept the beer stein that I'd given him for Christmas on a stack of Confederate memoirs, and the scent of Obsession lingered in the air. Eventually, I fell asleep in the chair, secure in the knowledge that I had defeated my enemy and all was well in my world.

I had to leave for school before Crane came off duty, so I didn't see him in the morning.

Last night, he'd said, "I'll pick you up at six sharp tomorrow, and we'll be at Snow Lodge in time for a late dinner."

"I'll be ready," I said.

That gave me about an hour after school to make a few visits. My first stop was Henry's white Victorian on Park Street. I was finally ready to talk about our mutual apparition.

I'd only been inside Henry's house once. At that time, the rooms had very little furniture in them, and the sadness was almost palpable. During the past month, Henry had added personal belongings, and the old haunted place was beginning to look like a home. In front of the bay window where I had first seen the phantom Christmas tree, Brownie lay chewing a rawhide slipper.

Henry had acquired another dog. A brown and white collie with a blaze and a graying muzzle lay by the fireplace next to his rocking chair. Walking slowly, wagging his tail, the dog came up to greet me. I had never seen Luke before, but I would have known him anywhere.

Gently I stroked his head. His dark brown eyes were trustful, and his fur was soft and warm from the fire. I didn't see any signs of hardship or abuse.

Brownie looked up from her slipper and watched me gravely as I stroked Luke's head. I saw a flicker of friendliness and longing in her eyes, and when I reached over to touch her, she didn't shy away. Lila had transformed Crane's frightened little stray into a happy pet. As for Luke, he was a miracle of a different kind.

"Good Luke," I said. "You came home, just like your master thought you would. What a clever dog you are!"

Henry's blue eyes were bright with happiness and excitement. "That's only part of the story," he said. "The impossible has just happened, and I can't wait to share the news."

He pulled up another rocker for me, a newer and smaller version of his own. "Sit down, Jennet, and I'll tell you all about it. It's quite a story. Did you see the *Banner* today?"

"No, I came here straight from school."

He picked up a paper that lay on the floor near his chair and handed it to me. Winter and I were the day's big story. I read the headline: 'Collie Turns Tables on Dognapper'.

"It's all here," he said, "except for your name and Winter's."

I skimmed the story, hoping to learn something new:

A collie and his owner, a female resident of Foxglove Corners, escaped death last night at the hands of Alfred Grimes who later confessed to the Christmas Day strangulation murder of local veterinarian, Dr. David Randolph.

Also arrested as a result of Grimes' capture was Rudy Zoller, owner of the Rocking Horse Ranch and alleged leader of a dognapping ring that has been operating in Foxglove Corners.

"Rudy Zoller!" I exclaimed. "So he was the dealer."

The writer didn't mention the rolling pin, but the bite Winter inflicted on Grimes' shoulder was described in detail, for that was what had enabled the would-be victim to subdue her assailant.

While it was true that neither my name nor Winter's appeared in the account, the description of Winter's unusual head markings would be familiar to anyone who had ever seen him.

"The story makes you sound like an Amazon, Jennet," Henry said. "Like Xena."

"I'm glad they didn't use my name, though."

I laid the paper down, wishing there were more. "This doesn't say why Grimes killed Dr. Randolph."

"Turn the page," he said. "Read on. Grimes confessed that he went to the Randolph house to search for stolen evidence that would implicate him and Zoller in the dognapping ring. He didn't think the vet was home. When Dr. Randolph threatened to have Grimes arrested for breaking and entering as well as dognapping, Grimes killed him."

"Grimes wasn't very bright," I said. "He should have made sure that Dr. Randolph was at the animal hospital before he broke into his house."

"Maybe the deputy sheriff will know more. Now, let me tell

you about Luke."

As Henry related the story of Luke's homecoming, I couldn't stop the tears that were trickling down my cheeks. This true Christmas miracle was more moving than fiction. It didn't matter that it was a month late.

Luke had been one of a batch of dogs who were slated to be trucked out of the state, with a research lab as an ultimate destination. One of Rudy Zoller's workers, who was in charge of feeding the dogs, took pity on Luke and spirited him away to her own house. She tried to alert Dr. Randolph to what was going on at the Rocking Horse Ranch, but before the doctor could intervene, Grimes murdered him.

When the worker heard that Grimes and Zoller were in custody, she brought Luke to the animal hospital, and Dr. Foster identified him.

During Henry's narrative, Luke had reclaimed his place near Henry's rocker. He was sleeping, and I had a feeling that he would stay close to his master from now on.

"I'll admit that I didn't think your story would end happily, Henry," I said. "We lost hundreds of dogs to the dognappers, but a few came home. Winter and Brownie must have been in one of Zoller's batches, too, but we'll never know for certain. The dogs can't talk, and I suspect that Grimes and Zoller won't have much more to say either."

"The police will get them to confess," Henry said. "And that Deputy Sheriff Ferguson. He's a persuasive fellow."

"The story doesn't say anything about Emil Schiller," I said. "I'll ask Crane about him, but for now, I need to talk about my own affairs."

Then I told him how the timely appearance of the phantom tree and Winter's bravery had enabled me to overpower Grimes.

"Imagine that!" Henry said. "Maybe that's why the tree

appeared to you, to save your life. For myself, I haven't thought about the past lately. I don't think I'll ever see the tree again. I've been helping the girls at the shelter some, and now I have Brownie to take care of and my Luke, too. In some mysterious way, evil was turned into good."

That sounded right, and I realized that I needed no further explanation of the apparition.

When I left Henry, I drove to the animal hospital, where Alice was hanging red balloons in preparation for the grand reopening. She knew more details about the dognapping affair. We made ourselves comfortable in her office for one last meeting.

She handed me a cup of coffee. "You're a heroine, Jennet. I'm glad we're on the same team."

"Winter is the hero. He kept Grimes occupied while I hit him."

"Camille brought him in this morning. He's going to be fine. It was your lucky day when you rescued him."

"And you found Luke, against all odds. What do you know that I don't?" I asked.

"I didn't really find him. Someone brought him to me. The informant was a girl named Michelle, also known as Shelley, who worked for Zoller at the ranch. She knew what Zoller was using the old barn for and hated being a part of it, but she was afraid of him and Grimes.

"Michelle was determined to break up the dognapping ring, so she phoned David in November, telling him what was going on. She stole Zoller's records and sent them to him at the animal hospital. They were full of inaccuracies and falsified information. She hoped that he would be able to stop Zoller without involving her. David must have searched our files and used Zoller's records to compile his list of dogs."

"At some point after that, your former receptionist found the list and sent it to the *Inquisitor*," I said.

"I'm sure that's what happened. David made a trip to the ranch, caught up with Zoller, and asked him some pointed questions that he couldn't answer.

"When Zoller discovered that his papers were missing, he suspected that David had taken them and sent Grimes to try to recover them. He didn't want that information to be made public. He didn't know that Michelle had taken pictures of the dogs when they were still inside the old barn. Those three dates were the times Zoller's truck was scheduled to transport the stolen dogs out of the state.

"After David's murder, Zoller distanced himself from Grimes. When Grimes was caught in the act of trying to steal the shelter dogs, he cut ties with him permanently."

I said, "So Grimes thought he had some justification for his vendetta against me."

"Zoller is a Class B dealer. He has been for years," Alice said. "He'll stop at nothing to make profits. Dealing in stolen dogs is only one of his illegal activities."

"That won't set well with the voters. I heard that Zoller was planning to run for mayor. And to think I thought he looked like Santa Claus."

"A demented Santa Claus, maybe. He'll be in jail, not the mayor's office. The man is corrupt to the core. He used sleigh rides and line dancing as a front for his illegal activities.

"Michelle brought Luke to me this morning and told me what she'd done, and I filled in the gaps. I recognized Luke from Henry's poster and took him home. That was a reunion right out of *Lassie Come Home*. I wish you could have been there. Oh, one more thing. Michelle told David that her name was Mike."

"She called herself Shelley when I visited the ranch."

"Whatever her name, she's left Foxglove Corners now.

Even with Grimes and Zoller in custody, she's still afraid of them."

"One piece is still missing," I said. "Do you know what happened to Emil Schiller?"

"I have no idea. Michelle didn't say anything about him, and he's not under arrest."

"Maybe he's gone, too. Emil is good at slipping out of town when things get hot." I remembered the time I'd seen him with Susan at the Carnival. Poor Susan. Her brief romance had an unhappy ending, but maybe it was for the best.

"Well, we're ready to reopen the hospital," Alice said. "We've hired a new receptionist, someone I think we can trust."

"So it's on to the future. With two dogs, I think I'll be a more frequent visitor. Now I have to say goodbye. I'm going out of town for the weekend."

"And I have more balloons to blow up. Have fun."

I left Alice to her decorating and headed home. Except for Emil, who was a loose thread, the mystery was neatly wound up, as was my spare first hour. When I reached my house, I found a strong new kitchen door in place and the power back on. I had about fifty minutes before Crane came to whisk me off to Snow Lodge.

Whisk me off. The phrase kept echoing in my mind, while I took my long-delayed bath, changed into one of my favorite red dresses, and fastened my crystal bracelet around my wrist, making all the old, familiar preparations for a wonderful new experience.

All I had to do now was feed the dogs and alert Camille that we would be bringing them by as soon as Crane arrived. That left ample time for dreams.

~ * ~

He was there at the stroke of six, stamping the snow from

his boots, examining the new door to make sure the workmanship was acceptable, throwing Halley's penguin for her, and smoothing the fur on Winter's neck the wrong way. He seemed to do all of these things at once. My house was electric again, and not only because the power was back on.

The light from the Tiffany fixture shone on the silver strands in his hair, and his gray eyes were warm. It always seemed that I was seeing him for the first time. I couldn't wait to kiss him and be kissed properly in return.

Instead, I asked, "Do you know what happened to Emil?"

"When we got to the red barn, the grooming van was there, but Schiller was gone. He'll be around again, probably in more trouble before long. We found thirty dogs locked in the barn. Every one of them has already gone home.

"That's an end to the mystery finally," he said. "Come here. I'm not on duty tonight. I can give you a real kiss. Since I came to your rescue last night, I think I'm entitled to about a hundred kisses as a reward."

"At least that many," I said.

I was so happy that I didn't point out something we both knew. I had needed the police last night, but not a rescue. I had managed Grimes very well on my own, as well as any Amazon. As well as Xena. Henry McCullough had said so.

But this was no time to talk, for Crane had taken me captive in his strong arms and was bending his lips to meet mine in one of those long, crushing kisses I yearned for when we were apart.

The scent of Obsession drifted over me, and I found myself surrendering completely to the power of this man who had held me in thrall for so long that I could scarcely remember what the world was like without him.

When he released me at last, all he said was, "Are you ready, honey? We have a long drive ahead of us."

"My suitcase is in the closet," I said. "There's not a single thing left to do except drop the dogs at Camille's."

"Let's go then."

He took my suitcase and shepherded Halley and Winter out to the Jeep, while I locked the door behind me.

When I turned around, I looked toward the woods. They were dark and filled with snow. Even though Crane was just ahead of me, I thought I saw him again, as I had first seen him, holding an antique gun in his hand, with the summer sun turning his fair hair and gray eyes to silver.

As I hurried to catch up to Crane and the dogs, I touched my crystal bracelet once. For luck.

~ * ~

We were in the dining room of Snow Lodge, finishing a late dinner. Our table was placed in front of a window with a breathtaking view of the freshly fallen snow that wrapped around the lodge like an unfolding bolt of white velvet. By the light of the moon and the stars, the new ground cover sparkled with a sprinkling of glitter.

Upstairs we had a sleigh bed, a fireplace and candles— everything I could desire for this night with Crane that I had thought would never come.

"At last," he said. "I was afraid we'd never get here, honey."

Across the table, he raised his tall champagne flute up to the uneven circle of light cast by the candles. The crystal came to shimmering life, and his hair and his eyes were touched with light.

"To us," he said.

Holding the stem of the flute as if it were a talisman, I touched my glass to his.

"To us."

Meet Dorothy Bodoin

Dorothy Bodoin lives in Michigan near the fictional setting of Winter's Tale with her black collie who appears in the book as Halley. She has a Master's Degree in English from Oakland University in Rochester, Michigan, and taught secondary English for several years. Now she writes full-time, alternating between cozy mysteries and novels of romantic suspense with Gothic elements. Her first published novel was Darkness at Foxglove Corners.

Dorothy is a member of Sisters in Crime and Romance Writers of America. At present she is working on another Jennet Greenway mystery.

*VISIT OUR WEBSITE
FOR THE FULL INVENTORY
OF QUALITY BOOKS*:

http://www.wings-press.com

*Quality trade paperbacks and downloads
in multiple formats,
in genres ranging from light romantic comedy to
general fiction and horror. Wings has something
for every reader's taste.
Visit the website, then bookmark it.
We add new titles each month!*